The Summer of 1964

LEO MOUNT

ISBN 978-1-64300-339-9 (Paperback)
ISBN 978-1-64300-340-5 (Digital)

Covenant Books, Inc.
11661 Hwy 707
Murrells Inlet, SC 29576
www.covenantbooks.com

'To Mom and Dad, who taught us unconditional love'

JUNE

National League Standings June 1964

TEAM	WON	LOST	WON-LOST%	GAMES BACK
PHILADELPHIA	25	15	.625	-----
SAN FRANCISCO	26	17	.605	0.5
ST. LOUIS	25	20	.556	2.5
MILWAUKEE	23	21	.523	4.0
PITTSBURGH	23	21	.523	4.0
CINCINNATI	21	21	.500	5.0
LOS ANGELES	21	23	.477	6.0
CHICAGO	19	22	.463	6.5
HOUSTON	21	26	.447	7.5
NEW YORK	14	32	.304	14.0

Chapter 1

Row Home Heaven

City Hall towers above the city of homes.

M artin McAlynn, Jr. was fourteen years old and having the greatest summer of his life. His favorite team, the Phillies, for decades the most hapless team in major league history with only a few brief flurries of success like in 1950 with the Whiz Kids and the Grover Cleveland Alexander-led 1915 National League championships, were in first place in the very competitive National League. The senior circuit had many potential pennant winners from the pitching-rich LA Dodgers (who swept the powerful Yankees in last year's World Series) and the Willie Mays-led SF Giants on the West Coast to the Midwest with the talent-studded Cincinnati Reds headed by the slugging duo of Frank Robinson and Vada Pinson and the well-balanced St. Louis Cardinals with hitting stars like Ken Boyer and Bill White. Even the more middle of the road teams like the Chicago Cubs had powerful sluggers in Ron Santo, Billy Williams, and the legendary Ernie Banks. In comparison to these league powerhouses, the Phillies had mediocre ability, but somehow the team was still very competitive. Everything seemed to be breaking in the right way for the Phillies.

The Phillies were particularly bad in the past decade. They were so pathetic that one of their managers, Eddie Sawyer, quit after only one game into the 1960 season. Asked why he threw in the towel so early by several reporters, he admitted he was fifty years old and wanted to live to be fifty-one. At the beginning of the 1960s, the Phillies lost over one hundred games two years in a row. In 1961, the team set the major league record of losing twenty-three games in a row. Certainly not promising material for the future.

On top of all this futility, the Phillies had the misfortune to play in a very well-balanced and talent-rich league. Just about every team in the National League had recently been in the World Series. The Milwaukee Braves led by hammerin' Hank Aaron and the ageless lefty Warren Spahn were in the Fall Classic two years in a row in 1957 and 1958. The Pirates won it all in 1960 as did the LA Dodgers in 1963. The Cincinnati Reds and SF Giants were the National League pennant winners in 1961 and 1962 respectively. Although the St. Louis Cardinals were not recent pennant winners, they were always competitive. The only NL teams worse than the Phillies were the new expansion teams, the Houston Colt .45s (soon to be changed to the more futuristic Houston Astros) and the NY Mets. Both teams were only in their third year in the league. So the stiff competition from the Senior Circuit made the Phillies season even more impressive.

The Phillies did have some advantages this year. The team had the hands-down probable rookie of the year, Richie Allen, a young slugger whose prodigious home runs rivaled Babe Ruth and Mickey Mantle in distance travelled. The team's right fielder was the rocket-armed Johnny Callison, who stood out defensively in a league chock-full of talented right fielders, including the great Roberto Clemente. Callison was having his best year at the plate and was prominent in discussions about which player would be the league's Most Valuable Player. The Phillies' pitching staff was young but full of promise with two possible starting pitching stars in Dennis Bennett and Ray Culp. Both players showed great potential in 1963 winning twenty-three games between them and posting excellent ERAs. The starting pitching improved tremendously with the off-season acquisition of veteran Jim Bunning from the Detroit Tigers of the American League and the surprising emergence of lefty Chris Short into another Sandy Koufax.

Perhaps their greatest asset, however, was that the club was led by the smartest, most baseball-savvy manager in the major leagues with the "little general," Gene Mauch, a fiery hard-nosed personality who toiled for many years in the Minors learning the craft of baseball. Like many mediocre ballplayers, Mauch made the most of his lack of playing time by learning the game while sitting on the bench and observing the ebb and flow of America's pastime. Not many big league managers could match Mauch's peerless knowledge of the game.

Marty actually was at a game in which Mauch did the unthinkable and forced an umpire to overturn a home run. Eddie Matthews hit a long ball that landed in the Connie Mack Stadium right centerfield light tower. Since the ball did not careen off the wall, the umpires assumed it was a home run since technically the ball did leave the ballpark, but the wily Mauch came out of the dugout and asked the second base umpire where the ball actually landed. The honest umpire admitted the ball hit below the yellow line of the light tower. Mauch then triumphantly opened the rule book and pointed out that the rules state that a ball that lands below the yellow line is considered a ground rule double. The umpires had no choice but to signal for the slugger to come out of the dugout and head to second base. Not many managers can claim to change an umpire's mind, but Mauch was living proof this rare event could actually happen. This is just one of the instances where Gene Mauch's matchless baseball knowledge benefitted the team.

Under Mauch's leadership and the addition of a few key veterans, it really was shaping up as a magical once-in-a-lifetime season for the Phillies.

"The stars are aligning perfectly in the universe," said Marty's dad, Martin Senior. "Let's face it. It's only fair . . . we have more than paid our dues. Our fans have suffered long enough."

That was as good a reason as any to explain how the Phillies, a team that set a major league record with twenty-three losses in a row only three years earlier, could be outplaying the Reds, the Cardinals, the Dodgers, and the Giants with a far less talented roster.

"This is a rare treat, so enjoy it," said his dad, Martin Senior, to his five sons. He also had five daughters, but they had no interest in sports with the exception of eighteen-year-old Catherine. His wife, Veronica, kept the girls busy with dolls and homemade clothes. Veronica was talented with her hands and used this skill to make doll clothes for the entire neighborhood. She could also take some old rags and transform them, like the Fairy Godmother in Cinderella, into the prettiest dresses—a much-needed budget-stretching skill in their household with ten kids and a sprightly grandfather and two parents, a grand total of thirteen people living in a three-story row home deep in the heart of South Philadelphia.

The McAlynn children's ages ranged from almost college age to preschool. The oldest were the eighteen-year-old twins, Catherine and Kathleen, similar in appearance but worlds apart in personality. Marie was sixteen, cheerful and kind but a real concern to her parents because she was mentally handicapped with Down Syndrome. Fourteen-year-old Martin Junior, the oldest son, was known as

Marty to everyone in the family and neighborhood, except the nuns at school who always formally called him Martin. His Irish twin brother, Mark, was thirteen and more of a rascal than the studious Marty.

Two more sons were born barely a year apart—Tim was twelve, and Ted was ten. Joseph was the youngest son at age eight, and then two more daughters graced the household—Theresa aged six, and the baby of the family was little Margaret who was four. This made the family five times a rich man's family if the old adage still held true.

Veronica, tired of hearing all the negative comments about her abundance of children in grocery store checkout lines and shopping aisles from inquisitive gossipers, had finally crafted a reply to their annoying nosiness. Veronica would look the women straight in the eye and say, "Yes, all these children are mine, and I wish I could have had five more!" This direct approach soon eliminated further comments from the self-appointed and obnoxious Planned Parenthood types.

Although the two older sisters, Catherine, aka Cassie, and Kathleen, aka Kate, were twins, they seemed so completely different both in personality and physical appearance. Cassie had short curly hair, emerald bright hazel eyes, and somehow overcame her ghostly white Irish genes by tanning effortlessly without getting sunburned. Kathleen had long flowing jet-black hair with pale skin and luminous mountain-lake blue eyes. Both were tall for a girl and attractively slim but not too skinny. They looked different in full face profile, but if you viewed them from the side in profile, they looked exactly the same—gently sloping nose, delicately attractive lips, and a rounded smooth chin.

Their mom, Veronica, had trouble telling them apart when they were little, which probably accounted for their different hairstyles. Veronica's subtle influence undoubtedly caused the different look.

The most striking difference in Marty's mind was their starkly different personality. Cassie was more abrasive and demanding. She was bossy but did keep discipline and ran a tight ship when no parent was around. The mothers in the neighborhood adored her as a babysitter.

Kathleen was more ethereal and so much nicer, or at least, she did not yell as much as Cassie. Kate did somehow manage to keep control when she babysat, probably by her saintly example. No kid wanted to misbehave because it seemed God would get upset. Marty idolized Kate for her wholesome goodness. In his eyes, she could do no wrong, even when she burned the meatloaf or overcooked the eggs. Marty had to grudgingly admit Cassie was the better cook, but their mom did most of the cooking, anyway. The kitchen was Veronica's queenly domain. It was rare for her not to prepare dinner.

Their home was located in the middle of 15th Street, a block with forty homes huddled next to each other in about a football field's length (including the two end zones). Its congestion was not obvious to the children living on the block, who used the street as their own personal playground. Very few trees provided shade from the bright summer sun, but this did not distract the myriad of kids from cheerfully frolicking along the narrow street.

The street had a uniform attractiveness with a stately, late nineteenth century feel to it. Sherlock Holmes and Doctor Watson would have felt right at home strolling down the numerous row homes with their ornate gabled roofs, limestone steps, Romanesque rounded windows, and dull red brick houses stacked side by side. The sidewalks were about ten feet wide, and the gray macadam street was twice that size—enough space to park cars on both sides, which left enough room for autos to drive down the one-way street (southbound). Parking was a major problem, but in the early decade of the 1960s, not many families owned a car. Many breadwinners took the subway or bus to work. The street had a distinct architectural ambience from the reddish brown steps to the pointed rooftop facades that, with a little imagination, resembled Amsterdam minus the canals. Some of the surrounding side streets around the corner were even narrower with room for just one side for parking, which left a slender lane for a careful drive down the street always on the lookout for small children dashing into the street.

All kinds of games went on during the day, ranging from hopscotch and jump rope for the girls to ledge ball and half ball for the boys. Cars occasionally travelled down the street, but their infrequency did not interrupt the games. The narrow block forced motorists to cruise slowly through the area, and the neighborhood kids were alert to any oncoming cars. This was drilled into the youngsters by their cautious parents.

From the early morning, when parents groggily left home for work to the late evening when teenagers clustered to flip cards or engage in a weird game called buck buck (when kids jumped on another kid acting like a horse to see how many could fit on another kid's back, something like an adolescent version of the old college prank of trying to fit so many students in a phone booth), the block was always busy with activity, like bees hovering over a honeysuckle bush. If anyone bothered to add up the number of kids inhabiting this one small block, the figure probably would be well over one hundred children, and this was just a routine block in South Philadelphia in post-World War II America. Children were not confined to this one street. Neighboring blocks were equally as fertile. The term Baby Boom Generation was not an exaggeration in this typical corner of blue-collar Philadelphia. The McAlynn family proudly claimed the title as the largest family in a half-mile radius of their 15th Street address.

Chapter 2

A Continental Grandfather

The McAlynns' maternal grandfather, Adolph Hammacher, was quiet but a benevolently satisfying presence in the home—feisty but unobtrusive. His daughter, Veronica, idolized her dad and wanted him to live with her young, growing family. His old neighborhood in North Philadelphia was changing for the worst. Crime and grime sullied the formerly pristine German neighborhood. One could practically eat off of the freshly scrubbed sidewalks due to the fanatical cleanliness of the German matrons living on the block. Sadly, this was no longer the case.

All kinds of disorder crept into the neat row home-lined blocks—fluttering paper trash, broken bottles, discarded cardboard pieces, plastic straws, and even unsightly graffiti scribbled on the brick walls with incoherent messages and symbols, marring the Little Vienna ghetto that Adolph raised his family of twelve children, seven boys and five girls, an even dozen as he proudly claimed. His own father owned a farm in Austria, right outside of Vienna, and one of Adolph's household chores as a boy was to store eggs in neat and orderly stacks of twelve. The old dozen egg stacker grew up to rear a dozen children. Adolph liked the symbolism, or was it a foreshadowing?

So as the old neighborhood deteriorated, his youngest daughter, Veronica, insisted her father move in with her own family in South Philadelphia. Adolph did not put up much of a fight. Most of his other older children escaped the densely packed urban streets to the former farmland and open spaces of the newly growing northeast section of Philadelphia. There was ample parking there, and even some garages (a rare but welcome convenience in a city that was built for nineteenth-century travel) as well as front lawns and a backyard.

It was not that Adolph needed a car. In fact, he never even bothered to get a driver's license. He literally walked everywhere.

Often, he would leave his 2nd Street and Allegheny address and visit some of his children's families in the Northeast Philadelphia sections of Mayfair, Lawncrest, and Burholme—a one-way distance of four to six miles, round-trip it could turn into a trek of eight to twelve miles. Many times, his children or grandchildren would be aghast at what he did and offer to drive him back to his home. Adolph did not mind the extra miles, but his family did, thinking it unsafe and dangerous, especially with the changing demographics of the city.

Adolph walked these routes well into his seventies, but now that he entered his eighth decade, his children worried even more about his welfare. However, Adolph did not acknowledge what the fuss was all about since he routinely walked to work every day in his younger days from his North Philadelphia home at 2nd Street and Allegheny to the western edge of Center City Philadelphia near the Drexel University campus at 33rd Street and Chestnut. Once there, he worked a ten-hour shift at the Philco manufacturing plant assembling radio parts.

Long-distance hiking was not one of his Teutonic-bred passions or hobbies but a practical necessity. This task saved him a lot of money on bus and trolley fare (a transfer was involved), gas, and a used car purchase. He was a hard worker but not a wealthy one.

Although he missed the old German restaurants, corner bars, and general cozy atmosphere, he was not as sentimental about the old neighborhood since his beloved wife, Elizabeth, died and all the kids moved out.

Adolph really enjoyed being around Veronica's large family. This rekindled fond memories of his own child-rearing days in his old family's cramped but cozy north 2nd Street row home.

He thought it was so nice to actually live with, interact, and converse with his youngest set of grandkids. Adolph enjoyed his visits

15

to the other grandchildren in the Northeast, but they were normally short in duration. By living in the same house with Veronica's children, Adolph could counsel and influence them for the better with his hard-earned worldly wisdom and hopefully prepare them for life's ups and downs, misfortunes and joys. He relished the thought and also wanted them to become faithful Catholics in an increasingly godless world, as he sadly viewed the state of contemporary society.

Another reason was to restore the grand old name of Adolph, now a term of derision and horror. He often complained how "that failed house painter and Austrian corporal ruined such a glorious name."

Adolph would then enumerate to his grandchildren all the great men that bore the name of Adolph, especially the wonderful saints like the pious and charitable Bishop of Osnabruck, the "Almoner of the Poor" who fed his hungry diocese with food as well as spiritual wisdom. Another St. Adolph was one of the martyrs of Cordoba in ninth-century Spain. The proud old grandfather would also list musicians, composers, princes, kings, and industrialists that had Adolph as their Christian name.

Despite his age, Adolph did not seem to slow down to any significant degree. He might not have been walking ten to twelve miles a day, but he managed to stroll five miles on a daily basis.

There was one drawback to his move to South Philadelphia. It was a solidly strong Italian enclave with a sprinkling of Irish and Polish sections but very few Germans. The ethnicity did not bother him, but Adolph felt hemmed in by the narrow confines of South Philly with the sprawling Navy Yard to the south and on the east by the Delaware River and in the west by the Schuylkill River. The only expansive walking area was to the north into the neighborhoods he had escaped from. However, this direction also led him into one of his favorite haunts, Center City. It was a near perfect five-mile round-trip jaunt into Philadelphia's historic areas of Independence Hall and the Liberty Bell. Adolph could also stroll into the many large department stores on Market Street—Strawbridges, Gimbels, Lit Brothers, and the granddaddy of them all-Wanamakers. He tried to have his grandkids accompany him on these walks on the weekend, but so far only Marty was interested and enthusiastic enough to join him on his uptown jaunts.

Grandpa Adolph always mentioned how the Phillies and he were the same age. They were both born, or in the Phillies' case, established in 1883. Despite the Atlantic Ocean separating their birthplace from each other, Adolph felt a special kinship with the club. He experienced the Phillies only two World Series appearances in 1915 and 1950. He never expected another one, which was another reason 1964 was so special.

In a weird quirk of fate, Adolph was fond of telling his grandkids that the Phillies were destined to win the National League Pennant in thirty-five-year increments. The senior circuit was founded in 1880. The Phillies were in the 1915 World Series. Adolph was thirty-two years old, married, and the father of two small children. Thirty-five years later, the Phillies made their second World Series appearance in 1950, and Adolph was a proud grandfather.

Based on this coincidental numerology, Adolph figured the Phils were not due to be in the Fall Classic until 1985, another twenty-one years to go. Adolph would be 102 and, more than likely, moldering in his grave.

"I never thought I would live to see another pennant run, but can you believe it, the Fightin Phils have a great shot."

Grandpop Adolph's excitement was as infectious as a sneeze in a black pepper factory and easily transmitted to his impressionable grandsons. This feeling brought added joy to the McAlynn household.

Only Martin, Sr. was immune to the growing optimism surrounding Philadelphia's baseball team.

His skepticism was well honed over the years.

"Something bad always seems to happen to our sports teams. I don't know why, but we always seem cursed at the chance for the big championship prize. Look what happened with the Warriors two years ago. Despite Chamberlain's historic year, we still fell a few seconds short against the Celtics. I'm still wondering how the Eagles won it all in nineteen sixty. I guess the Dutchman, Norm Van Brocklin, had some special magic. Look what occurred a year later when the birds had a chance for a repeat when the Cleveland Browns receiver,

Mel Renfro, dropped a certain TD pass from Milt Plum that would have forced a tie with the New York Giants and a championship play-off in nineteen sixty-one, although I doubt anyone could have beaten the Green Bay Packers that year."

So Martin Senior was not ready to pop the champagne yet; he had experienced too many heart-wrenching failures. This pessimism was passed on to his second oldest son, Mark, who was usually pretty negative while watching any sporting event, especially baseball.

Remarks such as the following were typical from Mark:

"Allen won't get a hit. He will strike out for sure."

"The relief pitcher, Baldschun, will blow the lead. You just wait and see."

"Chris Short is pitching too good this year. The law of averages will soon catch up to him."

In past years, Mark's negative comments were often sadly prophetic but not this year. The Phillies seemed to be living a charmed existence. The year 1964 continued to be a magical season. This was perfectly illustrated one blazing hot afternoon in Queens, New York, on the first day of summer (officially), June 21, 1964.

Chapter 3

Perfect Game

It was a torrid, sweltering first day of summer, the kind of day one wished for a refreshing, ocean breeze to cool things off, but Marty, his two oldest youngest brothers, Mark and Tim, their dad, and their grandfather were not outside enjoying the beginning of summer. They were seated, or lying as the case may be, in front of the family's Philco black-and-white television set, totally absorbed more than usual in the Phillies-Mets baseball game. It seemed as if something historic was happening right in front of their eyes.

"Bunning is really mowing the Mets down," said Martin Senior.

"Yes, like a dishwasher piling up the dishes in the sink," said Grandpa Adolph.

It was the bottom of the fifth inning, and the Phillies right-handed ace was hurling a no-hitter!

Could it really happen? cautiously thought Marty. He had never experienced a Phillies no-hitter, a rare event in baseball for any Major League team. The Phillies were recently the victim of a no-hitter by the great Sandy Koufax earlier in the month, but that was not a pleasant experience. Marty could not get his hopes up too high; after all, the game was barely half over. Bunning still needed twelve more outs. He came close earlier in the year with a one-hitter, giving up the lone hit in the fifth inning against the Houston Colt .45s.

There have been so many heartbreaking near misses in the past with pitchers needing just one more out for a no-hitter.

Martin Senior reminded his older sons of this fact.

"I remember that former Phillie, Harvey Haddix, once pitched a perfect game for twelve innings but gave up a hit and a run in the thirteenth inning and wound up losing the game. So you never know. You should never count your chickens until they hatch."

The Phils had a 4–0 lead, so there was little chance of Bunning experiencing another tough loss.

Marty and Mark were doubly excited about actually watching a possible no-hitter on TV. They were viewing potential history from the very first pitch.

As the game moved briskly on, there was one very annoying glitch. The Phillies expert analyst and color man, Richie Ashburn, kept calling attention to the fact that Bunning was on a roll. "Now that's sixteen in a row . . . that is, number seventeen," and so on.

"He should not be saying that," said an increasingly annoyed Martin Senior. "It is bad luck to mention a no-hitter while it is in progress. Richie shouldn't be so obvious. He really should know better."

Adolph agreed. "It is not a good idea to tempt the baseball gods and keep reminding the world of a no-hitter in progress."

When the game reached the seventh and eighth inning, Richie Ashburn kept bringing it up. "Now that is twenty-one in a row . . . now twenty-two . . ."

Martin Senior just shook his head and said, "Maybe he just doesn't want a no-hitter to happen. Richie was a hitter and a damn good one. He was a career .300 hitter. Not many big leaguers can make that claim, but I think I read somewhere once that he doesn't like pitchers very much. After all, a pitcher's job was to get him as a batter out."

Marty desperately hoped that Richie Ashburn was not jinxing Bunning.

Marty breathed a little easier when the game reached the ninth inning.

The Phillies had a commanding 6–0 lead. Little chance they would blow this large a lead so late in the game, especially against the last place Mets. The only suspense left was if Bunning could get three more measly outs. What made the game even more thrilling was that

Bunning was pitching more than a no-hitter. He was hurling something even rarer in baseball—a perfect game! The Phillies ace faced all twenty-four Met hitters, and not one reached base. No hits, no walks, no errors.

Tension built to unbearable levels in the ninth inning.

"Don't get your hopes up too high. There are no guarantees, even this late in the game," cautioned the ever realistic Martin Senior as he tried to soften the blow if the Mets got a base runner, even on an error, to spoil Bunning's bid for immortality.

But luck still seemed to be in Bunning's corner despite Richie Ashburn's violation of one of baseball's unwritten rules. Bunning had no problem retiring the last three Met hitters he faced. To cap it off, Bunning struck out the last batter to cap off his perfect game gem.

"Boy, everything seems to be going the Phils way this year. Well, it is about time," said Martin Senior, who followed the team through enough losing seasons over the past forty years.

To add more luster to the day, the Phils won the second game of the double header, 8–2, behind the pitching efforts of Rookie Rick Wise, who would ironically seven years later pitch a no-hitter himself to remain in first place in the National League.

The great day continued later in the evening when Jim Bunning made a surprise appearance on the Ed Sullivan Show to celebrate the first regular season perfect game in over forty years. There was Don Larsen's perfect game in 1956, but that occurred in the post-season, during the World Series. Bunning's perfect game was only the seventh one in National League history and only the fifth since the modern era began in 1900.

Bunning's performance gave a great sense of pride to the city, and Marty and his family basked in the shining glory of it.

Chapter 4

The Count Dracula Society

The Frankenstein Monster mask.

Since Marty was the initial organizer of the local South Philadelphia chapter of the Count Dracula Society, a group dedicated to the discussion of monster and fantasy movies, including science fiction, there was another important reason Martin Junior was enjoying the summer of 1964. Marty was making his very own home movie, a task that was gratifying to his budding creative interests. He wrote the script, directed the movie, and produced the whole shebang as far as he could tell. His mom was the cameraman or camerawoman, especially when filming the indoor scenes in the house basement. A couple of his brothers would also do some filming with the Kodak eight-millimeter handheld camera, but they all did it under Martin's overall direction, so he reasoned that made him the director.

Marty enjoyed making up stories to his friends and younger brothers and sisters. On walks home from school and around the neighborhood, Marty would create tall tales, mostly about monsters and invasions from outer space and spin them to his friends. Marty told stories about lizard men, transistor radios with human blood, ghosts haunting an alleyway, ghouls roaming around cemeteries, giant insects invading Center City Philadelphia, and man-eating gophers. His imagination was fired up by the many stories he made up to entertain his school friends.

Marty started telling scary stories to his younger brothers and sisters, but when they started screaming in the middle of the night with nightmares, his mom and dad warned him that he had to stop. Marty found it hard to believe his little brothers and sisters were actually frightened by his stories. Marty actually toned them down to fit his young audience. After all, weren't Grimm's Fairy Tales terrifying to a young mind with ugly witches, poisoned apples, fire-breathing dragons, and hairy trolls? But Marty did not want to be the cause of any conflict in his comfortably happy home, so he acceded to his parents' wishes.

His friends all thought the stories were good enough for Hollywood, so Marty decided to take their praise seriously and actually attempt to put his thoughts down on paper. Marty decided to write the script for a movie about his two favorite monsters, the tortured man-beast better known as the Wolfman and the oddly sympathetic man-made monster created by the mad Dr. Frankenstein.

Marty hoped the movie project would reignite some of the flagging spirits of his friends in the society. Some of his longtime pals were now becoming more interested in Brigitte Bardot than Boris Karloff. It was getting harder and harder to drag them to the latest Vincent Price AIP film based on an Edgar Allan Poe story or the most recent Peter Cushing Hammer movie about vampire brides, especially when the competition was Raquel Welch or Sophia Loren. When Marty announced his plans for the movie project, the Count Dracula Society members were briefly enthusiastic, but the zeal soon flagged when *And God Created Woman* hit the local theaters. Marty sadly realized his time with the society was soon coming to an end much earlier than he anticipated. Too many of his buddies were bailing out. This gave Marty an added impetus to make the movie.

Marty used his Christmas savings to finance this dream project by purchasing the eight-millimeter film and also paying to send it by mail for processing. The Kodak camera was already paid for. His dad purchased the movie camera six years ago to film family memories.

The motion picture projector was a Christmas gift from his mom and dad and was the only additional expense. Costumes, sets, and makeup were improvised from everyday household items. The movie title was *Return of the Monsters*. Marty's projected film was basically a remake of Marty's favorite movie, *Frankenstein Meets the Wolfman*. In addition to his writing, producing, and directing duties, Martin Junior was also playing the role of the Frankenstein monster. His oldest youngest brother, Mark, would portray the tormented soul of Larry Talbot, the Wolfman. The rest of the cast would be filled in with various neighbors, friends, and younger brothers and sisters. This is one of the key advantages in coming from a large family.

Some of his friends wondered how Martin could stand having so many brothers and sisters, but Martin did not mind. He could ignore all the fights, the football scrimmages, the flying baseballs bouncing off the living room walls, and the constant yelling. He was able to tune out all the noise and somehow concentrate on schoolwork. It must have worked. He was an honor student at St. Monica

School in South Philadelphia. All the nuns doted on him and kept saying what a fine priest he would make. Marty appreciated the comments, but he had other career goals.

Right now, though, Martin's sole career ambition was to become the Walt Disney of monster movies. He planned to become a moviemaker and became a jack of all trades in the film business. Martin wanted to do it all: makeup, direct, write, and act. Basically, his fondest dream was to become a combination Lon Chaney, Sr. (the man of one thousand faces in silent films), Boris Karloff, Bela Lugosi, and Val Lewton, the famous director of horror movies in the 1940s.

Due to budget limitations, Martin was using a rotting Frankenstein monster mask with painted rubber black hair and green skin. The mask was well used and was marred by a gaping hole in the left eye and a torn chin. It was cheap-looking, but when he began filming the movie, it was the best prop Marty had. Fortunately, most of the early scenes did not feature Frankenstein in it very much. His mom suggested, quite rightly, that the monster stay deep in the background when he needed to be in a scene. No close-ups were needed to see the torn mask.

This glaring problem was rectified when Martin used his recent birthday money and some of the money earned working an occasional part-time job at St. Monica's School auditorium by cleaning up the school hall after Wednesday night bingo. His cousin, Jack, and two of his older younger brothers, Mark who was thirteen, and Tim who was twelve, would sweep, take down tables and put them away, pick up trash, and generally make the place presentable for the next day's school events. For two hours of hard work, the job paid $10 plus a bologna sandwich, a soda, and a piece of cake. Not bad considering the minimum wage in 1964 was barely a dollar an hour.

The only drawback was that it took place at eleven on a school night, but Marty was used to staying up late anyway. Besides, this job was only an occasional, every-now-and-then job. The pay was worth the lack of sleep.

His mom, however, dreaded waking up Mark and Tim the next morning. They were heavy sleepers and had to be practically dynamited out of their bunk beds, but Martin could wake up with the softest call from his mom's voice. Another motivation for Marty was to get to the bathroom quick. In a household with thirteen people, bathroom availability was always tight in the morning, especially with five sisters who hogged the bathroom to an unreasonable extent. So when Martin heard his mom tell him it was time to wake up, he quickly bolted to the bathroom when it was free for his morning constitutional.

So with the extra money he earned as a bingo cleanup man at the church school, Marty was able to save enough cash to send away for a genuine bona fide Universal Studio-approved Frankenstein mask. It was full-faced and covered the entire head. The mask was placed over the head like an astronaut's space helmet. The mask even had matted black hair, red scars, bolts, and clamps, but the greatest bonus of them all was that the face resembled Boris Karloff's version of the Frankenstein monster. Boris was Martin's favorite actor. He thought no other actor came close to Boris's portrayal of the monster. This would give his movie the extra jolt it needed for authenticity.

The mask came in with the mail on a Friday afternoon in early June, which added even more joy to Martin. He could actually enjoy the moment more knowing he did not have school the next day and had the entire weekend to play with it.

Friday nights were without doubt the best night of the week in the McAlynn household. Since it was Friday and no meat was allowed, his mom ordered pizza for dinner.

Mark expressed it better than anyone could when he remarked, "If a greater food than pizza was ever invented, I'd like to know what it is," said Mark as he bit into the gooey cheese and savory red sauce of the slice. Martin couldn't agree more!

Pizza for dinner and no school the next day—what could be better!

Mark would sometimes complain that Saturday was not completely a day off because there was confession. His common complaint was, "We never get a whole day off . . . we have to go to confession on Saturday and Mass on Sunday and school from Monday to Friday. Us kids never get a break . . . it's just not fair."

Keep in mind Mark was always a world-class complainer.

"You are never happy," his mom would say. "You would complain about winning the Irish sweepstakes." His mom would imitate Mark's trademark whine. "If you won one million dollars on the sweepstakes, you would complain that it was not two million. You really need to count your blessings, Mark."

Marty would try to cheer Mark up by telling him confession was short and was in the late afternoon, around four, so Mark could sleep in on Saturday mornings. Of course, Sunday mornings were different. A late sleep was not possible because the family had to get up early for Mass. Leisurely, Sunday mornings were not possible in the large, busy McAlynn household. Mass was attended in two shifts with the younger kids attending church with their mom and dad, while the older children were deemed responsible enough to choose the Mass time on their own. St. Monica Church had numerous opportunities and enough Mass times to satisfy all comers ranging from five in the morning to noon. There were really no excuses to miss Mass on Sunday, and both Veronica and Martin Senior took their baptismal responsibilities very seriously, and the children knew this, so no slacking was permitted.

Chapter 5

The Joy of a Couch Potato

Martin was excited about the new TV schedule on Saturday night. At 11:30 in the evening, Double Chiller Theater was on Channel 6. Two horror movies would be on back-to-back. The first one was not the best, normally a late 1950s science-fiction and horror film combination with cheap special effects and wooden acting. That film mercifully only lasted about an hour and a half, so at one in the morning, the really good movie would play, an old Universal classic with one of the big three: Lon Chaney, Jr, Bela Lugosi, or Boris Karloff. It was well worth staying up for.

As an added bonus, another horror movie came in at two thirty or three in the morning, a pretty decent one, maybe a Val Lewton or Robert Wise psychological thriller about cat people or body snatchers. This movie would end around four thirty in the morning. This worked out perfectly because there was a five-thirty Mass at St. Monica, so Martin and two of his older younger brothers, Mark and Tim, just needed to stay up another thirty minutes so they could walk to church and fulfill their Sunday obligation by attending the early Mass.

The five-thirty Mass would usually be a quick service, less than thirty minutes, especially if Father Coniglio said the Mass. It would last a little longer if the very pious Father Murphy was on the altar. He was much slower and probably more reverent. At any rate, no matter which priest was the celebrant, Martin and his brothers would be back home around 6:10 at the latest. They could be in bed before six thirty in the morning. They could sleep until eleven, plenty of rest for growing boys.

To make matters even better, their mom would have a special Sunday morning breakfast: bacon sandwiches on a fresh Italian roll, rich soft dough with a crisp outer shell that was crunched easily with your front teeth and mouthwateringly tasty. During the school year, the early Mass left enough time to finish some homework before the sporting events, normally baseball or football, came on around one in the afternoon. During football season, the family would watch the Eagles on TV if the team was playing away, but if the Eagles were playing at home at venerable Franklin Field, they could listen to Bill Campbell's vivid broadcast on the radio. His excited rendition put you right into the action like a seat at the fifty-yard line. It actually was better because Bill Campbell's detailed descriptions were similar to a TV camera close-up. Even a fifty-yard line seat was not perfect. It was tough to see plays on either goal line. Listening to Bill Campbell's vibrant play-by-play was almost like having the best seat in the house, without obnoxious fans and foul weather.

Baseball season had the Phillies, which normally was kind of depressing, but 1964 was so much different. Since a baseball game is played almost every day during the 162 game season, the weekly buildup, unlike football, was not as intense or heavily anticipated, but a sports event always took the priority in the McAlynn household with the influence of their father, Martin Senior. Since there was only one TV, Veronica and the daughters were shut out, but Mom ruled on the afternoon for her daytime soaps. Veronica had free reign to watch while she did laundry, folded clothes, and prepared dinner because the kids were in school and Dad was working one of his two full-time jobs. Somehow it all seemed to work out for the entire family. There were no fights about what to watch on TV. Of course, there were only three channels at this time in the country, so variety was quite limited in those pre-cable and Internet days.

Chapter 6

Sticks and Stones May Break My Bones

One day, Ted came rushing through the door with tears in his eyes. He was crying uncontrollably as only a ten-year-old boy could; it was more in rage than in sorrow. Ted slammed the front door and ran up the steps, taking two at a time. His agitation was hard to ignore.

Veronica was cooking supper: meat loaf with brown gravy, string beans, and mashed potatoes. One of her older daughters, Cassie, was helping. Veronica interrupted her kitchen routine to walk into the middle room that was designed as a dining room but was far too small to accommodate the McAlynn brood.

She was carrying a brown towel and spotted Marty, who was laying on his back in the living room watching a *Superman* rerun on TV. He was really enjoying it. His brothers were always crashing through the house angry and upset. Probably lost a game of half ball. Marty more than likely thought that was why Ted was so annoyed. Marty did not give it another moment's thought.

But he saw his mom approaching with a concerned look, and she quietly asked Marty, "Go on upstairs and see what the matter with Ted is. Marty, can you do that for me, please?"

Marty was more than willing but was hoping he could wait until the next commercial break. This was one of the better *Superman* episodes when he put his superpowers to good use, even using his Super Breath in this episode.

Marty instinctively knew this was not going to happen. He couldn't delay too much longer, so he slowly, very slowly, got up to his knees and then his feet and gradually stood up. This action, plus his verbal willingness to help, brought Marty some extra time but not long enough to wait for the next commercial.

Marty knew his obvious delaying tactics were not going to be successful. Marty stopped watching the TV and then zipped up the steps to the middle bedroom where Ted shared a room with two other brothers.

Marty came up to the top step and hesitated before knocking on the open bedroom door. He didn't want to be too obvious about doing his mother's bidding at first but then soon realized it was only natural as a big brother to inquire why one of his little brothers was so upset.

"Ted . . . what happened? Did you get into a fight?"

Kids on the block were always getting into minor scrapes, even among the best of friends. A minor, even silly, disagreement could potentially lead to a rumbling fistfight.

Marty remembers breaking up a fight between his brother, Mark, and Joey Cantrello that started with a disagreement on a close call at first base during a pickup baseball game at Marconi Plaza. Joey was convinced he was safe and beat out a slow ground ball, but Mark, playing second base, was totally positive his quick throw to Marty at first base nipped Joey before his left foot hit the bag. Marty, as the first baseman, caught the ball but couldn't really tell if it was on time to get Joey out since his back was turned to the runner and the first base bag.

That's why baseball has umpires, Marty thought as Mark and Joey started screaming and shouting at each other. Marty wished they did have a neutral observer to make the call to stop the combative argument between the two boys. And to top it off, Joey and Mark were the best of friends who lived on the same block and were constantly at each other's home. Marty hated to imagine how bad things could get if they were playing kids from a different neighborhood. *World War III starting at Broad and Oregon. Not a pretty prospect*, pondered Marty at the time.

31

Mark had a vicious temper. He cooled off quickly but not at first. When his Irish fuse was lit like a firecracker, his anger was incandescent. It could light up the entire city of Philadelphia if it could be bottled. Mark would lash out and say a lot of mean things that he never really meant. Joey was equally explosive. His Italian temperament burst out in wild hand gestures and jerky body movements. This little argument was developing into a real war. Marty had to do something before the two friends did or said something they would soon both regret.

The only way to defuse the tension was to make a generous gesture. Since Marty and Mark were not only teammates but also brothers, Marty thought he had to do something that Mark would not like.

"All right, guys. Cool down! Joey was safe. Let's keep playing."

"What? No way!" screamed Mark.

Marty knew Mark would expend all his anger at himself. He was used to it and was often the recipient of previous outbursts. Marty absorbed Mark's vein-popping outrage by adopting his customary stone-cold look of indifference. This nonreaction to Mark's insults soon cooled off Mark, and he soon gave up trying to goad his older brother. Mark had tried too many times before with little effect. After a few minutes, Mark gave in, threw up his hands, and walked back to second base, still muttering under his breath.

The game resumed without further incidents, and after the game ended, Mark and Joey acted as if nothing happened and became the best of friends again. They even shared an ice-cold bottle of Mountain Dew from the soda machine in front of the neighborhood Acme supermarket on 15th Street.

Based on previous experiences, Marty naturally thought Ted got into a fight with one of his neighborhood friends, but Ted's answer completely surprised Marty.

"No, I wanted to fight Jimmy Dee when he called me a Kraut, but the remark hurt me too much, so I turned around and ran home. I didn't want anyone to see me crying."

"He called you a Kraut?"

Well, technically this was true. The McAlynn family was pure Irish on their dad's side but totally German on their mom's side of the family.

However, to call someone a Kraut was quite an insult to an American kid in 1964. All the big movies were set in World War II with the Nazis as the villains in most of them except for the occasional Pacific Island war film with the Japanese as the bad guys. The popular TV show, *Combat*, with Rick Morrow as Sgt. Saunders and his American infantry squad showed they were always fighting against the Krauts. So for a young boy who was immersed in the popular culture and playing war games in the streets, it was quite an insult to be labeled a Kraut. For the most part, the neighborhood kids no longer played Cowboys and Indians. The modern version pitted the American soldier against the bad guys, the Germans.

"All the Germans were not Nazis," said Marty. "Look at Grandpa . . . he was born over there in Germany and still speaks with a German accent. You can't meet a better man than Grandpa."

"I thought Grandpa was from Australia?"

"No . . . well, Grandpop was really from Austria, not Australia, but the Austrians are really German. They speak the same language, listen to the same music—Beethoven, Mozart, Bach, and all those guys."

"So we really are part-Austrian and not German." Ted's heartbroken spirit was reviving right before Marty's eyes.

"Yes, technically. It is kind of like us and the Canadians. We are basically the same people. We just live in two different countries."

That seemed to make Ted feel much better.

"Wait till I tell Jimmy how wrong he was," said a much happier Ted.

With those words of comfort, Ted regained his composure and went downstairs to run outside and tell Jimmy the real truth of his heritage. He was not a Kraut; he was an Austrian!

Marty was glad Ted felt better, but he didn't have the heart to tell Ted that Adolf Hitler was actually an Austrian also.

Marty thought it would be a good idea and was planning on talking to Grandpa Adolph about having the old man give a pep talk to the family about the glories of German history and culture.

This might make things better for the younger brothers. Marty went downstairs and was about to lie back down on the floor to watch what was left of the *Superman* episode. His mom came in and thanked him for helping.

"Well, I see you worked your magic again and calmed Teddy down."

His mom always overpraised him. It was kind of embarrassing. What he did was no big deal. All he did was talk to Ted, but his mom always acted as if he parted the Red Sea like Charlton Heston in the *Ten Commandments* movie.

Marty thought his mom acted that way toward him because he was not a wise guy. He never talked back to her like Mark and never gave her any lip or sarcastic comments. Plus he was a good student, and the nuns always overpraised him as well, which added to his rapidly growing halo in his mom's eyes.

His big sister, Cassie, was more skeptical. She was the oldest kid in the family, along with her twin sister, Kathleen. She was a big help to her mom in the kitchen and helped clean up the house, but she could be very mean. She was always telling her younger brothers and sisters to clean up after themselves. She was probably right, but she could have said it in a much nicer way.

Plus she always annoyed Marty by calling him the teacher's pet, which was unfair. Marty minded his own business in class as well as at home. He didn't deliberately seek after the approval of his parents or the nuns. It just came natural to him. He was just doing his job and not trying to be a nuisance. Marty never sought praise for his actions. He never wanted to be a troublemaker like Mark, who was always in hot water by talking back to the nuns and his mother but never to his father or grandfather.

Speaking of their grandfather, everyone loved Grandpa, but Marty had a very special regard for the old geezer. Marty especially admired his grandfather's legendary walking feats (no pun intended).

Grandpa Adolph, during his prime working days, would walk from the family row home at 2nd Street and Allegheny in North Philadelphia, an old German neighborhood, to his place of work in West Philadelphia at 33rd Street and Chestnut Street, a distance of five or six miles. He also walked back again for a grand total of almost twelve miles. Grandpa Adolph did this just to save trolley fare and bus fare. Back in those days, the trolley fare was only ten cents, but a dime could buy a loaf of bread and a gallon of milk to feed his large brood of twelve children.

To top it all off, Grandpa was a blue-collar worker to boot. At work, he didn't sit behind a desk in an air-conditioned office (of course, in those days, air-conditioning was not really invented yet), but he toiled in a workshop and was a blue-collar worker who scarred and scratched his fingers and hands to make tubing and coiled parts for radios. He also did some maintenance work, so he had to perform some painstaking manual labor for ten hours after walking six miles just to begin his workday. In addition, Grandpa Adolph, after a tough day job as a manual laborer, could look forward to another six-mile trek through the concrete canyons of West and North Philadelphia. What was an even more miraculous act was that he was never jumped and mugged by some of the youth gangs as he strolled through their neighborhood turf. Maybe they respected his blue-collar work ethic.

In addition and what was even more admirable, Grandpa Adolph possessed an infectiously cheerful and positive attitude. He always had a pleasant and kind word for everyone. He also gave out candy to his grandkids when he asked them to help out on an errand. The candy was little, maybe a piece of gum or cough drop, but coming from Grandpa made it extra special.

In addition to his hard work and his long walks and raising twelve children in a small row home, Grandpa Adolph had to nurse an invalid wife who suffered horribly from arthritis and gout. Her screams of pain were very trying to her children. Fortunately, his five daughters stepped up to the plate and helped comfort their mother in her long-suffering illness.

Marty had never known his maternal grandmother, Agatha. She died before he was born. In fact, most of his brothers and sisters never knew her except for Cassie and Kathleen, but they were small toddlers when Grandmother was still alive.

Both of Marty's older sisters did not have a strong memory of her either. Cassie recalled seeing her always seated in the living room chair. Because of her infirmities, she could not move around the house much.

On a more positive note, Grandpa was a fervent Phillies fans, which he always claimed helped toughen him to the unfairness and tragedy of life. But despite the Phillies' pathetic record since they were first founded in 1883, which was also the year Grandpa was born oddly enough, he was a fervent fan. This may explain why he preferred the sad sack Phillies over the more successful Philadelphia Athletics in the American League under their legendary manager, Connie Mack. Grandpop Adolph was a loyal follower, and some of his fondest memories were the Phillies' first National League pennant in 1915 with Grover Cleveland Alexander as the Phillies' ace and also the pennant-winning Whiz Kids from 1950 with Robin Roberts.

"That's a lot of time between World Series appearances," he would often say.

By a strange quirk of chronology, Grandpa would say the Phillies get to the World Series every thirty-five years since the founding of the National League in 1880. If that odd fact held true, the Phillies' next appearance was not supposed to happen until 1985.

"The 1964 Phillies are twenty-one years ahead of schedule," he excitingly told Marty. "I can't believe it. What a great stroke of fortune. Maybe God is allowing me one more chance to see the Phillies in the fall classic before I die since I will be over hundred years old and well into the grave in 1985."

"Don't say that, Grandpa," answered Marty. This kind of talk always upset Marty. "You are so healthy. Look at all the walking you did in your life. You are in great shape."

"Well, I used to do a lot more walking, but my knees are really bothering me . . . probably arthritis. Something I think runs in the family. We have to face the facts."

Marty did not like to think of his energetic old grandfather six feet under the ground, so he always tried to emphasize his seemingly great health.

"The Phillies play the Cards tonight. The game will be on TV since they are away in St. Louis. Are you going to watch it, Marty?"

Grandpop changed to a more pleasant topic to get Marty's mind off death and moldering in a grave.

"Of course!" said Marty, who took the bait. Marty was something of a couch potato, although he rarely sat in the chair or couch while watching the TV. He normally lay down right in front of the screen. He said this gave him a better view. Marty would soon find out that he was nearsighted and would need glasses, which explained why he sat so close to the screen. When he went to a Phillies game at Connie Mack Stadium, he had to squint a little to see the players a little more clearly. Marty was noticing he also had to do this squinting action at the movies. This was another reason he sat so close in the front rows in the movie theater, which annoyed some of his brothers who had better vision and did not like sitting so close to the big screen.

Grandpa then asked a question that Marty hoped he would not ask.

"I heard Ted crying earlier. What was the problem?"

Marty was going to tell a white lie and claim Ted fell or got hit by stickball bat. He wanted to spare his proudly German grandfather any pain but couldn't think of a falsehood quick enough.

"Well . . . uh . . . uh . . ." Marty hesitated but finally said Ted was called a name and hoped his grandfather would not probe any deeper.

But his grandfather was more perceptive than his grandkids gave him credit.

"What kind of name?" Grandpa persisted.

"Well, Ted was kind of being made fun of because of us being half-Irish and half-German."

Again, Marty was hoping to spare any hurt feelings and hoped Grandpa would think the family's German heritage was not being mocked.

But his grandfather knew the neighborhood was three-fourths Italian and the rest mostly Irish with a few Polish thrown in. There were very few Germans in this section of South Philadelphia.

"So what exactly did they call Ted—a Hun, a Nazi . . . a Barbarian?"

"Not that bad . . . he was called a Kraut." Marty tried to lessen the sting by adding that the popular TV show, *Combat*, was always calling the enemy Krauts, which was why the name was used so much. The movies also said the same thing.

"Well . . . I've been called worse," said Grandpa, who pursed his lips and looked downcast on the floor for a brief moment. Grandpa then had a more determined look in his eye as he raised his chin.

"Before supper, I want to talk to all you boys, especially Ted. It is time they realized there's nothing to be ashamed of by being German. That damn Hitler! He ruined so much . . . he completely destroyed Germany . . . a land that he claimed he supposedly loved . . . and we are still bearing the terrible brunt of his madness. I want to set the record straight. I want all you kids to be proud of your German heritage. We all were not Nazis! The German people tried to kill that lunatic a dozen times. Too bad all those plots never succeeded . . . and another thing, who do you think led the Allied effort against the Third Reich? General Eisenhower! You can't get a more German name than that."

Marty could see that Grandpa was stepping high upon his soapbox about the glories of German culture. He heard some of it before and agreed with just about everything that Grandpa talked about, so Grandpa Adolph was preaching to the choir.

The rest of his brothers needed to hear the speech, so Marty gently interrupted his grandfather and suggested he save his energy for the supper speech, which was only an hour or so away.

"I will tell everyone that you want to talk to us before supper, and I will make sure everyone is around and that no one is outside playing so they don't miss all the good stuff you have to say. No sense repeating yourself twice, Grandpa."

"Yeah, that makes sense. Thanks, Martin." Grandpa was always formal with his name. He was Martin and never Marty like the rest of his family called him, including his mom and dad. Marty then turned around and went downstairs to put out the word to the rest of the family, but as usual, no one was home; most of the kids were playing outside or over at some friend's house.

Chapter 7

Liberty Cabbage, a Meal Formerly Known as Sauerkraut

Dinnertime in the household had to accommodate the thirteen members of the family ranging from little Margaret, a four-year-old toddler, to the octogenarian patriarch, Grandfather Adolph. Since the kitchen table was not big enough to accommodate everyone at one time, the youngest kids took their place in the living room to eat their dinner and at the same time watch *Popeye* cartoons, and the Three Stooges on TV hosted by Sally Star, a blonde cowgirl, or Chief Halftown dressed to the hilt as an American Indian complete with an enormous feathered headdress.

This was a welcome treat and a great advantage in being the little ones of the family. They did not have to eat at the small kitchen table and listen to adult conversation. They could enjoy their meal while watching Moe slap, poke, and kick Curly and Larry all over the small screen. Dinner was a kid favorite—meat loaf with brown gravy, some deliciously creamy mashed potatoes, and string beans expertly marinated in vinegar.

Some of their aunts and uncles thought the Three Stooges were a bad influence and gave impressionable minds a green light to poke someone's eyes or slap faces and not cause anyone real harm. But Marty and his brothers and their friends never imitated the Three Stooges slapstick antics, so they did not see what all the fuss was about. Besides, the comedy trio have been around for over thirty years when their own parents were young. Didn't they grow up watching the Three Stooges in the movies, and they turned out all right, didn't they? This is what Marty and Mark thought and argued to the concerned adults, and their dad had to concede the lucid logic of it.

The older kids, including Marty, Mark, Catherine, and Kathleen, were stuck sitting at the kitchen table, which could comfortably seat six. Today was a treat, however. Martin Senior was not working at the firehouse so he could eat with the family. This was not always the case since Martin Senior often had to work the night shift at the firehouse and normally had to leave before supper at the McAlynn household was ready. Martin Senior had seniority with almost twenty years as a Philadelphia fireman and was fortunate to settle at a firehouse close to home at 13th Street and Shunk, just a few blocks away. Martin would walk since parking spots were more precious than gold in the tightly narrow neighborhood streets of South Philadelphia when the homes were built around the turn of the nineteenth century, and the streets were designed for horse and buggy travel and not automobiles.

To give up your well-earned parking spot for frivolous reasons was taking a huge gamble, especially if one was fortunate enough to get a spot on the same block where your family lived. Sometimes a frustrated driver would circle the neighborhood in a seemingly endless and futile quest to find a nearby parking spot. The string of profanities uttered by the driver would make a longshoreman blush. It was almost easier to dynamite someone out of their parking spot, and the parking situation kept getting worse with no relief in sight. In addition to the frugality, the pain of parking was one of the major reasons the McAlynn family did not own a car.

Martin Senior remembered the disbelief and anger the previous Philadelphia mayor generated when he suggested the residents would have to soon pay to park their cars. The former Mayor Richardson Dilworth was almost run out of town when he suggested residents might need to pay for parking on the city streets in their own neighborhood.

The mayor was the marquee perfect, old Philadelphia patrician Richardson Dilworth, whose chiseled chin rivaled movie star Kirk

Douglas in its granitic splendor. The resulting uproar of the citizens was enough to dim his chance to secure the Presidential nomination for the Democrats in 1960. The eventual nominee, John F. Kennedy, considered Mayor Dilworth to be his most potent threat in the nomination process. Dilworth had a tremendous resume-managerial competence, matinee idol handsomeness, mature sophistication, and heroic war record as a US Marine in both world wars. But his blunt outspokenness didn't endear him to his constituents. Martin Senior never cared for him since he was a Democrat, and the McAlynn family was solidly Republican, but he had to ruefully admit Dilworth was ahead of his time and probably right about the coming parking nightmare, especially in South Philadelphia.

"What an outrage! Who does he think he is?" said Marty's uncles repeatedly in their rage at the suggestion. But something had to be done. Looking for a close-to-home parking spot was always a frustrating adventure for South Philadelphia residents.

That was one of the key reasons Martin Senior did not buy a car. Where could he park it in the dense brick and macadam canyons of South Philadelphia? The other reason was financial; raising a family with ten kids on a fireman's salary forced him to keep a close watch on the family budget. A car was not an absolute necessity.

Shopping was an annoying pain at times with no automobile, but this was when all the extra kids came in handy. Veronica had each one of her younger children carry one bag, the older boys could hold two bags for the long three-to-four-block walk back home from the local Acme supermarket. With everyone's cooperation, the McAlynn family could take ten fully loaded paper shopping bags home. If things were really in sync, some of the neighborhood kids could also help, which meant no one had to carry more than one bag. Mrs. McAlynn would reward the extra help with some Kool-Aid ice cubes that were a thirst-quenching delight in the summer. The group looked like a pied piper march down 15th Street with all those children carrying brown paper bags.

This chore was a biweekly hassle usually around payday on Thursday. Mike's corner grocery store down the street helped fill in the food gaps in between the Acme runs. Mike's was on the corner and an easy half a block walk if an emergency bread or milk run was needed.

But if the family went on an extended trip, which was rare, Martin Senior would look around to borrow a car. He also came from a large family, so there were plenty of brothers and sisters who could be relied upon to lend him a car. Some of them moved out to the suburbs of Bucks or Delaware County where a car was a practical necessity.

So Martin Senior rarely had a car, and if he did, he dared not move the old, barely functioning car. Martin gladly took the short stroll to the firehouse. He also would shake his head in wonder and admiration at how far his father-in-law, Adolph, would walk every day back and forth to work during the Roaring Twenties and the Depression-wracked thirties.

Martin Senior had tremendous affection for his wife's father with his impeccable manners and dignified old European courtliness. He had absolutely no problem with acceding to Veronica's request to have her dad move into their home.

Adolph Hammacher was a lonely widower. His wife had died thirteen years before, and most of his children moved out of the old North Philadelphia German enclave to greener pastures in the great Northeast and beyond. Some of his children eventually ventured into the bucolic charms of Bucks and Montgomery County.

Adolph's old home was in the middle of the deteriorating neighborhood in North Philadelphia. He still loved to walk, and his daughter, Veronica, worried about his safety. It did not take too much persuading on her part to have the old Viennese gentleman move out and permanently stay in their home. Martin Senior also thought he would be a great influence on the kids. Martin genuinely admired his father-in-law's dignified reticence. Martin lost his own dad, Patrick, to a sudden heart attack a dozen years ago, so he thought it would be great to have the children get to know one of their grandparents. Traditions needed to be passed on, even if they were German and not Irish.

Veronica told her husband that dinner was just about ready. She just had to put more butter on the steaming hot string beans to put the finishing touches on the grand supper. She told Mark to get Grandpa, and Veronica also had Marty Junior round up the younger kids and get them inside the house to eat dinner.

Marty drew the short straw. This was one of the tougher jobs their mom could hand out. Grandpa was on the third floor; it was a steep climb, but no guesswork was involved. The old gentleman was probably sitting in his rocking chair and reading some religious book or saying the rosary in German. Mark gladly bounded up to the third floor to relay the news that dinner was ready.

Marty had to hunt down some of his younger brothers. Two of them were playing hide-and-seek in the narrow alleys between Carlisle Street and 15th Street. Marty had to physically go into the trash-strewn and narrow passageway and grab hold of his two younger brothers, who were well concealed near the alley's lone tree—a sad, withered spruce tree. Another brother was playing in Donnie McGraph's backyard. Actually, it was more like a small concrete open-air lawn and was barely big enough to accommodate two lawn chairs on a summer night. This area of South Philadelphia had no front lawn or backyard. The good thing about this was that it meant nobody on the block had any need for a lawnmower. Marty was grateful for that because some of his cousins in the Northeast and Bucks County often had to mow the grass as one of their family chores. No worries there, thought a grateful Marty. That was another one of the advantages about living in the cramped confines of South Philly.

A couple of neighbors put potted plants outside to add some rustic charm and a dash of color to the dull grayish brown paved sidewalks, but they were the exceptions. The backyards and alleys only had one useful function for kids playing outside, and that was plenty of hiding places for a game of jailbreak or hide-and-seek.

Marty Junior was able to finally lasso his wild roaming siblings scattered throughout the neighborhood and herded them all back inside for supper.

But the time he got them inside the house, Grandpa Adolph was in the living room standing next to Martin Senior, who said, "Before we all eat, Grandpa wants to say a few things."

The distinguished old European cleared his throat and asked Ted what upset him so much earlier in the afternoon.

"I was not that mad about it," said Ted. "But Jimmy Dee called me a Kraut, and that really bothered me because in the TV show, *Combat*, the good guys are always calling the bad guys Krauts."

"Okay, Tim. I understand your point, but you can't blame all the Germans for the horrible crimes of the Nazis. There were a lot of plots to kill Hitler, but he seemed to have a devilish version of a cat with nine lives. One of these plots really came close on July 20, 1944. If that succeeded, so many lives would have been saved, especially in all the concentration camps. It really is a shame the bomb just missed Hitler. He was badly hurt and lost a lot of his hearing, but he survived. But it took a lot of guts to even attempt to assassinate a crazy dictator."

Martin Senior winced at Adolph's use of the word *assassination*, especially with President Kennedy's recent death still resonant upon the nation's consciousness, which was not even one year ago. This terrible event was still sadly uppermost in the whole country's mind, especially the kids. It seemed to cast a black cloud over the entire country. Only very recently did the dark oppression start to lift, and the nation's mood rose a little higher and lighter.

Martin Senior still couldn't believe the awful crime. Many of his fellow firemen would often say he even resembled the first Catholic President a little. They both had wavy brown hair, sparkling lake-blue eyes, and a sunny Irish smile. Martin Senior even voted for him. He felt a little guilty about that. He feared his rock-ribbed Republican dad was rolling in his grave knowing one of his sons voted for a Democrat. Martin Senior had to admit the main reason he voted for Kennedy was that he was a Catholic and secondly because he was Irish. Martin Senior vividly remembered stories from his old grandfather, Patrick, about looking for work and seeing the dreaded NINA posters in front of the plant: "No Irish Need Apply."

Martin Senior thought even his own dad might have cast a vote just this one time for a Democrat because Kennedy was, at least, an Irish Catholic. Martin Senior's reminiscence was brought back to the present when Grandpa continued his speech.

"The retaliation by Hitler's brutes was terrible. They strung these heroes up with piano wire to die a slow, painful death."

Veronica was listening but quickly stepped in to spare her children the gory tales of torture and humiliating death perpetrated by the vengeful Nazis, particularly just minutes before sitting down to a well-cooked meal.

"Pop . . . why don't you emphasize more of the good and positive blessings of German culture? The meal is getting cold."

"Okay, Veronica . . . now . . . where was I . . . well . . . it was so sad that all these brave Germans died trying to get rid of an evil tyrant. You can tell your friend that the next time he calls you a name, Ted."

Grandpa was just getting started.

"Also tell him all the good things Germans have given this country. Think about this . . . what are America's favorite foods? Hot dogs and hamburgers . . . right! Guess what, they were named after two German cities, Frankfurt . . . get it, Frankfurters, and hamburgers were named after Hamburg, which is another town in Germany. And let us not forget, of course, beer . . . You guys are too young to enjoy it now, but you will love it when you're older.

"Look at all the amazing music—Brahms, Beethoven, Handel, Mozart, Haydn. Let us not forget the scientific genius of the Germans and all the great inventions they have given us. And of course, there is the magnificent genius of Goethe, a true Renaissance man, artist, poet, writer, and statesman. He even helped run the government. Everyone brags about Shakespeare, but old Herr Goethe gives the Bard a run for his money in the literature department in my humble opinion."

Grandpa knew everyone was getting hungry. In truth, his stomach was also beginning to rumble, but he wanted to add one more blessing from the Germans to America.

"We also have built some beautiful churches. Many saintly priests and nuns have plowed through the wilderness of New York, Pennsylvania, and the Midwest. Look at Bishop Neumann where all you boys will be going to high school, which is named after that great soon-to-be saint. He will be the first canonized American male saint."

The older half of the family was very familiar with Bishop Neumann. There is an interesting shrine and museum dedicated to his memory in North Philadelphia that the family would often visit. There were some fascinating facts in his life and interesting details about the miracles in the museum that proved he, indeed, was a holy man of God and saint. His body was visible upon the altar, which creeped out Kathleen and some of the younger kids, but Marty Junior found it very interesting. It almost looked like the saint was in one of Vincent Price's most famous movies, *The House of Wax*, a film that Marty Junior and his friends all recently watched at the Broadway Theatre. He had a sacrilegious thought about pounding on the saint's face to see what was beneath the mask, but he quickly chased it out of his mind. That was no way to treat such a great and holy bishop.

Mark, as ever the wise guy, remembered the visit to the shrine very well and mentioned, "But, Grandpa, wasn't Bishop Neumann born in Czechoslovakia? How does that make him German?"

Martin Senior winced and did not want to have his father-in-law answer. He hoped to distract everyone in the family from the impertinent question and said, "I think it's time to eat."

Grandpa Adolph was undeterred and did not miss a beat.

"Technically, you are correct, Mark. Bishop Neumann was born in Bohemia, but he was of German descent like you guys, and he spoke fluent German and administered and served the thousands of German immigrants in the snowy wilderness of Wisconsin and in the urban cities in New York and Baltimore. Keep in mind that when he was born, Bohemia was part of the Austro-Hungarian Empire, which had a strong German presence. Actually, my family hails from Vienna, the great and beautiful capital of the Austro-Hungarian Empire."

His eyes reddened a little and were about to tear up at the thought of the empire's destruction and breakup at the end of World War I. He never forgave Woodrow Wilson for his cavalier dismissal of the magnanimous, devout, and stalwart last emperor of the Austro-Hungarian Empire, Karl von Habsburg. His early death at such a young age (he was only thirty-four) left his wife, the Empress Zita, with eight young children. This event still shocked Grandpa even after the passage of four decades.

His daughter, Veronica, rescued her dad from tearing up completely and choking up in front of his grandchildren and forcefully but joyfully told the entire family, "Pop, that's enough history and culture for the kids. We really need to eat before it gets too cold. Cassie made the brown potatoes exactly as you like them."

That cheered up Adolph, and he smiled and turned around to walk toward the kitchen with his grace and dignity intact. The rest of the family broke off into their respective rooms to enjoy Veronica's delicious dinner.

Chapter 8

She's Not Heavy, She's My Sister

Martin Senior worked a couple of extra jobs to keep the family finances afloat. Luckily, his shift work as a Philadelphia fireman enabled him to work another full-time job as a maintenance man in Fairmount Park and left enough time to work an additional part-time job cleaning houses for rich people in Delaware County. Although Martin Senior worked several jobs, he always seemed to be available for his family.

Martin Senior was an optimistic man for the most part. He had a pleasant disposition and a genuine zestful joy for life. He enjoyed playing baseball with his sons and his one tomboy daughter, Cassie. Martin cheerfully took his more refined and spiritual daughter, Kathleen, to father-daughter dances and trips to various shrines in Philadelphia—Bishop Neumann, of course, but there was also the Mother Drexel shine on the northern outskirts of Philadelphia in Bensalem. The common opinion among those in the know was that Mother Katherine Drexel was another budding saint that graced the City of Brotherly Love—one a male saint and the other a female saint. Not many American cities could make that claim. There was no official confirmation, but all the signs of potential miracles pointed to a canonized duo for Philadelphia.

Martin Senior enjoyed roughhousing with his younger kids: getting down on his knees on the living room floor and having his sons jump all over him and ride him like a horse.

Martin Senior regretted he could not play with his youngsters more often since his shift work at the firehouse forced him to work several nights, and his other full-time job as a Fairmount Park janitor took up a lot of his other free time, but Martin made the best of the situation. The family was large enough that they could always play among themselves. In addition, the block they lived on was chock-full of kids that his sons and daughters could spend time with. The postwar baby boom generation was still very fertile and noticeable in this quiet corner of South Philadelphia.

But there was one melancholy problem that worried Martin incessantly and caused his irrepressible Celtic enthusiasm to border on despair.

His third (or second, depending on how one took into account the twins) oldest daughter, Marie, was a Down syndrome child. It broke his heart when he thought of her future.

Who will take care of her when Veronica and I are gone? he would often think. Marie did have several brothers and sisters that could help, but soon they would forge ahead with their own lives and families. Their potential future help was comforting but still a major worry.

Marie was a happy, easy-to-please child. Her pleasantness was heartwarming, but how was she going to support herself in the future? Martin's two oldest daughters, the twins, Cassie and Kate, had good motherly instincts, but a lot depended on whom they would marry. Would their husbands be so open to add a mentally handicapped woman to their own family circle? It would not be fair to jeopardize their future marital prospects, so Martin was more and more inclined to lay the responsibility for Marie's future welfare upon his oldest son, Martin Junior.

"Marty, you know someone will always need to take care of little Marie. Your mom and I won't always be around. Your older sisters will want to take care of her, and that's only natural, but if Kathleen becomes a nun and Cassie marries, you never know where they might wind up or know what part of the country they will live in. It all depends on whom they would marry and their job opportunities. No guarantee they will stay put here. I know South Philadelphia seems to be the center of the universe. Certainly, it is the center of our world, but I want you to pay special attention to Marie. You're the oldest boy, so that gives you a lot of responsibility. Life is not always fair, but that is your cross. You need to bear that burden, but it is a light burden as our Lord said in one of the Gospels. Marie will always need a protector, and you need to make sure she's taken care of, Marty."

Marty Junior was impressed that his dad thought enough of him to confide some of his deepest fears. Marty Junior solemnly accepted his father's charge and wish.

"Don't worry, Dad. We will always be on the lookout for Marie's welfare. You can count on us to always have someone to care for her."

Marty Junior felt some pride that his father confided in him. He was determined not to let his dad down.

Martin Senior tried to lighten the mood. "Well, the Phillies are on TV tonight. Bunning is pitching, so we should have a good shot at winning. We will order some tomato pie from Pizza Shack down the corner and enjoy the game."

"Sounds good, Dad."

Marty Junior always enjoyed when Bunning pitched. He rarely got bombed and always kept the Phillies close. Marty would have been a little more confident with the Phillies' chances that night, except for one thing. The Cardinals also had an intimidating pitcher hurling tonight—the great Bob Gibson.

Marty always enjoyed watching the game with his dad. It was a rare treat with his father often working night shifts at the firehouse.

Even when his dad worked at night and could not watch the game together, they could always talk about it later. They both believed it would create a special lifelong bond.

Marty had very special father-son memories two years ago when Wilt Chamberlain had his unbelievable statistical year of averaging fifty points per game during the 1961–1962 NBA season. His dad and older younger brothers, before the Philadelphia Warriors played a game that night, would each make predictions on how many points Wilt would score during the game.

For example, Marty would say on that particular night Wilt will score fifty-six. Mark said fifty-one. Tim predicted fifty-four, and their dad would sometimes say, "I think he is going to have an off night tonight and will only score forty-three points." This give-and-take added some special interest to the upcoming game.

One of Marty's biggest thrills in sports happened during that 1962 basketball season. Marty and his older younger brothers, Mark and Tim, actually listened to the historic game when Chamberlain scored one hundred points. Many years later, many fans claimed they witnessed the event in person. One quick way to determine if they actually did see it live was to ask them one simple question: where did the game take place? If the fan answered Philadelphia, you knew they were either lying or sadly mistaken.

The Philadelphia Warrior-New York Knickerbocker game was not held in Philadelphia's Convention Hall but actually took place in Hershey, Pennsylvania, in a small arena that only housed four thousand spectators.

Marty made no such claims, but he did listen to every minute of Bill Campbell's exciting radio broadcast. Marty and Mark knew something special was going to take place when Chamberlain scored eighteen points in the first quarter. At the time, the record for most points in an NBA game was held by Chamberlain himself who scored seventy-eight points, breaking Elgin Baylor's previous mark of seventy-one points. If Wilt kept that pace up with eighteen points per quarter, he will come very close to establishing a new single-game scoring record. A quick calculation of four quarters scoring eighteen points would make seventy-two points, so Marty and Mark and Tim were especially interested in what might happen that night.

The Warriors built up a good lead, so it seemed like a sure victory. Another good omen that it was going to be a special game was the astonishing fact that Wilt Chamberlain was actually making a lot of free throws. Foul shooting, for some reason, was Wilt's Achilles' heel. He was a great athlete. In addition to his impressive basketball skills, Wilt excelled at track and field in college and possessed prodigious strength. There was even some talk that Chamberlain would take on the heavyweight champion of the world, Cassius Clay, later known as Mohammed Ali, in a boxing match. Wilt had a nice touch shooting from the outside in his early career, and, in fact, he didn't invent his patented dipper dunk until a few years ago. Despite all his great gifts and amazing skills—his remarkable rebounding and shot blocking—Wilt had trouble making a simple foul shot.

But not on this night, March 4, 1962! Chamberlain was on fire, and during the second period, Wilt scored even more points, twenty-three, which gave him forty-one points at halftime, and was well on pace to break the single-game scoring record.

Marty and his brothers did not want to miss a minute, and Wilt outdid himself in the third quarter with twenty-eight points! Now he had sixty-nine points. There was a whispered caution in Bill Campbell's voice—could Wilt actually score one hundred points?

"Too bad Dad is at the firehouse. He would really like to hear this game," said Mark.

"Yeah, that would have been nice," said Tim. "But as long as there are no homes on fire tonight, Dad is probably listening to the game at the firehouse."

That thought was comforting to the three brothers. They were enthralled by the electric play-by-play over the radio by Bill Campbell whose stirring and smooth delivery of the action put a listener directly at center court. Early in the fourth and final quarter, Wilt easily broke the old mark of seventy-eight points in a single game. Now the real suspense was how close he was going to get to the mythical century mark.

One of Chamberlain's teammates, two-time NBA scoring champ and former Marine Paul Arizin, noted for his patented line drive jump shot, which was developed in the cramped low ceilings of inner city CYO courts, once scored eighty-five points in a college game when he played for Villanova. Another college player, Frank Selvy, once scored one hundred points for Furman in an NCAA game, but no pro basketball player ever scored one hundred, so the excitement was building to a high level.

The opposing team, the New York Knicks, knew what was at stake and had no intention of letting Chamberlain reach the century mark. It was a matter of pride. So they fouled other players to prevent Wilt from getting the ball, and when guards, Guy Rogers or Al Attles, did manage to get the ball into Chamberlain's hands, the Knicks, well aware of Wilt's poor foul shooting, flagrantly committed foul upon foul on the Warrior center.

But this tactic did not work. Wilt was almost perfect that night making his shots at the foul line. He sank twenty-eight out of thirty-four, a remarkable percentage even for a gifted foul shooter. There was no defense in the game. The Knicks, led by Rich Guerin, were also piling up point after point, but they were still twenty points behind.

Finally, after a tense few minutes, Chamberlain netted a patented dipper dunk with less than a minute left and reached the historic figure.

Mark and Tim let out a big cheer. Marty gave a nod of his head in what he thought was ecstatic jubilation. Marty did not want to get too excited about things outwardly, but inside he was on cloud nine.

"I can't wait to read about this in the *Bulletin*, the *Inquirer*, and the *Daily News*," said Tim as he mentioned all three of Philadelphia's daily newspapers. All three brothers once again wished their dad could share in the historic excitement.

"Well, we can talk about it tomorrow morning when Dad gets back from the firehouse and before we go to school," said Mark.

That was a pleasant memory from the 1961–1962 Philadelphia Warrior NBA basketball season. It ended in heartbreak in the decisive seventh game of the conference championship when Sam Jones hit a bank shot in the final seconds to allow the Boston Celtics to once again advance to the NBA finals against the LA Lakers.

Mark cried uncontrollably. His dad tried to comfort him, but he was also a realist. "Get used to it, Mark. As a Philadelphia sports fan, prepare to have your heart broken and your guts torn out. Our town's teams rarely win anything."

The three older brothers put that sad memory deep in the recesses of their memory bank. The year 1964 was shaping up as a magical year with the Phils still miraculously in first place. They all looked forward to the baseball game in St. Louis tonight. Their dad was not at the firehouse, so that made the night even more special.

Chapter 9

The Greatest Food Ever Invented

Mom's homemade pizza- good to the last bite.

S ince it was Friday night and no meat was allowed in those pre-Vatican II days, Veronica finally threw in the towel and adjusted her Friday summer routine into reality. She used to make fish cakes on Friday since it was a day of abstinence for Catholics, but she got tired of all the complaints from her children.

"Ugh . . . not fish cakes again, Mom. I can't stand the smell!" This seemed to be the universal sentiment from the entire family. Even Marty Junior who rarely complained couldn't stand the bland non-taste and repulsive smell of fish cakes.

"What is the younger generation coming to? What else can we eat on Friday? They all know we cannot have meat," she often complained to her husband. "We can only eat so many grilled cheese sandwiches."

Like his wife, Martin Senior was used to fish cakes. Their respective families stoically suffered the unappetizing non-delights of fish cake. What choice did the family have? They tried to be good Catholics, and meat was verboten as her dad, Adolph, always said with sad resignation. Grandpa was also a proud carnivore.

Veronica and Martin were resigned to the meatless Friday routine and expected their children to also suck it up.

"Offer it up to God," said Veronica, "and get some poor souls out of purgatory. Make your suffering and complaining count for something. There is nothing worse than useless suffering. Do you realize how many suffering poor souls I have helped with my arthritic hands and poor feet?"

Veronica had more bunions on her feet than a bus full of tourists in Center City Philadelphia. It caused her great pain, but she bravely offered up the pain for purgatory's suffering souls.

The McAlynn household did not look forward to Friday's supper or lunch, and this almost ruined the other glory of Friday during the fall and winter months—no school the next day! The bland tasteless fish cakes dampened what should have been a joyous day. But one day, Mark came up with an idea that made up for all his mischief and sarcastic barbs.

"Why don't we just have pizza every Friday? Everyone in the whole world loves pizza, or at least everyone in their right mind!"

Sometimes a simple suggestion can change the world. Mark's idea was like Alexander the Great cutting the Gordian knot.

What a great idea, thought Martin Senior who always enjoyed a nice piping hot slice of tomato pie. It was something he looked forward to but only indulged in rarely. The more he thought about it, Mark's simple but grand idea had tremendous merit.

So after Mark's suggestion, the McAlynn family made each and every Friday night pizza night and restored Friday to its rightful place as the greatest day in the week.

When the Phillies-Cardinals game started, there was still another forty-five minutes of daylight left, so the younger boys were still playing outside on the block with their neighborhood friends. The older boys, Mark, Tim, and Marty Junior, were already inside and all set to watch the game. Grandpa was sitting in his favorite chair. This was also Martin Senior's favorite, but he ceded the most comfortable chair in the house to his honorable father-in-law.

He really didn't mind making the small sacrifice. He figured Adolph had paid his dues in life with his hard work at the factory and taking care of an invalid wife. Grandpa Adolph was an octogenarian now, and he deserved what few creature comforts the row house offered.

The game was a pitchers' duel as expected with Jim Bunning and Bob Gibson squaring off against each other. Ken Boyer hit a two-run double in the fourth inning. Richie Allen, the Phils' powerful rookie, smashed a long two-run homer in the fifth. The score remained 2–2 until the bottom of the eighth. As usual, Bunning pitched late into the game, but with one out in the bottom of the eighth inning, Bunning gave up a cheap infield hit, and the next batter bunted the runner over to second. Bunning struck out the next hitter, so there were two outs and a runner in scoring position. Things still looked good for the Phillies pitcher to get out of the little jam, but the Cards catcher, Tim McCarver, was up next.

Marty Junior was a little worried.

"McCarver is dangerous. He always seemed to get the clutch hit when his team needs it."

"He is only the number eight hitter. Bunning should get him out with no problem," said Mark.

"I don't know. McCarver always comes through with a hit when the Cards really need it."

"He is only batting about .260. He can't be that great," continued Mark, who was not unusually so optimistic.

McCarver worked the count to three and two and then fouled off five pitches in a row. He was really making Bunning work hard to get the final out.

Bunning's next pitch was a low strike, but the resourceful McCarver golfed a ground ball that bounced over the shortstop Bobby Wine's head into left-center field for a run-scoring single. The Cards took the lead, 3–2, and held on for the hard-fought win.

"I don't know why it is like that," said Marty. "But McCarver must hit .400 against the Phillies."

"What a shame. Bunning pitched so well. He's such a hard-luck pitcher," said Martin, Sr. "He should easily win twenty-five games this year, but as things stand now, Bunning will be lucky to win twenty. I have never seen a pitcher hurl so well and still not get the win. Even Robin Roberts was not that unlucky."

Even with the loss to the Cards, the Phils still had a decent lead over St. Louis in the pennant race. The Cardinals, despite a slow start, were still one of the Phillies' biggest potential rivals in the National League with their solid starting pitching of Bob Gibson, Curt Simmons, and Ray Sadecki, all potential twenty game winners, and all-star hitters like Ken Boyer, Bill White, Lou Brock, and Curt Flood.

Chapter 10

The Wolfman Cometh

The Mask of the Wolfman.

Marty was planning on filming a key scene in the movie when his brother Mark's character, Larry Talbot, changes into a werewolf. Marty had an inspirational idea and told his brothers, Mark and Ted, to go to the local barbershop to sweep up the already cut hair from the floor and collect it all. The hair would be used to paste on Mark's face as he transformed into the Wolfman.

Tony, the barber, was incredulous but grateful when Tim and Ted offered to sweep up all the hair from the floor of his barbershop. He offered to pay the boys for their work, but they chivalrously declined. Tony was an immigrant from Sicily and said in broken English, "You are such nice boys . . . many say the world is going to the dogs, but you kids show there's still a lot of good . . . you boys are living proof . . . thank you very, very much . . ."

Mark thanked him for his kind words and distracted Tony, while Tim and Ted placed the swept-up hair into a brown Acme paper shopping bag. The boys really didn't think Tony would mind taking the hair, but why take chances? The barber might have thought it a bit strange. Mark did not want to give a weird impression to Tony, especially after he praised them to the high heavens.

Mark brought the Acme paper bag back to Marty Junior who opened it and congratulated Mark and Ted and Tim on a job well done. Marty looked inside. Most of the hair was black and brown, but there were a few tufts of gray. All mixed together, Marty believed it would create a terrific Jack Pierce/Lon Chaney, Jr. scary-looking Wolfman.

"That's one hurdle down . . . now we have to figure out how to get the hair to stick to your face," said Marty.

"We can ask Mom," said Mark.

Marty didn't really want to do that. His instincts told him that their mother would not approve of sticking other people's hair on her son's face. She might think it a little too dirty. Marty didn't want to take the risk that their mom would get upset, so Marty thought it over and figured Elmer's glue would work. It was not that sticky, and the smell was not too bad. Marty did not think using model glue would be a good idea because its adhesiveness was too strong, and it had a cold nasty smell. Marty also recalled that adults claimed never to sniff this type of glue because its fumes could destroy your brain. Marty thought this was a precaution well worth taking.

"We do not have to tell Mom about this. We will not need to have Mom film the scene. I can do it since the Frankenstein monster is not in this particular shot. This will be our little secret."

Marty was really looking forward to this moment. He had it all figured out. Mark would see the full moon and start to get a pained expression on his face like he just ate some liver and onions. Marty would stop filming and then put some Elmer's glue on Mark's cheeks, chin, and forehead and then add some hair. Marty would resume filming, and Mark would make some more painful expressions. Marty would stop the camera and add more hair. Marty also put some black makeup on Mark's nose to add some fierceness to his boyish face. He would do this a few times, and the result would be movie magic. The final scene would show Mark being transformed from a pasty-faced boy into a raging and terrifying werewolf. At least, that's what Marty envisioned and hoped how it would look on film.

The big transformation scene took place in the dark and dank cellar of their row home. The bare solitary lightbulb would stand in for the moon. Marty cut out a cardboard circle and put it close to the lightbulb and hoped on film the effect would kind of look like a full moon.

At last, all the props were in place, and they were ready to film. Mark pretended to look at the full moon and sank to his knees, writhing in great pain. Marty filmed this as a medium shot, taking in Mark's whole body.

Marty stopped filming and put the Kodak movie camera very close to Mark's face and resumed filming with the close-up. Mark gave a pained sneer. The filming stopped, and Tim and Marty put some more glue on Mark's face and added some clumps of hair to Mark's cheeks. Marty stopped operating the camera and added more hair to Mark's face. This process was completed three or four times until Mark had a face full of hair. Marty had Mark put on fangs to complete the man to werewolf transformation.

The final effect looked really good. Marty got a nice close-up of Mark as a hairy, ferocious-looking Wolfman. Good thing he got that great shot because in a few seconds, some of the hair started falling off of Mark's face and landing on the cellar floor.

"Quick," said Marty, "give a growl and turn around. The hair is starting to fall off."

On cue, Mark curled his lips and wisely put his hairy gloved hands up to his face to shield the disintegrating pasted-on hair and turned around with his back to the camera and, in his best Lon Chaney, Jr. manner, hunched over and swayed his arms and loped into the darkness of the back basement.

Marty filmed Mark fleeing into the blackness and stopped the camera. Mark came out of the rear of the cellar, and even more hair had fallen off. He looked like a poorly shaven hobo. Worse yet, his face started itching and turned a bright apple red. The glue was really bothering him.

That was all the filming they could do today. Marty had planned for the werewolf to attack one of the little brothers, but without much hair, the werewolf would look ridiculous.

Mark was itching like crazy, and Marty tried to wipe away as much glue and scarce remaining hair as possible. But the glue was still sticking stubbornly to Mark's face. As much as Marty hated to, he soon realized that they had to tell their mother. Marty hoped to keep his idea about using glue and old barber-cut hair away from his mom, but Mark was turning a bright blotchy red and needed expert help. Only a mom knew how to get glue off of a thirteen-year-old's face.

Needless to say, when Veronica found out, she was not too happy.

"You did what!" she yelled. "Don't tell me you used dirty hair from a barbershop floor. What were you thinking? Marty, I thought you had more sense than that!"

It was a rare tongue-lashing from his mom. Marty usually avoided getting into trouble, but he was in hot water now. Marty figured he deserved it.

Veronica was able, with much effort, to get the Elmer's glue off of Mark's face, but it was still red and blotchy. Mark must have been allergic to the glue.

In future filming, Marty had to figure out how to make Mark look like a werewolf without resorting to glue and human hair. He thought it over, and much as he disliked the thought, Marty realized he needed to dig into his pocket and raise the budget of the movie by purchasing a Wolfman mask.

Marty had about $30 still saved over from Christmas when his aunts and uncles gave him money instead of a gift. They realized he was too old for toys. There was some concern his relatives might buy him some clothes for Christmas, but thankfully that did not happen. Marty would now put that money to good use.

Marty looked in the back of his latest issue of *Famous Monsters of Filmland* and saw a decent werewolf mask that included genuine black hair attached to the rubber face. He immediately sent the money in the mail for the now indispensable mask. This would further delay the filming, but what choice did he have? As the writer, director, and producer of the movie, he had awesome responsibilities. At least, they did get the werewolf transformation scene on film before Mark's face broke out and most of the hair fell off.

The summer of '64 was not all caught up with the Phillies' surprising play. The British invasion, with the Beatles leading the way, still created quite a stir. There were many other music groups other than the Fab Four that made an impact from across the pond—the Dave Clark 5, Herman's Hermits, Chad and Jeremy, and of course, the Rolling Stones. It seemed all the top ten hits were from the British rock groups. However, the US musicians were still a potent force on the airwaves with the Supremes, the Four Seasons, and the Beach Boys.

Marty liked the Beatles; after all, what young person didn't? But he was glad when the Four Seasons finally broke the Beatles' grip on number one hits with their smash single, "Dawn." The Four Seasons were one of Marty's favorite groups, next to the Beatles, of course. Plus, it was nice that they were Americans. As entertaining and melodious as the British invasion's influence was, it was encouraging to see an American band break through. There were actually a lot of good American groups singing at this time. Motown was especially huge with the Temptations, Martha and the Vandellas, and the Four

Tops, but solo artists like Roy Orbison, Mary Welles, and the versatile Dean Martin were also chart-toppers, but it certainly seemed the British flood had completely inundated the airwaves.

The Beatles had quite an impact on his older sisters. It appeared teenage girls formed into Beatle teams based on their favorite Beatle. Paul was the "cute" Beatle, and he was Cassie's favorite since she was always so visual. Marie—bless her soul—liked Ringo the most. Somebody had to. Kathleen preferred George, the "quiet" Beatle, because she liked his pensiveness, believing it denoted a hidden spiritual quality. John was considered the "intellectual" Beatle, but his braininess held no attraction for the McAlynn girls.

Marty, Mark, and Ted didn't have any favorites. They just liked to listen to the music as a whole. Even their mom, Veronica, liked their music. She didn't like their physical appearance with the shaggy hair, but they sure dressed right in their neat tailored suits. Veronica was initially turned off by the Beatles but softened a bit when she was told by Kathleen that two of the Beatles, Paul and George, were baptized Catholics. Martin Senior was a little mystified by the Beatle's popularity. He still preferred Bing Crosby over Frank Sinatra and maintained a lingering strong streak of sentimentality when he remembered Der Bingle singing "White Christmas" during World War II when he was serving on a Navy destroyer during the Battle of the North Atlantic. The Irving Berlin song still brought a misty tear to his eyes whenever he heard it played during the Christmas season.

Martin Senior's anti-Beatle resolve started to crack a little when he read somewhere at the firehouse that all the Beatles were actually of Irish extraction. The more he dwelled on their names—Sharkey, Lennon, McCartney, Harrison—the more it seemed plausible. Being something of an Irish chauvinist, Martin started nursing a little warm spot in his heart for his fellow descendants from the Emerald Isle.

Although Marty Junior liked the Beatles music, he couldn't stand the teenage girls' reaction in the audience when the Beatles played. Their screaming, crying, and jumping up and down were very annoying. He could not picture his older sisters doing that. Maybe Marie, who was a happy-go-lucky person to begin with.

Cassie seemed too no-nonsense and serious, and of course, Kathleen was too dignified and reverent. Based on his three older sisters, he could never understand why so many teenage girls lost their composure while listening to four British musicians sing.

Chapter 11

A Pacifist Defends His Role(s)

Marty Junior always considered himself to be very peaceful. He avoided fights by ignoring any potential conflicts by looking the other way and took Jesus's admonition to turn the other cheek very seriously. He rarely, if ever, got into a fight with his younger brothers, who were always wrestling or slapping each other playfully around. As the oldest son, Marty thought he should set a good example. Besides, he was bigger than they were at the time and didn't think it fair to start pummeling the little guys just because they might start to irritate him.

Marty tried his best to avoid any fights with kids from the neighborhood. He minded his own business and looked the other way or ignored any insults that a kid might yell at him in an attempt to instigate a quarrel.

Marty desperately hoped to avoid the Army and prayed he had flat feet so he would not need to get drafted. Marty never liked war movies and only sat through a military movie when it was the first half of a double feature, and thus had no real choice.

Marty's budding self-imposed pacifism and fight avoidance were severely tested one afternoon when he went to the bakery to buy some rolls for his mom. Marty picked up a dozen and a half fresh soft rolls from Cacia's, the Italian bakery located a block and a half from his family's home. The delicious smell of hot, right-out-of-the-oven rolls was intoxicating. Marty took another deep breath of the savory fragrance before leaving the store.

Marty only took four steps outside before he was violently pushed to the concrete pavement. Luckily, he previously folded the top of the paper shopping bag, so no rolls spilled out onto the ground, even though he dropped the bag when he fell.

Marty stood up and tried to ignore the kid who pushed him, figuring if he did not make eye contact, the ugly situation could diffuse. Marty could pretend it was an accident, just an overly rambunctious kid who accidentally bumped into Marty as he came out of the bakery.

Marty's strategy did not work when he went to pick up the bag of rolls. The overly aggressive kid came up to Marty with a broken coke bottle that was jagged and menacing and pointed right at Marty's face.

Marty couldn't avoid the aggressor. He immediately recognized the kid as the neighborhood psycho, Sammy Bongiovanni, aka Sammy the Demon or Sammy Igor. His nickname said it all. Sammy was a real troublemaker, constantly creating mischief within a six-block radius: ringing doorbells at midnight, pulling little girl's ponytails, knocking down trash cans, and generally inciting fights with other kids who just wanted to mind their own business.

Marty managed to avoid him for the most part. Sammy went to the local public school, so Marty and his siblings had very little contact with him. When Marty walked around the neighborhood, he discreetly went out of his way to avoid Sammy. Marty would spot Sammy two blocks away and would either cross to the other side or walk completely around the corner, anything to steer clear of Sammy the Demon and his posse of "wannabe" bad kids.

Marty stared at the broken glass. His mind and hand coordination must have somehow melded into a smooth functioning machine. When Sammy thrust the bottle at Marty's face, he luckily was able to grab Sammy by the wrist and deflect the blow. Much to Marty's surprise, his grip was concrete hard and prevented Sammy from lifting his arm again. Marty was able to just use one hand to keep Sammy from trying to cut him. He still had the bag of rolls in his right hand. Fortunately, Marty was using his stronger arm, his left, and was able to push Sammy against the brick steps of the house next to the bakery.

Marty held on for dear life and somehow was able to keep Sammy pinned against the steps with just his left hand. He kept Sammy at bay for what seemed like several minutes. Marty's arm started to ache, but he kept pushing, and Sammy was powerless to escape.

Maybe the fact that he refused to drop the bag of rolls again and looked forward to its soft chewy freshness when he got home kept Marty supremely focused. Sammy grimaced and tried to push his way out of Marty's grip, but he failed to dislodge it. Marty did not know how much longer he could hold on, but he was deathly afraid to let go of Sammy's arm.

"Hey! What's going on here?" yelled a grown-up man passing by.

Thank the Lord, thought Marty. An adult was intervening. Salvation was at hand!

"Let's break this up. Right now!"

Marty did not want to loosen his grip yet. He still did not want to get cut, not after fighting off Sammy for so long.

The adult came closer, and Sammy dropped the bottle to the ground. Marty eased up, and Sammy shook off the grip and ran away north up Hicks Street toward Snyder Avenue.

Marty felt great relief. He still was carrying the bag of roles. The adult, a graying, middle-aged Italian-looking gentleman, quickly sized up the fight and knew who was at fault. He asked Marty if he was okay, and Marty shook his head up and down since he couldn't say any words at first. His close call had not worn off yet, and Marty could not formulate any words in response.

Marty took a deep breath and was finally able to say something. "Thanks," he told his unwitting savior and walked back home. The rolls still felt hot inside the bag. They would taste especially good as he sat at the kitchen table.

Marty was still shaking off the shock he felt after the broken bottle attack by Sammy. Why in the world would Sammy want to pick on Marty? He was completely mystified. Marty never made fun of Sammy's intensity. He did not run in the same circle and had very little peripheral contact. None of his brothers or sisters did either.

Marty always minded his own business with close friends and his family. His mom was constantly telling Marty that he was too quiet. "What's on your mind, Marty? Keep me in the loop, please," she would often say.

In point of fact, there was not a whole lot going on inside Marty's mind. He was a good student, but it was more because of his sense of duty, treating school like going to work and doing your job. His brothers, Mark and Tim, thought he was a brain, but Marty was not a natural student who could breeze through school without much effort. He just did his homework and studied hard. There were no deep dark secrets with Marty. What was on his mind nowadays were two things primarily: following the Phillies' magical season and making and completing his Frankenstein battles the Wolfman movie.

Marty was pretty much a clear person. He was as transparent as a pane of glass. It just so happened that his two current obsessions— the Phillies and his monster movie—were going along smoothly. Things couldn't be any better, which is why Sammy's assault was so disturbing. The attack came out of nowhere and was completely undeserved. Marty had a well-honed Irish Catholic conscience, so when things went bad, he felt he did something wrong. Marty wracked his brain to see if he did, indeed, deserve some ill fortune. He really couldn't figure it out. He never gave his mom any trouble. He was not a "wisenheimer" as his grandfather would say and got right up in the morning during the school year, and even made his own bed. It might not have been Marine Corps precise, but for a freshly minted teenager, Marty thought he was saving his mom some work.

Sad to say, this was the only chore he did to help out his mom around the house. Wasn't that what big sisters were for? At least, Marty was not a troublemaker like Mark, who could be a royal pain to his mom.

Thinking about Mark, Marty started to believe the whole Elmer's glue and barbershop hair incident that he used to turn Mark into a Wolfman was his transgression against God's law.

Mark was breaking out pretty badly with unsightly red blotches and pimples. In addition, Marty misled his mom about it. *That was probably it*, he thought. *Well, lesson learned.*

Marty resolved to be more honest and forthright in his future dealings with everyone, especially his mom. He might even tell her a few things about what was going on his mind. Mothers seem to like that sort of thing.

The shock of the crazy fight was beginning to wear off. Marty's initial annoyance and guilt was giving way to a strange growing sense of pride. Marty may not have won the brief scuffle, but he did not lose it either. It was like the Korean War that he just learned about in school. In fact, the more he thought about the fight, the more Marty started changing his opinion. In many ways, he actually won the fight. After all, Sammy did not cut him with the broken bottle. Marty held the crazy kid at bay. Sammy had the initial advantage and surprise on his side, and still Marty prevented Sammy from hurting him. All in all, Marty did pretty well. He felt really good about it upon further reflection. Marty finally stood up to a bully!

Being a budding pacifist, Marty avoided neighborhood fights. He might not have been a ninety-eight-pound weakling, but Marty was not a Muscle McGurk type either like his cousin, Ray, who looked like Steve Reeves as Hercules-solid muscle built upon more muscle.

Marty never had much confidence he could win any fight. He had only two brief skirmishes in the past. One time, a kid from school jumped Marty from behind and pinned his arms. Marty was carrying a brown paper bag filled with groceries. Marty recognized the kid from the neighborhood and was surprised and perplexed when the boy asked for some change. Marty's stunned reaction of disbelief must have given the kid some second thoughts. The kid mumbled something and let Marty go and then ran away. It could have turned into a case of "All's well that ends well," except that there were a dozen eggs that broke when Marty dropped the shopping bag. It created a terrible mess when it mixed in with the lunch meat and bread that were also inside the brown paper bag.

Marty was honest when he returned home and explained that some kid jumped him.

"Are you okay?" said his mom in a worried and concerned tone.

"Yeah, he didn't hit me or anything, so I'm not hurt in any way. Sorry about the eggs, Mom."

"That's fine, Marty. We can always buy more eggs. It's more important that you are okay."

When his dad heard about the incident, Martin Senior started to give Marty some boxing lessons and introduced Marty to some self-defense techniques.

"Marty, it is always good to be able to defend yourself. Like the Duke, John Wayne, does in his movies. Don't pick a fight, but be ready to fight back and win so you don't get bothered again. I've always found that bullies are basically cowards. If you stand up to them, the bully will back down like a scared dog. Initially, you just have to have the guts to confront the bully, which is not always as easy as it sounds, but it needs to be done!"

Marty took a slight interest in self-defense skills. He saw their utility and initially really wanted to learn them, but his heart just wasn't into it. He had no interest in fighting and avoided any inklings of a conflict.

Maybe Marty was lucky. Considering his many daily wanderings throughout his South Philadelphia neighborhood, he was rarely the object of any ridicule. The only other time Marty was ever bothered was when Marty and his friend, Jimmy Mac, were enjoying a walk along Passyunk Avenue during a late March surprise snowstorm. The freshly falling snow blanketed the grimy streets of South Philadelphia with a pristine, charming mantle of white, which covered the gritty streets and narrow sidewalks with a forest fresh coating that seemed to magically clean up the neighborhood.

Marty and Jimmy were relishing their late winter stroll near the Bowling Alley shopping complex on Passyunk Avenue when five aggressive teens emerged out of a secluded alley and ambushed them. They pushed Marty and Jimmy to the ground. Fortunately, the two-inch snowfall cushioned their fall, and they slid on the street a few feet. Marty always remembered the long skid mark their bodies made across the white road.

The attacking kids just basically chased Marty and Jimmy out of the neighborhood. It never escalated to more than just a one-sided shoving match.

Marty and Jimmy did nothing to retaliate but slithered away with their tails between their legs, figuratively speaking. It was humiliating, but Marty was not cut or injured, so they figured it could have been much worse.

So the more Marty thought about his battle with Sammy, the more he actually felt better about the result. Marty did not run away. He stood up and held his ground and, in many ways, triumphed over the neighborhood wacko. Of course, Marty was not going to become overconfident. Marty did keep his eyes peeled for any signs of Sammy whenever he walked around the area. He dearly hoped his dad was right about standing up to bullies!

JULY

National League Standings July 1964

TEAM	WON	LOST	WON-LOST%	GAMES BACK
SAN FRANCISCO	45	28	.616	-----
PHILADELPHIA	43	27	.614	0.5
PITTSBURGH	38	32	.543	5.5
CINCINNATI	38	34	.528	6.5
CHICAGO	35	34	.507	8.0
MILWAUKEE	36	37	.493	9.0
ST. LOUIS	36	38	.486	9.5
LOS ANGELES	34	38	.472	10.5
HOUSTON	35	40	.467	11.0
NEW YORK	22	54	.289	24.5

Chapter 12

Waiting for the Wolfman

Practicing for the big fight scene.

Since Mark could not be filmed as the Wolfman until his face cleared up and the new full face Werewolf mask arrived in the mail, Marty had to regretfully delay the movie for a short while. In order to take advantage of the slight delay, Marty and Mark decided to more fully rehearse the most exciting part of the movie—the climactic battle between the Frankenstein monster and the Wolfman.

Marty believed the final battle between the two monsters was great in the original movie. The Frankenstein monster and the Wolfman both furiously threw each other against laboratory machines and tossed chairs and operating tables at each other. There was one spectacular scene when the Frankenstein monster grabbed a lab console that the Wolfman was perched upon, ready to pounce, and the man-made monster effortlessly flung it aside. The Wolfman crashed to the floor, along with the machine. It was a stunt that amazed Marty, and he wondered how the moviemakers could pull the shot off without harming the actors involved. Marty's fondest dream was to outdo that spectacular scene.

In order to get ready for the climactic battle, Marty and Mark practiced for the fight scene in the kitchen. They choreographed different stages of the big battle. The two brothers only went half speed so as not to hurt each other, but their actions caused the kitchen chairs to crash against the stove and refrigerator. The kitchen was a little cramped, so Marty and Mark could not let their vivid imaginations run wild.

Veronica probably would have complained about all the rattling of kitchen furniture, but Saturday was Mom's night out with either her husband (as long as he was not working his shift at the firehouse) or her dad. Her sister, Ann (who also lived in South Philadelphia unlike their nine other siblings), and Veronica would sometimes take their father out for the evening to a restaurant. The tough part was getting someone to drive the two sisters, who had no driver's license between them, to travel the twelve miles from South Philadelphia to Rising Sun Avenue in Lawncrest for the numerous German restaurants in the area.

South Philadelphia had plenty of Italian eateries but very few German restaurants. The problem was solved when their brother,

Tom, offered to make the drive to pick up his two sisters and their dad, Adolph, so they could enjoy some sauerbraten and Paprika schnitzel. Tom worked as a PTC/SEPTA bus driver, so he drove all over the city and didn't mind helping out his family. This only happened once or twice a month.

"That is what families do," Uncle Tom would always tell Marty when he came in the front door to pick up his dad and two sisters. "We should always be there for each other no matter how inconvenient." Uncle Tom also got a free meal out of the deal, as Adolph picked up the tab. Uncle Tom married an Italian girl from the Burholme section of Northeast Philadelphia, so as great a cook as she was in her own Tuscany specialties, she never mastered the satisfying stomach stuffing joys of German meals.

Once their mom was out the door, Marty and Mark began their rehearsal. The only other potential hurdle they had to overcome was Cassie if she stayed in for the night. She would not tolerate all the commotion and banging of chairs and tables in the kitchen. Luckily, Cassie usually was out with some friends or was doing some babysitting for some extra cash.

Marty and Mark practiced several grappling moves. The Frankenstein monster would use his best killing technique—strangulation—and try to grab the Wolfman's throat. Mark as the Werewolf would use his superior speed to deflect the monster's deadly grasp. They practiced these moves a few times to make it smooth and exciting.

Another well-rehearsed move was to have the Wolfman jump on the monster's back from the table. Frankenstein would then flip the Werewolf off onto the floor. Marty and Mark rehearsed this risky move a few times to get it just right. Most times it went off without a hitch until one particular Saturday night in early July.

Marty was too enthusiastic and tossed Mark a little too far off his back, and Mark bounced off the kitchen table and knocked a couple of glass cups off that fell to the floor and shattered into pieces on the floor. As Marty saw the glass smash on the floor, he instantly realized too late that they should have cleared the table before the rehearsal.

Bad move! What made this oversight even worse was that Mark also slid off the table and fell hard to the floor. Mark tried to break his fall, and his hand landed on top of some broken glass. Mark screamed in pain, and blood came spurting out in terrifying amounts. Marty and Mark looked at each other in stunned silence for a few seconds.

Mark was bleeding pretty badly. Marty did not know what to do.

Both of their parents were not at home, even their two older sisters were out. What Marty would not give to have Cassie home right now. They could use her overbearing but take-charge personality.

Mark recovered somewhat. He was not crying in pain but was really worried about all the blood. Marty still did not know what to do. He went over to Mark and started picking pieces of sparkling glass out of Mark's bloody hand. He also got one of the kitchen towels and told Mark to wrap the cloth around the cut hand. Maybe that will stem the bleeding, he desperately hoped.

The wound looked bad enough for Mark to need hospital attention. The Methodist Hospital was the closest, only a short drive, about three blocks, but there was no family car, or any eligible drivers.

Then Marty realized Grandpop was upstairs on the third floor. Surely he will be able to help. Marty ran past the middle room into the living room and went halfway up the stairs to the second floor and yelled out, "Grandpop, we need help! Mark cut his hand real bad!"

Grandpa Adolph answered quickly in a strong and reassuring voice, "Don't worry, boys. I will be right down!"

Adolph, despite his advanced years, was still in excellent shape and calmly but quickly came down the steep flight of steps.

He strolled into the kitchen, looked at Mark's cuts, and calmly said, "I have seen worse."

Adolph used his long ago training as a World War I medic and gently took Mark's hand over to the kitchen sink and washed off the blood and any remaining pieces of broken glass.

He told Marty to go into the bathroom and get iodine. Marty quickly retrieved the bottle from the cabinet and handed it to Grandpop.

"This will sting a little," he told Mark, "but you are a tough little guy."

Grandpop poured the red liquid over the wound. Mark winced slightly but did not cry out. Adolph got a fresh clean towel and wrapped it around Mark's hand.

"The key is to keep the cut clean and stop the bleeding, one of the four life-saving steps. Keep the towel wrapped tight. I'll check in another half an hour. You are very lucky no veins were cut. Otherwise, Mark, you would have been in very serious trouble."

Grandpa Adolph told Mark to sit down and keep pressure on his wrapped hand. He started to walk away but turned around and said to both of his grandsons, "No more pretend fights, okay?"

Marty and Mark both nodded affirmatively and vigorously, grateful that the old man was home on that particular Saturday night and not having dinner with three of his own children in the Northeast, as he sometimes did.

It all turned out fine, as Mark's cut hand stopped bleeding and looked so much better. There were no obvious scars, so they guessed that Grandpop was right again, as usual. It appeared to be a lucky fall—no lasting damage to Mark's hand. To top it off, there was no lingering sting or sharp pain. Marty and Mark were grateful they dodged a potentially bad bullet.

On a typical Saturday night during the summer, Adolph's normal routine, provided he was not eating out with his son and two daughters, would be to watch the Phillies on TV or listen on the radio if it was a home game.

The Phils were still in first place, and Grandpa Adolph was still in a pleasantly stunned state of disbelief.

"Something is out of whack with the universe. The Phillies are not due to win the pennant for another twenty-one years. Don't get me wrong, I am eternally grateful. It affords me one last chance to listen to a World Series game with my favorite team actually playing in it. Maybe they will actually win it all this time."

Marty said this was only fair after all the suffering years of last place teams Grandpa endured over the past several decades.

"Look at it this way, Grandpa. All your prayers for baseball success have finally paid off."

Grandpop Adolph would have none of that way of thinking.

"No . . . no . . . God doesn't care who wins a baseball game. Don't you think there are a lot of Cardinal, Reds, and Pirate fans praying for their teams? God has more important things to be concerned with, like having your Uncle Tom pick up a dinner tab every now and then . . ." He joked.

Grandpop then winked and said, "Of course, I have slipped in a lot of aspirations over the years in my daily prayers for a key Phillies hit or strikeout every now and then."

Marty smiled at Grandpa's jokes as always. Adolph often did that. It looked as if he was going to say something profoundly serious and then added something humorous to put a smile on your face.

Lately, Marty was a little apprehensive that Grandpa was not as enthused about the Phillies' unlikely success this season and seemed somewhat restrained. It gave Marty an uneasy feeling that Grandpa had an inkling of some future disaster. He had to respect his grandfather's judgment. The old gentleman had seen so much of life and overcome so much hardship—a refugee from Bismark's Kulturkampf, a bedridden and ailing wife, and one son killed in World War II. Despite these tragedies and heartache, Grandpa was always a positive person, pleasant and fun to be around with, not a gloomy old crank. This made it all the more disturbing about his recent worry about the pennant race.

But this pessimism soon disappeared when game time approached, and Grandpop Adolph resumed his sunnier disposition. It certainly helped that Chris Short was on the mound to start for the Phillies.

The potentially disastrous evening turned even better when Chris Short pitched a shutout gem for a solid Phillies win, beating the Pirates and their ace hurler, Bob Veale, 2–0, and left them comfortably on top of the National League.

Marty and Mark's evening became even better. the *Werewolf of London* was on TV that night scheduled at one in the morning. Henry Hull was not as good a werewolf as Lon Chaney, but Marty and Mark looked forward to the 1935 film to gain further insight into making a good werewolf movie.

There was one downside to the evening. Before they could enjoy the *Werewolf of London*, the two brothers had to sit through a cheesy, late 1950s junky horror movie. It was something they had to endure, like in the old days when they had to eat fish cakes on Friday. The best movie in the Double Chiller Theater program was usually the second feature. Marty was beginning to think the TV station did this on purpose to force monster movie fans to keep watching the channel because if the station showed the classic Universal movie first, every fan would then turn off the TV before watching the second, lousier movie. Marty was gaining insight into the power of television advertisements.

Both Marty and Mark were still wide awake when the *Werewolf of London* came on at one fifteen in the morning. They got a few good ideas from the film, especially the transformation scene. Instead of concentrating on the face, the director gradually changed the actor from man to wolf as the werewolf walked past a series of stone columns; each succeeding pillar brought a further change and made the werewolf hairier and less human. It was a great idea, and Marty resolved to do something similar. Already his creative wheels were churning. Marty believed Mark could walk from tree to tree in the woods and have a gradual change from man into the werewolf mask. This could avoid pasting on hair with glue, the previous recipe that proved a disaster. *Something to chew on*, thought Marty.

The movie ended at three. The next film was an old Boris Karloff movie, *The Devil Commands*, in which Boris played another sincere but mad scientist trying to communicate with his long dead wife. He was not evil, just misguided. This was one of his more sympathetic roles and required no makeup. Boris looked like a dignified, gray-haired gentleman. In many ways, his appearance reminded Marty of his own grandfather, except that Grandpa had less gray hair and a more thinning pate. This movie ended at five in the morning, and the two brothers washed their faces to prepare for church and to help stay awake.

Both Marty and Mark were scheduled to act as altar servers for the five-thirty Mass with Father Coniglio. They both volunteered since they were staying up late anyway watching Double Chiller Theater. Father Coniglio really didn't need two altar boys at the early Mass, but he appreciated their perceived dedication and devotion, not realizing the boys had an ulterior motive.

Marty and Mark walked out of the house onto 15th Street and into the midsummer early morning air. There was little humidity, and the sun's heat was not glaring overhead. Dawn was slowly casting its dim light over South Philadelphia. It was unusually silent, and birds could be heard chirping in the few trees dispersed along the block. It was a good time to walk before the sun rose higher in the July sky. They walked up the wide steps of the church, an imposing limestone and granite gray masterpiece with two Norman Gothic towers. It was just a neighborhood church but beautifully constructed. The interior was equally compelling with magnificent stained glass windows imported from a Munich studio and further enhanced with brightly painted scenes of the apostles on the ceiling and various saints converting pagans in the wilderness. The altar had a depiction of heaven and the Holy Trinity. All this visual beauty was designed to foster a spirit of awe and holiness for the average pew sitter.

The church was even more impressive when one realizes it was built with the contributions of poor immigrants from Ireland, Italy, and Poland, a testament to their great love and devotion. The five-thirty Mass was designed to accommodate workers on shift work, both the midnight and early morning variety, and not for teenagers staying up all night to watch three horror movies. Marty and Mark made this Mass time work best for their schedule, especially during the school year when Saturday night was their primary time to relax.

They were pros at this and had little trouble remaining awake. Occasionally, the brothers would splash water on their faces and do some push-ups. Little brother Ted tried to keep up with his older brothers but had a tougher time and usually fell asleep at two in the morning on the couch. Marty and Mark let him sleep there. Maybe next year, he will be more ready for the all-nighter. Both boys did not eat anything after midnight because as altar servers, they would be expected to receive the body and blood of Christ at Holy Communion. It was a routine they were accustomed to and prepared for by eating several ham sandwiches and piles of potato chips before midnight.

Father Coniglio said a quick Mass due to his rapid-fire presentation. There were no songs, and the Communion rail was sparse. There were not many Mass attendees at such an early time. The Mass ended before six in the morning, and Marty and Mark would walk the half mile back home and arrive at 6:10 and be in bed by six fifteen. They could sleep until eleven in the morning. At that time, their mom would be back from the 10:10 Mass and be cooking for their breakfast, a much cherished bacon sandwich on a fresh Italian roll.

Marty had a leisurely Sunday morning and afternoon all planned out. He could mix business with pleasure. The Phillies were playing at one thirty. Before that, Marty and Mark could work on the film script and try to emulate the werewolf transformation scene they had just conceived after being inspired by the late-show movie.

Chapter 13

Defense of Marie

Marty was taking a walk one sunny but not too humid summer afternoon in early July. No pickup baseball games were scheduled with the neighborhood kids, so Marty ambled north toward Marconi Plaza to indulge himself and enjoy this small slice of urban greenery that added some country charm to the ever present brown and gray atmosphere of row homes and paved streets.

Marty walked past Millie's Hoagie shop and was tempted to buy a creamy vanilla milk shake, but this pleasant thought was interrupted when he saw little Marie walking fast near the corner with her head down and crying uncontrollably.

Marie did not venture outside the house alone very often. Her two big sisters, Kate and Cassie, would normally accompany her on some jaunts around the neighborhood for some fresh air. Veronica always worried about Marie walking too far and getting lost if she was by herself. However, Cassie and Kate mapped out a safe and easily remembered route for Marie so she could enjoy a secure dose of much-needed independence. The route was bounded in the east by Broad Street and St. Monica's Church in the west and the busy thoroughfare of Oregon Avenue to the south, enough space for an easy half-mile stroll for Marie.

Marie was safely within the boundaries of this walk, so Marty wondered why Marie was so upset. She was only a block and a half from home, and her Aunt Betty lived on the same block, a home

Marie would often visit with her parents and family, so there was no way Marie thought she was lost.

The startling answer soon became sadly apparent when Marty heard some taunting from a group of kids that were following Marie.

"Where you going, you retard? Are you running home to Mommy? Come back, we want you for our neighborhood freak show." The insults were ugly and unbearable.

Marty felt he had to do something. This was the first test of his dad's recent talk with him about Marie's future and Marty's role as her protector when Mom and Dad were no longer around.

Marty hesitated. Should he just comfort Marie and walk her home and gently talk to her and try to make her forget the vicious insults? Or was something more drastic in order?

Marty tried to placate Marie and put his arm around her shaking shoulders and speak some soothing words, but the group of kids stayed close and did not let up their hurtful tirade. Marty's words of comfort could not drown out the dreadful verbal assault.

"What is wrong, retard? Are you so stupid you need your little brother to make sure you get home without getting lost? Are you that much of a moron?"

The words cut Marty like a sharp knife. Nothing he said to Marie could conceal the unrelenting horror that the words conveyed.

Marty had heard enough! He stopped walking and told Marie to wait by the nearby Pizza Shack. The savory smells might give her a degree of solace. Pizza was hands down her favorite food.

Marty's anger was overflowing like a flood spilling out of the banks of the Nile River. He was usually pretty calm, and his brothers often said his boiling point was 500 degrees, but his temper was about to explode.

Marty turned around and walked toward the posse of punks. He quickly figured out who was the ringleader and the most obnoxious. The kid was probably close to Marty's age, maybe a little younger. It didn't matter. The punk was about to pay for his treatment of Marie.

Marty prided himself on his pacifism. He took the inexplicable but inspiring saying of Jesus to turn the other cheek seriously despite some reservations. This was not the time to turn the other cheek.

Marty charged toward the group and grabbed the ringleader by the lapel of his polo shirt. Marty was tempted to wrap his hands around the kid's throat and start to throttle him like the Frankenstein monster did in so many movies, but he remembered his Uncle Mike, who was a World War II Army veteran. Uncle Mike served in the liberation of the Philippines and often demonstrated some self-defense techniques he learned in combat training to his nephews. Uncle Mike often cautioned about the throat and emphasized that it was not a part of the body to play around with.

"One good chokehold and you could cut off air to the brain and cause some serious damage. It may sound extreme, but don't ever use this technique unless you really want to hurt somebody."

These words came back to Marty as he grabbed the ringleader's shirt just below the neck. Marty bunched the shirt in his hands and stared intently at the kid's startled face. He almost felt sorry for the kid, but his ringing insults to Marie were still clanging in Marty's mind.

Marty pushed him against the mottled stonewall of the closest row home. Marty then twisted his arms and threw the boy down to the pavement. He was able to slow down the fall, so the boy did not hit his head against the concrete. Marty, despite his fiery anger, still had enough presence not to cause a concussion.

Marty wanted to say something dramatic and unforgettable but couldn't think fast enough, so he settled for a warning.

"Don't ever call my sister any names again. You got that! What did she ever do to you? She does not deserve such treatment, especially from creeps like you. Pick on someone that can actually fight back next time and let us see how brave you are then."

Marty was so furious that he did not think about the other kids in the group. They could have easily pounced on him when he pushed the ringleader to the ground.

Maybe they were too stunned. Probably the best explanation was his dad's constant reference that bullies are basically cowards and that if you confront a bully, they will scamper away like a frightened rabbit. Marty just reacted, and his boldness seemed to carry the day.

He let up the frightened ringleader, and true to form, the group ran away down 15th Street toward Shunk Street. Once they were a short distance away, the ringleader regained a portion of his dignity and turned around and shouted back to Marty.

"You don't scare us. We know about you. You are a mama's boy and the teacher's pet. My brother knows all about you."

As he said that, the ringleader was running backwards and tripped over a toy wagon. His parting words were rendered ridiculous by his Jerry Lewis pratfall.

Even Marie laughed at his false bravado. Marty looked up and said a silent thanks to the Almighty.

Thank God they are running away, thought Marty. He was afraid to think what might happen if they rallied around their humiliated ringleader, and gang-jumped Marty. Maybe he could have held them off long enough for some of Mark and his friends to come to Marty's aid. Word spread more quickly than the superhero Flash in their small community. But Mark's assistance was not necessary, so Marty walked Marie home. She was still amused by her tormentor's fall down the block. This fortunately kept her mind focused away from the terrible insults she recently suffered.

Marty continued to encourage Marie as they walked back home, hoping she would forget the worst part. It seemed to be working, as Marie continued to laugh about the gang leader's trip and fall and was in much better spirits.

"I think Grandpop will get a kick out of this story, don't you think, Marty?"

"Yes, Marie. I have no doubt he will. Why don't you be the first to tell him."

"Really, Marty! But you were so brave. You should tell everyone. You can say things so much better than me."

"No," Marty insisted. "I think this will be better coming from you."

Marty was a little worried about a future retaliation from the gang, if you could call them that, but dismissed the thought. He was actually more upset at being called the teacher's pet. That really got his goat. Just because he studied hard and never talked back to the nuns and teachers did not make him the teacher's pet.

As one can imagine, this was the big topic at suppertime in the McAlynn household that evening. Most of the family considered Marty the hero of the tale.

Veronica was more upset. The word she originally received was that Marty was strangling a much younger boy from around the corner.

"I knew watching all those horror movies were having a negative effect on you," she told Marty. "You can't go around choking kids no matter how serious the provocation."

To Marty's surprise, Cassie leaped to his defense.

"Come on, Mom! Marty just scared the little punk. There was no stranglehold. Marty just pushed the jerk around." Cassie instantly knew she said the wrong word.

"Cassie, watch your language! The younger kids are listening."

"Sorry, Mom, but you don't know all the facts."

"That's right, Mom, I never put my hands around the kid's throat, even though I really wanted to. You should have heard what they were saying to Marie."

Marty tried to explain himself better to his mom.

"Okay, Marty, I'll take your word for it."

Later that evening, when Martin Senior heard the story, he heartily approved of Marty's actions.

Chapter 14

A New Setting

The woods at FDR Park.

The werewolf mask arrived the next day, and both brothers were thrilled it only took about a week. Mark eagerly tore into the brown cardboard box and took the item out as shredded paper and other protective filler fell to the floor, creating quite a mess on the blue rug. Mark was too busy checking out the mask to be concerned.

Cassie noticed when she came into the living room and gave Mark holy hell for his carelessness.

"Make sure you clean it up before Mom sees it. Don't expect me to do all your dirty work. I'm not your personal maid."

"Yeah, yeah. Don't worry. Why are you making such a big deal? It will only take a few seconds to scoop it up."

"Because I'm the one that has to clean up after you slobs."

Mark was totally absorbed and rushed off to tell Marty.

Cassie just shook her head in a semi-disgusted manner. She was accustomed to Mark's thoughtlessness and proceeded to pick up all the strewn-about paper and throw it away in the trash can.

The mask really looked terrific and was full face like the Frankenstein mask. It had real-looking, dark brown hair on top and the back and had some wispy clumps along the chin, cheeks, and forehead. The eyes had a diabolical slant, and the mouth was curled into a snarl with sharp rubber fangs. Perfect!

The challenge would come with the transformation scene. Marty and Mark had to come up with the gradual change without resorting to glue and discarded barbershop hair.

After some serious thought, Marty and Mark decided the scene would be filmed in the most wooded section of FDR park in extreme South Philly. The only place further south was the Delaware River and the huge Navy Yard, the oldest naval base in the country; another one of Philadelphia's firsts, along with root beer and the first post card and soda fountain. The Navy Yard was one of the city's largest employers. Marty had several uncles and cousins working there.

The FDR park was also known to the locals as The Lakes. It was an extensive park with plenty of trees, a lake, a golf course, and a medieval-looking castle housing the Swedish American museum graced with grandiose, wide sweeping steps, and two cast iron cannons flanking the entrance. Marty was planning to make good use of the unique structure in the movie, thinking it would make a perfect Frankenstein castle/laboratory from the outside.

Some of the surrounding dense woods would be the location for the new werewolf transformation scene, which was inspired by the *Werewolf of London* movie they just watched last weekend. Marty and Mark figured they could use the numerous trees to make the gradual change from Mark's pale face to a dark, hairy wolf man face.

Marty mulled over how to make the small changes to Mark's face and remembered how his mom used burnt cork to darken the kid's faces with fake mustaches and beards for Halloween. It was a cheap costume and a nice budget stretcher during Halloween. Carbon paper had the same black effect without the heat.

Mark could transform and get darker from tree to tree as he walked through the forest—first his sideburns and then a beard and finally his nose. It should look like a subtle change into a werewolf. The camera would close in as Mark walked past the last tree, and—lo and behold!—the transformation would be complete. Mark would have on the Universal-designed Lon Chaney, Jr. wolf man full-face mask and then turn toward the camera. Marty hoped it would look good on film.

The camera would shoot medium shots as Mark walked from tree to tree. From that distance, the cork and carbon would look like hair. Marty thought this would give the illusion of gradually growing hair on Mark's face, and then the camera would close in and reveal the mask in shocking close-up.

Yes, this might work! It would take some practice, but Marty and Mark became more and more enthusiastic the more they thought about it.

The two brothers were anxious to film the exciting transformation scene very soon. They searched the area where it would take place, and concluded that the best spot would be a short distance from the Swedish American museum, which was near the lake and would give the shot a nice Central European touch. The wooded area was off the beaten path, so not many kids would be playing nearby. The only disadvantage was that it was near the park golf course, and by the look of all the lost golf balls scattered around, the young film crew had to be on the lookout for flying golf balls from the numerous amateur hackers.

Unlike basketball and boxing, Philadelphia was not a mecca for professional golfers. Even the famous Miracle Mile area of South Philadelphia centered around 17th and Ritner reared no famous golfers.

Marty's dad always pointed with pride to this small ten-block area of South Philly that fostered many sports legends like light heavyweight champion boxer, Tommy Loughran, who also fought heavyweight boxers like future champions Gene Tunney, Gentleman Jim Braddock, and Max Baer. He also gave heavyweight champ, Primo Carnera, a ferocious battle until finally succumbing to Carnera's superior talent and massive weight advantage in the later rounds.

Another local sports hero was Paul Arizin, the Villanova college basketball star and two-time NBA scoring champion who once scored eighty-five points in a college game. Martin Senior would often see Arizin shooting basketballs and practicing for hours at 17th Street and Porter, an old public school playground but now the site of Marty's grade school. Martin Senior often told this story to his sons to emphasize the virtue of perseverance and the grueling fact that "practice makes perfect."

"I saw Paul Arizin practice for hours and hours, even in a driving rainstorm. He was amazingly persistent. Everyone thought he was a little crazy and foolish, but look what he accomplished! He won two scoring titles and was on an NBA championship team. It just goes to show you what hard work can do for you. We can all learn from his example."

All fathers want to encourage their children to be industrious and not lazy. The Paul Arizin story gave Martin a concrete example to illustrate one of life's great virtues.

Marty and Mark had the good fortune to watch Paul Arizin in his final NBA season when their dad took them to Convention Hall to a Philadelphia Warrior game. His brothers and dad were heartbroken when the team moved out of Philadelphia to San Francisco.

"Now we know how the Brooklyn Dodgers fans and New York Giants fans felt when both franchises took up stakes and moved out to the West Coast a few years ago."

The Philadelphia Warrior team was unique in that the 1962 team had four out of five starters from Philadelphia: Guy Rodgers from Temple, Tom Gola from LaSalle, Paul Arizin from Villanova, and Wilt Chamberlain from Overbrook High School in West Philadelphia. Wilt did not attend a Big 5 college and attended college in Kansas, but he was a native Philadelphian. Ironically, the only non-Philadelphia born starter was a San Franciscan, forward Tom Meschery.

In the first decade of the fledgling NBA, the owners wanted local talent to boost attendance in the league. Its later worldwide popularity did not catch on until decades later.

Marty and Mark were satisfied with the new plan for the werewolf transformation and eagerly awaited the right time to carry out the new phase of the movie.

Chapter 15

An Unwelcome Shock

Marty took his customary evening stroll after supper. He stuffed himself as usual at dinner and decided to walk it off. Marty ate three pieces of thick succulent pork chops that were charred, almost burnt, just the way he liked it, and burnished with tangy fried onions. He also had a Matterhorn-sized portion of creamy buttered mashed potatoes and a half-plate size of string beans, also drizzled in melted butter. His mom asked if he wanted seconds, but as tempted as Marty was, he didn't want to make a pig of himself.

There were no good shows on primetime TV since it was the summer. They were just reruns. The Phillies were in Cincinnati, and the game did not start until eight thirty in the evening, so Marty had time to get some exercise before settling down to watch the team on the boob tube.

Marty had several choices for his evening exercise. He could head north to Snyder Avenue and East Passyunk Avenue toward Pat's King of Steaks, but he did not want to spend $.50 on a cheesesteak. He had to save money for the movie's increasing production costs.

Marty could walk south to Oregon Avenue and the wide-open spaces of Marconi Plaza Park where his brothers and the neighborhood kids often played baseball. If you walked a few blocks even further south, he could watch some of the movie at the outdoor drive-in theater on Broad Street near the entrance to the Navy Yard, but there would be no sound. It was kind of neat to see what movie was playing. He thought he read in the *Philadelphia Bulletin* movie page that a Dean Martin and Shirley MacLaine film was playing, *John Goldfarb, Won't You Please Come Home*. Weird title. It was probably a comedy, and so it was probably not worth Marty's time.

If it was not a horror movie, Marty had no real interest. His heart was broken to read about Peter Lorre's death a few months ago in March. It was even more of a shame because Lorre's career was reviving with his new movie partnership with Vincent Price. Boris Karloff, his favorite actor, was approaching eighty and was still pretty active and still making movies, so it was shaping up as a mini-golden age for horror movies, especially with all the Hammer Films coming out from England with Christopher Lee and Peter Cushing.

Another option Marty could take was to walk west toward 20th Street. This would take him past his old grade school at 16th Street and Porter. The homes west of 18th Street became less like his 15th Street row house neighborhood and more like an English country village featuring homes filled with porches, front gardens, and a wider street, amply shaded by tall leafy maple and birch trees. There was also some space between homes to park a car if the need arose. He could imagine himself overseas in this unique slice of South Philadelphia with its front lawns and columned porches.

A solidly ornate and relatively grand Carnegie library was also in this direction. Marty spent many hours cruising magazines and biographies in this place. He just finished Basil Rathbone's (Sherlock Holmes himself) autobiography and was interested in learning that Rathbone, even though he usually played the villain, was a World War I real-life war hero. One of Basil's relatives, Major Rathbone, was in the theater box with Lincoln in Ford's Theater when the president was fatally shot on that dreadful Good Friday evening.

Marty was also surprised to learn that Basil Rathbone was a more skilled swordsman than his on-screen nemesis, Errol Flynn, but since he normally played the bad guy, he had to lose his fencing battles with Flynn as the movie hero.

The westward walk also led Marty into a large shopping center, rare in South Philadelphia, which had ample parking spaces. There was also a bowling alley that Marty sometimes entered in order to use the bathroom. During dinner, he drank so much iced tea that he needed some relief, and thankfully the bowling alley was situated in the perfect spot.

Beyond the strip mall, which had a laundromat, a bookstore, and a Woolworth's 5 and 10 shop, and across 24th Street, Marty did not dare venture. There was a large housing project built north of Snyder Avenue, and his safety was not assured if he wandered under the solemnly dark and cobweb-filled I-76 Schuykill Expressway overpass into unknown territory. It was like passing from friendly into enemy lines in a war movie. Marty decided to take the more leisurely southern route and wander through the tree-shaded Marconi Park for some relief from the congested row home neighborhoods where he lived.

Marty walked down 15th Street and neared the grim Medieval-like Protestant Church on the corner. Its Gothic gloom reminded him of a recent Vincent Price-Lon Chaney movie, *The Haunted Palace*. The church was constructed of dark brown bricks. No outside lights brightened the glum exterior. Cobwebs could be seen above doorways and along the stained glass windows. Bats sometimes flew out of some recesses, and fierce stone gargoyles added to the building's Halloween spookiness.

Marty originally hoped to film some outside scenes for the film near this building, which could stand in for Frankenstein's castle provided the camera could be skillfully placed to block out the obvious Church areas. He salivated at the potential. As Marty finished looking up at the flying bats, he cast his gaze along the street level and was about to pass the church doors, which had some steps leading to a covered area.

There were always some kids hanging around there playing cards or flipping coins. There were also a few annoying couples hugging and kissing in the dark recesses near the door.

He tried to ignore the intertwined couples, but what he saw near one corner totally stunned and shocked him like a red-hot electric current zapping down from the top of his head to the soles of his feet!

Marty did a double take and looked again. He couldn't believe what he was seeing!

It couldn't be!

He walked a little closer, almost afraid to find out the truth or confirm this hard-to-believe reality.

Maybe his imagination was playing tricks on him. Marty sincerely hoped this was the case, but as he edged closer, he focused on the two bodies locked in a passionate embrace and desperately hoped it was not who the girl looked to be. Marty was a few feet away, and after the couple finished their necking and came up for air, there was no doubt who the girl involved was. It was Kathleen! His sainted sister! Why was she involved in such a tawdry exhibition?

Marty's shock soon turned into explosive rage. He walked up to the couple and angrily but gently separated his sister from her "lover boy" and then not-so gently swung his fist and punched the numbed boyfriend in the mouth.

This action really hurt Marty's hand. The pain was almost as intense as the shock of finding his sister engaged in such unusual behavior. The blow staggered her boyfriend, and he fell a few inches against the wooden church door. The boyfriend became intensely angry and was about to spring onto Marty, but he restrained himself, partly because Kathleen stood in front of her boyfriend and slowed down his natural instinct to fight back.

"Marty, what are you doing?"

Kathleen's words seem to wake up Marty from his shocked anger. A minute before, he was in an uncontrollable rage, but after hearing Kate's voice, he felt ashamed and pitiful.

Marty looked at Kate with wounded eyes and muttered, "I am sorry . . . I . . . I . . . I didn't . . . I . . . I don't think . . ."

Marty didn't know what else to say. He was deeply embarrassed and meekly walked away. He felt like running away to a dark cave and hibernate like a desert monk, but he just slowly walked north up 15th Street with his hands in his pocket, still in a dazed and deep shock.

The boyfriend, who received Marty's heartfelt but weak punch, was John Stanton.

"What gives, Kate? Who was that?" he asked as he licked his lips, which bled slightly. He rolled his tongue around his front teeth to make sure no teeth were missing.

"That was my brother Marty. I don't know what got into him. He's a little naïve and idealistic. I'm sorry, John. I'll talk to him. I'm so glad you didn't overreact."

"Overreact!" He almost shouted, but then he calmed down. "I'm six inches taller and fifty pounds heavier. I don't pick on people, especially kids, half my size. Give me credit for that, at least."

"Yes, John, you are a true gentleman." Kate couldn't help herself and started giggling.

"What's so funny?" asked John, but then he also saw the humor in the situation and also started laughing. Soon the couple dissolved into helpless laughter, which bonded them even closer together.

Marty was really upset at himself. What was going on in his mind? He was a budding pacifist, not an aggressive fighter. He hated war movies. He had no desire to go in the Army. He prayed he would have flat feet so the military would reject him. This was his third fight in the last couple of weeks.

The first fight was really just self-defense against Sammy the Psycho. He had no choice; otherwise, he would've been cut up too badly. The second one was in defense of little Marie who was insulted by some punk kids. Marty only wanted to come to her defense, but things escalated beyond what Marty thought. That fight was somewhat justified defending his family's honor.

But how could he justify this last fight? Well, it wasn't really a fight, just a punch. Fortunately, the guy, whoever he was, did not fight back. Marty would have been massacred. The other guy was much taller and bigger in every department.

Why did Marty throw the punch? In his mind, Marty was defending his big sister's honor, but Kathleen seemed willing and was enjoying all the hugging and kissing too much. Maybe that was what really bothered him.

Marty did not want to go home. His mind was racing too much. He could not sit still and kept walking. He was too upset and had an enormous amount of pent-up energy to burn. He walked north on 15th Street to Ritner Street and then turned left. He wanted to go on a really long walk, so Marty turned south down 16th Street and headed toward Oregon Avenue.

From that point, if Marty headed west, he could walk for miles. South Philadelphia was restricted to the east by the Delaware River and in the south by the massive Navy Yard. To the north, the neighborhood got worse, and then there was always a chance to get jumped by some street corner gangs.

However, if Marty walked west on Oregon Avenue, it soon linked up with Passyunk Avenue, a long diagonal street that stretched from 8th Street westward across the Schuylkill River into Southwest Philadelphia. This road had several walkable bridges to cross the river, unlike the much wider Delaware River to the east.

Once he was on Passyunk Avenue, Marty crossed the singing bridge near Jerry's Corner, a huge chaotic store, which had everything in it from books and groceries to clothes and toys and everything imaginable in between.

Marty could then reach 61st Street and then walk into Southwest Philadelphia and possibly into the suburbs of Delaware County. All this was feasible once he crossed the Passyunk Avenue Bridge over the river. There would be no remaining obstacles in his path, and Marty could safely walk out of the restricted confines of South Philadelphia.

Marty walked on Oregon and went by Murphy's department store where he often bought his movie monster magazines. Across the street was the massive Quartermaster complex, which employed thousands of Philadelphians including three of his aunts and his two older sisters. The place made uniforms for the military services, something Marty hoped he would never have to put on or wear.

Once Marty reached 21st Street and Oregon, the crowded row homes of South Philadelphia were few and far between. The area become less residential. The Schuylkill Expressway divided the area from the isolated Grays Ferry neighborhood. The looming oil refineries took up a massive amount of space. As Marty walked toward the Passyunk Avenue Bridge, he saw the menacing giant tanks and prayed none of them would catch fire and explode. They resembled gigantic squares outlined with iron bars.

His dad as a fireman always said a refinery blaze was his greatest fear fighting fires. The tanks' flammable mixture and explosive force could ignite into a horrendous tragedy. Several of his dad's fellow firemen perished in the blazes of a refinery inferno. Marty quickly sped up until he crossed the singing bridge over the dirty gray Schuylkill River. His dad gave the bridge that poetic name because when the car's tires crossed the metal grates, it created the rhythmic hum that, with a little imagination, almost seemed like a song. The bridge would not make a singing sound when Marty crossed the span by walking since the pedestrian lane was concrete Macadam. Only a moving car could produce the sound.

Marty felt better crossing over the river, which put more distance away from the refineries.

He looked to his right and saw the large, mostly empty parking lot of Jerry's Corner. Marty walked two more blocks to 61st Street. The area was extremely isolated and remote. The only businesses were filled with junkyards containing huge stacks of broken and decaying cars and tall columns of black tires. There was no pavement to walk on, just a three-foot wide grassy area filled with brown rocks and gray pebbles. Their sharp edges bit into Marty's Converse sneakers.

As he was about to turn on 61st Street, Marty almost jumped out of his skin! A loud growl from a snarling, sharp-toothed German shepherd, the largest dog Marty ever saw, jolted Marty from his daydreaming doldrums. Marty jumped back a few steps, but his fear lessened when he saw the cyclone fence, overgrown with uneven bushes, protected him from the barking dog. The German Shepherd leapt high against the fence, but the eight-foot-high metal grating had a comforting topping of sharp and jagged concertina wire. There was no way the dog could hurtle over the fence, and if it did, the animal would impale its stomach and paws against the sharp spikes.

The dog scare made Marty quicken his pace, and he made the turn on 61st Street with a sigh of relief. There were two more dog-guarded junkyards to pass, but he was better prepared and steeled himself against the barking and growling dogs. Their fierce movements and piercing rumblings did not have the same terrifying effect on Marty, but he quickly sped by the junkyards until he arrived adjacent to the 61st Street drive-in theater.

His dad had taken him and his brothers many times to this theater, mostly to watch the latest Vincent Price-Edgar Allan Poe movie from American International Pictures or the newest Hammer horror film with Peter Cushing and Christopher Lee. His poor dad had to seat through these horror movies just to please his sons, and all his dad really wanted to see was the latest Paul Newman or Charlton Heston movie.

As Brian looked at the marquee that displayed what the drive-in movie was showing that night, he saw the movie was a Cary Grant picture called *Father Goose* and also playing was *What a Way to Go* with Paul Newman, Shirley MacLaine (again), and Robert Mitchum. These mainstream movies made him think more of his dad, and a surge of homesickness hit Marty very hard. He started feeling very guilty. What was his mom and dad thinking? How worried were they? What did his sister Kathleen tell the family about what happened?

Marty did not want to face the family with what he did, and that was why he kept walking. How could he face Kate again? He thought so highly of her, and he did something so totally out of character. He didn't know the time, but it must have been around six or seven in the evening. The sun was still high enough for another hour or so of daylight. Marty thought he should turn around. He hated the thought of walking by the dog-infested junkyards at night. They were scary enough when the sun was shining high in the sky.

Marty had arrived into the more residential neighborhood of Southwest Philly. The open spaces of the drive-in theater and the junkyards were replaced by a nice set of row homes. Some even had porches and front yards. This area was built more recently than the row homes in South Philadelphia where his family lived. Southwest Philadelphia had wider streets, some homes had front gardens, and some even had backyards. It almost looked like the suburbs.

Marty walked to the wider east-west traffic moving Woodland Avenue, which was the commercial center of this Philadelphia neighborhood. The area even had a Murphy's department store, which was even bigger than the one he visited on Oregon Avenue. Marty decided he better turn around and head back home. But first, since he was so close, he knew there were two movie theaters nearby, the Benn and the Benson. He was curious what was playing, so he walked two more blocks to 63rd Street.

To his delight, he saw the Benson had a double feature, *The Gorgon*, with Peter Cushing and Christopher Lee and the *Last Man on Earth* starring Vincent Price. Marty missed these movies when they played at the Savoia and the Broadway movie theaters in his neighborhood. This was a good chance to catch them with his friends in the Count Dracula Society. It was too late to go now. He really needed to get back home, but maybe his friends could come tomorrow or in the next few days. They had to figure out a way to get there. It was about four miles away, a good hour-plus walk. Marty didn't mind the walk, but he could just hear the whines of his buddy, Jimmy Mac, about having to walk so far just to see a movie. Marty would worry about that later. He walked toward 61st Street and headed south. He walked faster in hopes of getting home before darkness descended on South Philadelphia.

Chapter 16

Facing the Music

Marty was so absorbed in his thoughts that he didn't realize how hot and humid the weather was. His T-shirt was thoroughly soaked, especially in the back, and his armpits were starting to chafe—another reason to head back home and face the music.

The sun was setting, and the shadows lengthened across 61st Street. Fortunately, there was still plenty of daylight when Marty scampered by the junkyards with the dogs. He kept his brisk pace until he reached Jerry's Corner and the foot of the bridge. A slightly cool breeze from the Schuylkill River felt refreshing on his sweat-drenched shirt. Once he got home, he would need to take a shower. Anything to avoid facing his family about punching his sister's friend. He dreaded what was to come.

He wasn't sure if his dad was home. He kind of hoped he was at the firehouse. His mom would probably not be as mad.

As Marty reached Oregon Avenue, he slowed his pace. He really wished it was tomorrow and the confrontation was over and done with. Marty walked by the free library on Shunk Street and wanted to enter and get lost among the rows and rows of books. He almost shuffled as he passed the St. Monica bowling alley. Anything to delay his night of reckoning. Home was now less than three blocks away: the moment of truth could not be delayed much longer.

Marty never bowled before, but he was ready to duck in and hide inside. It wouldn't be long now before he had to face the wrath of his family.

His little brother, Ted, spotted him and told Marty he had to get home right away.

"Where have you been? Mom and Dad want to talk to you. They are really worried and . . ."

"Okay, I'm on my way," he said. *Great*, he thought. His dad was home. No avoiding it now. In some ways, Marty felt better about that. Better to get it all over with and not have the consequences hanging over his head.

As he turned on Porter Street, where Marty was the corner safety at lunchtime during the eighth grade in happier days, Marty ran into Mark with the same news as Ted.

"Where were you? Everybody's looking for you. Mom and Dad are really upset. What in the world were you thinking?"

"I don't know. Did you talk to Kate?"

"Yeah, but actually she's not as upset as Mom and Dad."

Marty felt a little better about that despite what happened. Despite his stupidity, he still wanted Kathleen to think well of him.

Marty put his head down and walked the last block and a half to their sturdy 15th Street row home. He passed some kids playing stickball and buck buck, where one kid jumped on top of another kid, almost like a cowboy jumping on a horse. Marty never understood the game and went out of his way to avoid playing it. He was more of a loner and liked playing or walking with his older and younger brothers and close friends.

Marty walked by the Protestant church doors—the scene of the crime, so to speak, and the stage of his own personal humiliation.

It seemed to Marty that the whole entire street knew what he did. It looked like each and every kid stopped what they were playing and doing and stared at Marty as he walked down the block. It was like Gary Cooper in *High Noon* as he made the slow, lonely walk to his home to meet his fate.

It only took a few minutes, but to Marty, the time felt like an eternity. He reached his house and walked up the six reddish brown concrete steps to the front door and opened the double-windowed door and entered.

His dad was standing near the living room window with his arms folded across his chest. His mom was sitting at the dining room table with a worried look that changed instantly to relieved joy when she saw the humbled Marty come through the front door.

"What in the world were you thinking, Marty?" said his dad in a generally mystified tone.

"Let him sit down first, Martin." His mom interrupted. "He has to be tired from all that walking."

Marty did not feel like sitting, even though he was dog-tired from his eight-mile round-trip walk into Southwest Philadelphia. He actually thought his grandfather would be proud of his walk once he found about it.

His dad continued, "Marty, what has gotten into you? That makes three fights in about a couple of weeks. This is very unlike you!"

"I know, Dad." Marty tried a weak defense of his actions. "The first one with Sammy was not my fault . . . he attacked me . . . I had to defend myself."

"I know, but the other two, especially with Kathleen's boyfriend just now, what in the world happened there?"

Boyfriend!

Marty winced when he heard that term, and the word almost felt worse than a slap on the face. He still couldn't picture the sainted Kathleen with a boyfriend. In Marty's mind, Kathleen was a pure angel just waiting to be canonized after a holy life of charity and good works. How could she ever get herself involved with a boyfriend!

Marty still tried to meekly defend himself and avoid the real reason for the family conference.

"The second one . . . well . . . I was just trying to defend Marie from some nasty insults."

"We understand your actions that day, but we already talked about the right way to handle Marie and her detractors. Don't change the subject. You know what we are here to discuss. Why did you hit John Stanton?"

John Stanton! That was his name. I will have to do little background back on that guy, thought Marty, still evading the issue.

A short silence followed. His dad kept up the offensive. "Well . . . we are listening."

"I don't know . . . it bothered me seeing Kathleen hugging and kissing right out in the open. I didn't think she could do such a thing . . . it seemed . . . I don't know . . ."

Marty wanted to say it seemed cheap and tawdry but didn't want to insult Kathleen, so he just shrugged his shoulders and said, "I don't know. It just really bothered me."

"Just because something bothers you, it doesn't give you the right to fight someone. You should know better."

His dad began his lecture, which he heard several times before, but it was usually directed at his younger brothers.

All Marty could do was grin and bear it. He did deserve the dressing down for the most part, hard as it was to admit it.

After his dad finished his litany of admonishments laced with some encouragement, Martin Senior lowered the boom and told Marty Junior that he was to apologize to his sister and her friend, John Stanton. Martin still hated the thought of calling John his sister's boyfriend.

Marty didn't mind the thought of expressing sorrow to his sister. He sincerely wanted to express his regret. She was always nice and understanding. Despite what happened, Marty still thought Kathleen's charitable nature would reassert itself and restore his good relationship with her.

However, he hated the thought of apologizing to John Stanton. That would take some effort mainly because of Marty's profound embarrassment. He prayed that Kathleen would make the task a little easier

Well, first things first, thought Marty and realized it was best to apologize to Kathleen as soon as possible. Before Marty looked for Kathleen, he saw Cassie near the kitchen door with her arms folded like a schoolteacher listening to a student giving a homework presentation.

Marty thought she was about to say a smart remark, but to his surprise, she held her tongue and gave off a sympathetic feel for

Marty with a bemused but understanding grin, as if to say, "Don't feel too bad, Marty. Your heart was in the right place."

Marty was grateful Cassie was not being her usual biting sarcastic self.

What in the world came over her? thought Marty. It was not a case where Cassie was being overly nice; it was more that she was not being her customary mean self. Maybe there's more to Cassie than the front she constantly puts on, always claiming she has to be a second mom sometimes to all her younger siblings.

"Where is Kate?" asked Marty, determined to get the first stage of the unpleasant task over with.

"She's down the cellar doing the wash," answered Cassie.

"How mad is she?" Marty thought he had to ask this, although unlike Cassie, Kate was never known to raise her voice or get uncontrollably angry. He hated to think he was the cause of a family-shattering event.

"Kate was very tight-lipped, but she said she wanted to keep busy, and that's why she volunteered to do my usual chore of washing clothes in our dingy damp basement."

Come to think of it, Marty thought, it was odd that Kate was washing the clothes. This was normally Cassie's job. She always seemed to do the drudgery work—cleaning dishes, doing the wash, vacuuming, etc., whereas Kate did the more pleasant tasks like going to stores, playing with the younger kids, folding clothes. Marty was starting to see a pattern there.

Marty hesitated for a few seconds. Cassie spurred him on and told him, "Go on down. You'll feel better . . . you don't want this hanging over your head all night."

"You're right!" Marty replied and bravely opened the red basement door and walked down the rickety wooden stairs.

The cellar was partially finished. The linoleum floor was a recent addition. Martin Senior knew some of his fellow firemen who were handy with home improvement projects and held down second jobs in this field. He would get these craftsmen to work on the house for a bargain price. The basement walls were only half done with plywood. Rich Iannelli was the fireman working on that task, but on his day job as a fireman, he suffered a serious case of smoke inhalation, twisted his back, and was out of commission for about a month, so the wall paneling project was put on hold until Rich recovered completely.

A bare lightbulb illuminated the cellar. Before it was paneled, Marty and Mark used it as a graveyard scene in the opening shots of the movie. It was dark and creepy enough to stand in for spooky cemetery.

The basement was much cleaner-looking now, which was good for the family but bad for the movie. Fortunately, there were no more graveyard scenes that needed to be filmed.

Off to the right, Marty could see Kathleen taking clothes out of the Maytag washer and into the Sears dryer. She was intent in the task and did not see him at first. A popular Beatles song, "Do You Want to Know a Secret" was playing on the transistor radio on the table.

Marty took a deep breath and waded in. There was no sugar-coating what he had to say. So Marty just cleared his throat and said, "Kate . . . I am very sorry. I don't know what got into me. It just kind of . . . I don't know . . . it really bothered me."

Kathleen turned around and tried to put a serious pensive expression on her face. For a moment, she did not smile, but in an instant, she beamed the most infectious, heartwarming, more-dazzling-than-sunlight smile imaginable, and Marty felt immensely relieved. It was a feeling he often felt by studying hard for a test and knowing you aced the exam. All that needless worry was unfounded.

Kathleen said, "So my little brother is a knight in shining armor, sallying forth to defend my honor."

"Well, I wouldn't put it quite that way," said Marty.

"Okay. I admit I did get carried away. John is usually more respectful, but he told me he is leaving soon and . . ."

Leaving soon! Marty felt even better. Maybe this character will be out of Kate's life, and she can concentrate on more godly matters, but this brief hope was soon dashed when Kate continued.

"John is enlisting in the Navy and will leave in a month, so the sudden shock of the news threw me off, and we gave into the moment, and he told me he loved me . . ." She started to tear up. "So this news hit me hard. I know he wanted to go to Annapolis and was so disappointed he did not get the congressional appointment. I didn't realize how badly he wanted to attend the Naval Academy, so . . . oh, I'm sorry, Marty . . . I don't want to bog you down in details and tell you my troubles, but I do want you to tell John how sorry you are. Can you do that for me? He really is a good guy."

Marty knew he was getting off too easy, but he didn't realize how strongly she felt about John and how upset she was about his imminent departure. Marty was tempted to say, "Not soon enough," but he was slowly comprehending Kathleen's depth of feelings for the future sailor.

In the background, the transistor radio was still on, and the WIBG radio station broadcast Dean Martin's latest pop single, "Everybody Loves Somebody," which was a big hit this year. The song somehow seemed very appropriate, almost like a sign from God.

What else could Marty do? He readily agreed and told her yes, he would apologize and wanted to seek John out right away and apologize this very night to get it over with. He hoped it would make Kathleen feel better also. Marty was moved by Kate's brief tears. She quickly flashed another warm comforting smile and thanked Marty for admitting his mistake and went back to her laundry chore.

Marty had a bittersweet feeling. He was happy the initial ordeal was over but a little sad at Kathleen's melancholy mood at the prospect of John's imminent departure. It was around eight in the evening, the Phillies game was about to start. They were in Cincinnati. After the ordeal of the past couple of hours, Marty looked forward to relaxing and watching the first-place Phillies and not worrying about apologies and embarrassing reminders, but he also wanted to make a clean sweep, so he asked Kate where John was.

"Marty, you can wait until tomorrow. He's probably home watching the Phillies with his dad."

"No, I'd like to get it over with. Where does he live?"

"Right off of Passyunk, not too far from St. Maria Goretti. You sure you want to do this now?"

"Yeah, absolutely."

"Well, let me finish up, and I'll go with you."

Marty was doubly happy Kate would be going with him. This would surely make the apology so much easier.

Marty walked up the cellar steps followed by Kathleen.

Grandpa was settled in his favorite chair close to the TV. He had an ice-cold mug of beer in his right hand, his only noticeable weakness, and his dad was lighting up his pipe also comfortably snuggled into the lounge chair. Tim and Mark were lying on the floor, also very relaxed, and waiting for the first pitch.

Grandpop Adolph asked, "Marty, where are you going? Game is about to start. Should be a good one. Chris Short is pitching . . ."

"I won't be long. I'll be back soon."

"I know you had a tough night. Come on . . . just take a seat . . ."

"No, thanks. I really need to take care of something . . ."

"Okay . . . good luck." In truth, Adolph was glad Marty was getting it all resolved as soon as possible and did not try anymore to change Marty's mind.

Marty and Kate walked out of their home and stepped into the sultry evening air and headed east to Broad Street. Kate was keeping up a friendly chatter. Marty was grateful. She was making an awkward moment more bearable.

They walked by the block-long building of the Methodist Hospital. A loud ambulance siren blared as the vehicle turned into the emergency room entrance. Next door to the hospital was an impressive Gothic Presbyterian Church. Marty, always mindful of an appropriate movie set, considered using its exterior as an alternate plan for use as Frankenstein's castle with some strategic camera placement, but it was composed of bright white rocks, which gave off a too sunny appearance. Definitely not monster movie material.

The two siblings proceeded to walk by the huge two-block-long South Philadelphia (Southern) high school building where teen idols, Frankie Avalon, Fabian, and Jimmy Darren, went to school, which was a nice source of South Philadelphia pride. Marty hoped his name would be famously known as a moviemaker in a few more years.

Before Kate and Marty made it to the diagonal Passyunk Avenue, which sliced through the orderly streets of South Philadelphia, another movie palace came into view—the Broadway Theater took up half a block. On the marquee was another Vincent Price movie that Marty and his friends were looking forward to seeing, *The Masque of the Red Death*.

Kate and Marty walked by the two five-and-dime stores across the street from the movie theater. At McKean Street, the brother and sister made a right turn on Passyunk Avenue, which was the Italian restaurant heart of South Philadelphia. As they walked past the many cheese stores and their pungent odors, the overwhelming smell took Marty's mind off of the coming confrontation. He was especially glad that Kate was coming with him to ease his growing discomfort at the upcoming meeting.

Kathleen's customary good-natured and cheerful disposition kept Marty's mind engaged, but as they strolled closer to John's house, Marty's stomach butterflies kicked into high gear. He was starting to lose his courage and resolve.

Kathleen seemed to sense Marty's increasing nervousness and attempted to lessen it. "Don't worry, Marty, Johnny is a real nice guy. He took it rather well, all things considered."

"Did he? Really!" That helped Marty feel a little better.

"Yes. His parents are really nice also, and his entire family is very friendly. I know you feel awkward, but you're doing the right thing getting it all over with tonight."

They made a left turn and headed west toward Broad Street and entered the small narrow street where John Stanton's family lived. The row home was located in the middle of the block. Marty felt like he was walking a long plank in an old pirate movie. He had come this far, but the actual prospect of meeting his nemesis, John Stanton, face-to-face unnerved him, and he started walking slower, almost a lumbering shuffle.

Kathleen sensed this and tried to give Marty an added boost of confidence.

"Just about there, Marty . . . in a few minutes, it will be all over with."

Since his sister was with him at first, he didn't worry about meeting John a few blocks ago, but now he started getting nervous goosebumps, even though it was hot and sticky in the thick humid air.

How was he going to react? Marty did not fear a physical attack, but he couldn't bear any insulting tirade against him, especially in front of his favorite sister. It was an unbearable thought.

Kathleen kept up a faster pace, so Marty had to stop his slow gait to continue to walk alongside her. Before he knew it, they were at his front door. The die was cast! This was the moment! There was no turning back.

Kathleen made Marty knock. Probably a good thing, thought Marty as he walked up the squat four freshly scrubbed white limestone steps and unhesitatingly rapped on the double wooden door with frosted glass.

Marty and Kate waited for the door to open. He wished the front steps could swallow him up and magically take him home. John's little brother, Ed, answered the door. He looked to be the same age as Marty's brother, Tim. Ed went to a different school, St. Nicholas of Tolentine, so Marty did not know him. They lived less than a mile away, but in the densely packed urban wilderness of South Philadelphia, it might as well have been across the state in Pittsburgh.

Marty was about to ask, "Is John home?" but Kathleen cut through the awkward formalities and told Ed, "Can you have John come out, please? We need to talk, and it would be better outside here."

That was a relief to Marty. He really didn't want to meet the parents and John's other brothers and sisters. Coming here was tough enough.

Thank God Kate was cutting through the awkwardness in leading the charge to get this ordeal over with, thought an eternally grateful Marty.

As Ed went back inside the narrow brick row house, Kate continued to raise Marty from any doldrums he might be immersed in.

"It's okay, Marty, he won't bite. I figured you really did not want to go in."

As Marty waited at the bottom of the steps, some of the neighbors were sitting outside on the reddish brown stoops and listening to the Phillies game while munching on potato chips and drinking the beer of choice in the neighborhood, Ballantine beer. He heard some cheers and assumed the Phils must have been doing something good.

A tall figure wearing a white T-shirt and blue jeans came to the door. Indeed, it was John Stanton.

No beating around the bush. "This is it!" Marty muttered to himself.

Once again, Kate helped break the ice and said, "John, my brother, Marty, is here, and he has something to say to you."

Well, there was no turning back now for Marty, and he just plunged right into it.

"I'm sorry for what happened . . . I don't know what got into me . . . I don't know what else to say, except . . . I'm really sorry."

"Don't worry about it, slugger. In a way, I guess it is a compliment to your sister. That someone is looking out for her who really cares and wants to protect her."

Marty couldn't believe how nice John was being. All that needless worrying. He even kind of complimented Marty's punch, or was he being too kind? Marty never thought of himself as much of a fighter.

"Hey, kid. You pack a nice wallop . . . did you ever box in the Golden Gloves? You should give it some careful thought."

"No . . . I don't like fighting . . ."

"You should look into it. There is a good boxing gym on Passyunk Avenue just a few blocks away."

"Well . . . I don't know . . . well . . . sorry for hitting you. I'm really . . . kind of like a pacifist."

"Really! You could've fooled me. No way I'm a pacifist. Only the dead have seen the end of war."

"That's a sad statement. Not very hopeful for mankind."

"Sad but true . . . you know who said it?" John kept talking.

Marty volunteered, "General Patton?"

"Close . . . kind of. Douglas MacArthur said these words, but he was actually quoting the Ancient Greeks, Plato to be exact."

Douglas McArthur died earlier this year. He remembered all the fuss about the famous general's passing in the papers. By all accounts, he was an amazing figure. Marty remembered his "I shall return" speech in History class. One of his uncles served under MacArthur during his island hopping campaigns in the war against the Japanese in the Pacific. It was service his Uncle Tom was very proud of.

John was actually easy to talk to. Marty was almost enjoying the conversation.

"How come you are a pacifist? Don't you think we need to fight for our country, especially with the sad state of the world today? We can't let the godless Communists take over the world. Look how they suppress religion behind the Iron Curtain by nailing forks into priests' heads. A lot of horrible stuff going on over there."

Kathleen did not want John to get on his super patriotic soapbox, so she tried to help Marty.

"John, no need to get into all of that. We only just came to apologize."

"Okay, now I'm the one that is sorry. Hey, I hear you like to walk," said John, who tried to gracefully change the subject and still engage Marty on the same topic.

"Yeah, I like to walk around the neighborhood. It is kind of peaceful and relaxing."

"Well, you might actually like the Marines then. They walk all over the place, mountains, deserts, forests. It sure beats walking around this concrete jungle and a heckuva lot more scenic. The Marines go on twenty-five-mile road marches all the time like it is a walk in the park."

"They do!"

This piqued some interest in Marty. He always hoped he had flat feet so he would be rejected by the military, but he did love to walk, and his feet never really bothered him. Maybe there was something to the military after all. Marty would give it some more thought.

Marty was still a little puzzled.

"I thought you wanted to go in the Navy?"

"Well . . . kind of. Actually, I want to be a Marine. Many Marine Corps officers also go to the US Naval Academy. The Marines are part of the Department of the Navy. If I graduate from the Naval Academy, I have a good chance to join the Marines, which is what I really want to do."

"Well, I wish you luck."

"Hey, the Phils are still playing. Callison just hit a two-run homer. Chris Short is on the mound. Do you want to watch some of the game? It also gives me more time with your sister, Kate." He paused and gave Kate a wink. "I promise I'll behave and be a perfect gentleman."

"Well," Marty hesitated and looked in his sister's direction.

Kathleen smiled and said, "Okay, just a few innings. I'll call home and let Mom and Dad know."

The brother and sister entered John's house and met his family. There was room in the living room, so Marty and Kate sat down to watch the game.

During the top of the seventh inning, Kathleen and Marty thought they should return home. The Phillies had a solid lead. The game should be another win barring a late inning catastrophe. Normally, most Philly fans would expect the collapse, but this year was different. The Phillies were resilient, and luck seemed to be in the corner.

John Stanton seemed to embody this newfound optimism and confidence.

"Can you believe it! I have followed the Phillies for more than half my life, and they have been lousy. I've endured nineteen sixty-one and the twenty-three-game losing streak and all kinds of horrible games with poor pitching and hapless hitting. I've seen a fifty-year-old Phillies manager quit on opening day because he claimed he wanted to live to turn fifty-one. The only consistency about the team was their consistent lousiness, but this year is different. They have a tremendous chance of going to the World Series, and where will I be in October? I will be smack dab in the middle of my Navy basic training on one of the Great Lakes. I won't be here for all the excitement."

Marty asked, "Can you delay the Navy for a month or two and push back your reporting date?"

"No, I have already enlisted. I have a set date. No turning back. Besides, I want to be in the Naval Academy for the class starting next summer. I can't afford any further delay."

"Are you guaranteed a slot for the Naval Academy?" said Marty.

"Nothing is a lock, but I have a good chance. My grades were good in high school, and if I keep doing well at the prep school, my chances are excellent. This is something I really, really want."

Marty asked, "Why not just try to enter into the Naval Academy for the next class?"

"Well, you need a congressional appointment. I tried to get one this past year, but I was a third alternate, which meant there were four guys in front of me. The odds of all them bombing out the selection process are very slim. I didn't make it that way in my senior year. Next year, there will be fresh candidates from high school. By joining the Navy and getting into the Naval Academy prep program, this will increase my chances astronomically."

Marty glanced at Kathleen who appeared sad at the prospect of John leaving. Marty felt a little guilty at the thoughts running through his mind—that John's absence would make Kathleen forget this infatuation, but Marty was realizing Kate really seemed to care for John, and Marty had to ruefully admit that he really was a pretty good guy. Marty knew he was being selfish, and he should only wish his sister all the best.

"Well, we better get back. Let's go, Marty. John, we will talk tomorrow," said Kate.

"Okay, sounds good. Good night." John gave an impish smile and said to Marty, "Is it all right if I give my girl a little hug without getting slugged?"

"That won't be necessary, John," said Kate as if to spare Marty any more discomfort. She also thought John was being a little too cute.

But Marty said, "I'll step outside. I'll meet you out there, Kate."

Marty left without looking back. He liked John a lot better now, but he still didn't want him to show such outward affection for his sister. Kathleen seemed to sense this, and Marty was grateful. There was a lot to absorb today.

Marty stepped out into the sticky night air. The next-door neighbor let out a big cheer, so something good must be happening with the Phillies. It looked to be a sure win.

"Short just struck out the side," said the enthusiastic neighbor. Chris Short's transformation from mediocrity into full-fledged stardom was a pleasant surprise and a big reason for the Phillies' surprising success.

Kathleen came out and gave Marty a big hug. He tried hard to hide his embarrassment, but he thought this was a nice gesture of forgiveness from Kathleen to him.

Marty felt a tremendous sense of relief. He even considered giving the military another look. Maybe there's more to it than all the dumb movies he had to endure during a double feature that had a monster movie on as the second movie. Marty always hoped the movies could be reversed in order so he could walk out of the Army film. But he was becoming more intrigued.

The prospect of a twenty-five-mile hike and all that walking in all different types of environments was really starting to appeal to his sense of adventure. Marty tried to calculate what a twenty-five-mile hike would be in South Philadelphia terms. If he attempted the hike that started from his house, amazingly enough, he could almost walk to Delaware, a completely different state. If he crossed the Delaware River and walked for two consecutive days and headed east, he could wind up in Atlantic City, which excited him even more. There was certainly a lot to chew on that night. The lure of unrestrained wanderlust filled his heart and mind.

Marty felt a great burden had been lifted from his shoulders similar to how he felt after studying for a couple of tests the night before and doing well. The relief was pure bliss, and his mind felt clear, cleaner, and uncluttered.

Even better news awaited him at home. More eight-millimeter film arrived from Kodak. In the excitement of the afternoon, his mom never had a chance to tell him. Marty made plans to film the next day. It was supposed to be a nice sunny day with only a slight chance for a late afternoon thunderstorm—perfect weather for his planned scene of the Frankenstein monster wandering and being chased around the countryside.

Chapter 17

The Pit and the Thunderstorm

South Philadelphia was a congested urban neighborhood packed with wall-to-wall row homes. Despite this density, there was an unusual spacious, undeveloped, open pit area on Penrose Avenue near the Quartermaster Complex and the I-76 Schuylkill Expressway that had some dirt trails, a few trees, and a steep hill that led down to a clear semi-forested, almost rural area with no buildings. There was plenty of rubble strewn about. Since the area was a large open depression, no modern twentieth-century buildings could be seen that would interfere with the Central European setting that the movie was supposed to be set in.

Ironically, across the street from the depression was a busy twenty-four-hour diner that was always crowded with all kinds of customers, including big, noisy trucks. The area was a quick exit off of the I-76 Schuylkill Expressway, so it was popular with truck drivers and long-distance travelers. However, inside and within the isolated depression, the undeveloped area resembled the Black Forest in all its isolation.

Marty and Mark scouted out the area one day. They went to the nearby Dairy Queen and started walking off the pineapple sundaes they were eating. It was twilight, and the colorful, bright lights of the diner and the constant steaming headlights of the expressway were bright and prominent, but Marty and Mark noticed a dark unlit undeveloped blotch not far away like a large circle of darkness, and this caught their attention. When they saw the area was almost a football field long and wide, they realized, as budding filmmakers, this was a golden opportunity they should take advantage of and without much delay. They noticed a large sign with a DePascuale Construction logo, so in short order, the area would soon be filled, and something would be built on top of the pit.

"This would be a great place to have the monster being chased by some angry villagers. It has great potential," said Marty, practically salivating at the prospect.

"Yeah, but we better do it quick before some hotel, a restaurant, or something else is built here," answered Mark.

"As soon as we get new film, we will get going." Marty wanted to take quick advantage of the fortuitous find.

The film had finally arrived, and tomorrow would be the day to get the unusual location of inner city wilderness on film. Marty was too excited to sleep. He watched the end of the Phillies' game and started watching the late show movie, *Angels with Dirty Faces*. He was impressed. Cagney was a pretty good actor but not in the same league as Boris Karloff.

The one main problem they faced would be to avoid Sammy the Psycho. They would have to cut through his neighborhood in order to get to the big undeveloped pit. His unpredictability and wild mood swings worried Marty.

The next morning dawned bright and sunny, but Marty did not get up until ten thirty. The sky was still partly sunny, but the puffy white clouds were becoming darker and more ominous on the western horizon. His younger brothers were already awake and playing stick and half ball in front of their home out on the street, but they could not get going because Mark was still sleeping, so Marty tried to wake him up before the day became grayer. It was a task Marty did not look forward to.

"Mark, wake up! Mark, come on . . . wake up! We have to get going . . ."

Mark yawned a couple of sleepy "Okay . . . okay . . . I'm coming. I'm coming," but he still just lay in bed and did not even sit up.

Marty tried to emphasize the urgency, but Mark never stirred to get out of bed.

Now I know what my mom goes through every morning during the school year, thought Marty.

He tried very hard to get Mark moving, but to no avail. Marty looked out the front bedroom window and saw the sunlight gradually disappearing behind light gray clouds. He really needed to get Mark, his right-hand man, up and going. Everyone else was eager to film, or at least, that's what they told Marty. The boys seemed to be enjoying the neighborhood half-ball game, but they could play that at any time. The movie had to take priority.

Marty was getting desperate. Mark kept rolling away in bed and did not get up. He remembered his mom's threats during the school year about pouring cold water on Mark if he did not get up "this second." The warning actually worked because Marty never remembered his mom actually doing it.

Marty attempted to use the effective threat.

"Mark! I am going to pour water on your head if you don't get up!" Still no response.

Marty tried a few more times and finally became completely fed up, so he went to the bathroom and filled up the glass on the sink. It wasn't freezing cold but more a cool room temperature. Marty brought the glassful of water into the front bedroom and charitably gave Mark two more warnings.

"My conscience is clear," said Marty as he poured the water on Mark's still sleeping face.

"What is going on . . . what's happening? Help! I'm drowning!"

Mark was annoyed and started cursing at Marty, but he did finally get up and out of bed. *Mission accomplished*, thought Marty.

"Sorry, Mark, but you wouldn't budge. We were waiting on you."

"What was the big hurry?"

"We were all set to go, but you wouldn't get up, so I had to resort to drastic measures. Let's go! Just get dressed. We need to start filming."

Mark was greatly annoyed at first, but the wet dunking not only cleared his head but also invigorated him. He quickly recovered from the initial irritation and actually looked forward to the day's shooting schedule.

Marty and Mark assembled their crew. Their mom asked if they needed any help since so far, she was the principal photographer, but Marty said it was a long walk, and he would rather have her prepare supper.

"Okay, it will be meat loaf with tomato sauce, string beans, and mashed potatoes," she said as she wiped her meat and gravy-stained hands on a brown and white towel.

"Okay, good. We will be home in plenty of time."

Cassie was close by, folding some clothes in the dining room. She could not resist a parting shot.

"Okay, Marty, try to be civil. Don't go around punching kids and starting fights."

I guess the world has returned to its balance, thought Marty. Cassie has recovered from her earlier bout of niceness and resorted to her old sarcastic self. Marty ignored the barb and marched his five-man crew—all brothers and one close friend—down 15th Street toward Oregon Avenue.

Once they reached Oregon Avenue, a wide street with both commercial businesses and plenty of homes, the budding film crew turned right and walked west. This was virgin territory for his younger siblings, but Marty had trudged these streets for years.

He especially enjoyed the area around Christmastime. The area was a typical South Philadelphia Holiday Street scene with front and basement windows outlined in bright red, green, and blue lights. A few homes had white lights. Many Nativity scenes graced the front bay windows, and a few were set up in the basement windows. There were plenty of Santa Clauses also as well as numerous toy-stuffed sleighs driven by nine illuminated reindeers led by Rudolph's bright red nose.

But there was one street that really stood out and was truly remarkable, even by South Philadelphia standards. Smedley Street, which was a unique street because it was twice as large as the typical row home street, had a large grassy island in the middle of the road, about one-half of a football field wide. So in addition to the brightly lit individual homes, the street had a huge life-size Nativity complete with shepherds and farm animals and Santa's toyshop with elves and plenty of toys in the middle of this urban meadow. To add an even more festive touch, Christmas music was piped in over loudspeakers, so a wandering pedestrian could take in the colorful street scene and listen to the Yuletide music to get even more into the Christmas spirit. Marty especially enjoyed walking in this area on a Sunday night in December after an Eagles game. It was more fun with an Eagles victory to savor but still enjoyable no matter what the outcome.

The only drawback was that Sammy the Psycho lived a few blocks away, and their path to the Penrose Avenue outdoor scene would force Marty's group to enter Sammy's twisted domain.

Marty had a supporting group, but they were very young. Marty dreaded the thought of losing face with his youngest brothers if he ran into Sammy and he went on a rampage again. This would be a major problem. Marty fervently hoped and prayed the unwelcome confrontation would not happen.

As they approached 21st Street, Oregon Avenue became more commercial and less residential. They were getting uncomfortably close to Sammy's hangout. Marty hoped Sammy would not be around. He felt responsible for his younger brothers. They were out for a lark: a pleasant stroll to an isolated pocket of country in the city and also make a movie with their older brothers. They were thrilled. The clouds made the summer day more pleasant by cutting down on the sun's heat.

Marty didn't want their infectious good spirits dashed by a confrontation with a "wannabe" tough guy. Marty didn't want to lose face with his younger brothers and feared another fight with Sammy would do that.

Marty was lucky the last time he met Sammy and was able to hold off his attacker and his broken bottle weapon of choice. Would he be so fortunate a second time?

One plus was that he did have Mark with him, younger by only a year. Mark was pretty feisty and tough and would be a good wingman if Sammy attacked Marty again, and now he started feeling better if they ran into Sammy. Mark would be a big help. As long as Sammy didn't have a posse of punks with him, Marty became more confident Sammy could be neutralized.

When they passed Murphy's department store and turned northwest toward the busy intersection, Marty breathed easier. No sign of Sammy. He could fully concentrate on filming the movie scene. *Could be the greatest one yet, even better than the werewolf transformation scene*, mused Marty.

The rain looked like it was holding off, and the gray clouds would add an ominous air to the outdoor scene of the Frankenstein monster on the rampage among frightened villagers (all four of them).

Marty had a bag of different shirts to make it seem there was a bigger cast. Marty's monster would strangle one brother with a red shirt and kill the same brother with a yellow shirt to make it seem more villagers were being attacked by the man-made monster. With a small cast and budget, Marty had to do a lot of improvisation.

The adolescent film crew reached the edge of the depression. Marty visualized the various scenes to be filmed. The monster would kill a couple villagers who wandered into his hideout. The pit had a few clumps of bushes and small trees that would serve as a nice backdrop for the unsuspecting villagers.

The main dramatic scene would be the chase between the angry stick-waving villagers and the fleeing Frankenstein monster. There were some rubble-strewn trails in which the chase scene could take place. These dirt paths led to a steep slope upward out of the depression and back onto the Penrose Avenue area. The hill would be where the monster got tired of running away and turned to fight back. There were several small rocks along the rural hillside. Marty would have the monster pick up the rocks and hurl them down on the pursuing mob.

Marty was really excited about this action-packed scene, and his enthusiasm transferred to his four brothers and their two friends. The quick death scenes were filmed, and the thrilling chase scene began. Marty's exertions caused him to sweat quite a bit inside the full-face mask. He had to take a couple of breaks to wipe the sweat out of his eyes and forehead. Luckily, he bought a handkerchief and used it to wipe off the excess perspiration not only from his head but also the mask itself, which was getting soaked.

The wind started to increase and whistled through the bushes and small trees for a nice dramatic effect. Marty looked up at the sky, and his heart dropped. Dark thunderous clouds were building on the western horizon. No doubt a big storm was coming. Marty wondered why the storm was brewing so early. All the weather reports called for late afternoon and evening storms.

Marty hoped they could film the rock-throwing scene before the skies really let loose and exploded. Mark was the cameraman, and he set up at the base of the hill, and again began filming. Marty stumbled up the slope (it was tough to see through the narrow slits of the hooded eyes of the mask) and reached almost to the top. His pursuers would try to climb up after the monster.

Marty would start throwing the rocks, but he carefully aimed to avoid hitting anyone. Marty tossed the stones down. They rolled down theatrically, and his dodging and falling brothers and friends created a spectacular scene (or at least, he hoped so).

The rain held off for most of the scene but finally burst through the gray clouds. Mark kept filming. A couple of shocking lightning bolts slashed through the sky. Marty hoped some of the zigzagging streaks were caught by the camera.

The rain came down in heavy torrents and soaked the crew. The slope became muddier and difficult to climb up for the younger boys. Marty and Mark helped the younger brothers up the slick slippery incline. After a few slides and slips, everyone was back on top, and not a moment too soon, the heavens really opened up, and the lightning and thunder screeched louder and closer. Some of the boys started crying. Marty really couldn't blame them. He was really getting scared himself. He had never experienced such an intense storm, especially being exposed outside in the elements with nowhere to safely hide from its ferocity.

Marty, in another stroke of good fortune, took his mom's advice and brought along a couple of plastic bags for the props. Mark wisely put the eight-millimeter camera in one of the bags to keep it from getting wet. *Thanks, Mom, as always*, Marty thought.

But the wild weather was terrifying, and he had a couple of frightened youngsters to worry about. Where could they go?

There were very few homes and even fewer businesses in this area. The location was near the expressway, and there was no viable place to seek shelter. There were a few tall trees, whose wide leafy branches could shield them from the heavy rain, but Marty remembered hearing and reading that tall trees were a bad place to hide in a lightning storm.

Marty and Mark frantically looked left, right, and everywhere. There were no shelters close by. Then in a desperate flash of insight, Marty remembered how close they were to the Schuylkill Expressway. There were some overpasses that could protect them from the driving rain and intermittent lightning. The closest bridge was a few blocks away.

That was it! They would have to run a few blocks, but the activity would get their minds off of the storm's terror.

"Don't worry, we will be okay," said Marty. "But we need to run to the bridge a few blocks from here. Are you all ready?"

Marty looked at Tim, Joey, and Ted with their soaked clothes and scared faces. He couldn't tell if the drenching rain or their fearful tears caused most of the facial wetness. Activity and purpose would alleviate much of their alarm. So Marty and Mark took a firm hold of the camera and prop clothes on one hand and used their other free hand to grab hold of the younger brothers and keep them running at a fast pace and to ensure in their panic that they did not get hit by any car. Marty's mom would never forgive him if one of "her boys" were struck by a vehicle, especially since it was Marty's idea to come to this remote area in the first place.

A loud crack of thunder terrified Joey and Tim, and they rushed into Marty's arms. The rain, if possible, came down even harder. Marty felt like he was being hit with a powerful Atlantic Ocean wave with all his clothes on. The loud snap of lightning also terrified Marty. He looked at Mark, who was equally scared. His eyes were wider than a basketball.

Even though Marty didn't like war movies, he remembered a line from one of the better ones in which one heroic soldier (he vaguely remembered the actor might have been Richard Widmark) told his huddled group of frightened men, "There are two kinds of people here—those that stay here on the beach and die and those that get up and fight and survive." *Something like that*, he thought, so Marty gave more encouragement to his frightened siblings.

"Well, we are already soaked . . . we can't get any wetter. We just need to go past these two big trees, and we will be underneath the bridge where we will be perfectly safe. Okay, grab my hand and Mark's and stay with us. Don't run off by yourself! Is everybody ready?

Marty could see the gleam of hope in their eyes. The group started running. The first intersection light was still green. Marty hoped it would stay green so they could get to the expressway overpass quicker and not have to wait at a red light. The boys had a good pace going, and Marty wanted it to continue.

As they approached the busy thoroughfare of Passyunk Avenue, the light turned yellow. Marty looked at Mark and silently nodded to keep going. The group got halfway across the wide street, and the light turned red.

He knew his brothers had it drilled into them to stop at any sign of a red light, but they had to keep going. Tim was slowing down in obedience to his parents' warning, but Marty gave a hard tug to keep him running.

"Marty, the light is red. We have to stop . . . ," Tim dutifully said.

"Mom and Dad will understand. The cars will see us. Let's keep going."

Marty devoutly hoped the cars would stop. They were more than halfway across, so any normal driver slowed down, but the pouring rain cut down on visibility for everyone. He said a couple of Hail Marys for a safe crossing.

It worked! They made it across without any speeding car smashing into them. Now the overpass was closer, and no red lights could delay the group.

Marty stepped into a couple of big puddles. Now his shoes were completely saturated, along with his shirt and pants, but the group of boys kept moving, and they scampered safely underneath the high-way bridge and felt more secure.

The rain was not letting up, and frightful bolts of jagged light-ning zapped close by. The shocking explosions of thunder caused them to huddle closer together, but Marty reassured them that the bridge would protect them from any plunging lightning strikes. Now all they had to do was wait out the storm.

"How much longer, Marty?" asked a more confident and less scared Tim.

"Thunderstorms usually don't last too long."

Marty looked westwards toward the Schuylkill River and Jerry's Corner and saw a definite brighter set of clouds.

"Look! The dark clouds are going away. Maybe another ten minutes if we are lucky."

The thunder became more muffled and the flashes of lightning duller and less surly. The stormy weather was definitely breaking for the better.

With the improving weather, Marty was going to say, "Wasn't that fun!" but believed their soaked condition would get a definite negative response, so he talked about the Phillies' great win last night to get their minds off their misery. The ponderous gray clouds broke up, and patches of blue punched through the gloom. The storm finally lessened, and they started walking the nine blocks to home.

Marty shook off the heavy moisture from the yellow Acme plas-tic bag, which protected the precious eight millimeter Kodak camera. The angular feel of the camera brightened Marty's mood. The terri-ble storm and his traumatized siblings preoccupied Marty and almost made him forget the great film footage they had recorded.

The increasing sunny weather matched Marty's growing opti-mism. The sun's heat even started drying out their wet clothes. Things were definitely looking up! By the time the party reached 15th Street, their clothes were just about dry. The one glaring exception was their drenched socks and sneakers, which would need more than a sunny afternoon to clean and dry.

Marty wanted to downplay the mad dash at a red light across Passyunk Avenue in the driving rain. He hoped his little brothers thought the same thing.

They did. The quartet of brothers were so happy to be safe and dry in their secure home. The terror of the thunderstorm was fading, and the thrill of the adventure took over.

Their mom asked, "Did you get taught in the storm?"

Marty answered more positively than he originally thought. "Yeah, we did, but we rode most of it out underneath the overpass. Our shoes are still soaked to the bone. We stepped in plenty of puddles along Oregon Avenue. Glad we are now back safe and sound in our nice warm house."

Veronica told all the kids to take off their wet shoes, and especially the socks.

"I'll do a wash. Make sure I get all their socks. Have them change their clothes. Marty, it is your job to make sure they all take off their wet clothes. I don't want anyone getting sick. Get it in a pile and put them in the wash. Don't forget to include your clothes also."

Marty didn't mind making sure all his brothers changed out of their wet clothes. He really didn't even mind collecting them all into a pile. But putting them all in the washing machine was going a little too far. Wasn't that Cassie's job? Marty had never opened up the washing machine. He had absolutely no idea how it worked and what to do. Wasn't that what big sisters were put on earth for?

He was hoping Cassie would be in the area and take over when he collected all the clothes. Marty would gladly put up with her "wise gal" comments. Cassie had a smart mouth and dished out a lot of criticism, but Marty had to give her credit. She did get things done. Cassie cleaned around the house a lot and occasionally helped cook sometimes, although their mom was in complete control in the kitchen. It was her queenly domain. The older sisters could lend a hand here and there: cut up some tomatoes and onions or do some shopping. That was about it. Cassie also helped out a lot in other areas also, vacuuming and dusting and cleaning the bathroom. Cassie was a big help to her mom but a royal pain to her younger brothers.

Marty took out the Kodak eight-millimeter camera from the wet plastic bag. The bag was so drenched from the rain that large drops of water fell on his shoes and the living room rug. Cassie walked by and, of course, made a smart-alecky comment. But Marty just grunted and half-smiled. After all, Cassie, true to form, did take care of all the wet clothes and started the wash, so Marty gladly absorbed her wisecracks. Marty reached into the bag and held his breath. The outer bag was totally drenched. He dearly hoped the camera was dry as well as the precious film inside it. He grasped the metal sides and felt tremendous relief. The camera seemed pretty dry. When he pulled the camera out, it looked like it was inside a dry warm toaster oven instead of being outside in a raging thunderstorm.

Good old Mom, Marty thought. Thank God they followed her advice and brought the plastic Acme shopping bags. If the camera was dry, the film had to be just as dry. Marty thought the five minutes of film was their best effort yet and made plans to process the undeveloped film through the normal mail channels. He could hardly wait for the results.

AUGUST

National League Standings August 1964

TEAM	WON	LOST	WON-LOST%	GAMES BACK
PHILADELPHIA	59	41	.590	-----
SAN FRANCISCO	59	44	.573	1.5
CINCINNATI	56	47	.544	5.5
PITTSBURGH	53	45	.528	5.0
MILWAUKEE	53	48	.525	6.5
ST. LOUIS	53	49	.520	7.0
LOS ANGELES	50	50	.500	9.0
CHICAGO	48	52	.480	11.0
HOUSTON	45	60	.429	16.5
NEW YORK	32	72	.308	29.0

Chapter 18

Family Vacation and a Heavenly Surprise

North entrance to the Wildwood boardwalk.

August rolled around. The good news was that the Phillies were still in first place. The news became even better when the team acquired slugger Frank Thomas on waivers from the Mets.

"He will be a welcome addition. He has some power and will give the Phils extra jolt in the lineup," said Martin Senior. Marty Junior remembered that Frank Thomas led the Mets in home runs in their first season just two years ago. The Mets were terrible, setting a major league record with 120 losses, so that might not look too impressive, but he did hit thirty-four home runs and knocked in almost one hundred runs. Not bad for such a horrible team. The whole family was excited. They all believed this could only help the Phillies in their quest for the pennant.

The bad part about August was that it meant the month of September was next, and then the start of a new school year was closing in, and summer vacation was drawing to a close.

"Summer's over," moaned Mark, who always looked to the negative side of things. If the Phillies had a five-run lead, he would say it should have been eight runs if Wes Covington didn't strike out with the bases loaded.

"Not really," replied Marty, trying to be more positive. "We still have another solid month of summer vacation. Let's make the most of it. We can finish the movie. We'll keep practicing the final fight scene. Hopefully, we can film it on the steps of the Swedish American Museum. I really believe that is our best bet to use as Frankenstein's castle. I also think it will be even better than what we just shot on Penrose Avenue."

That seemed to motivate Mark a little more, but what really pepped him up was that during the second week of August, the whole family was going to the Jersey shore and a fun-filled week in Wildwood.

Martin Senior was able to get a week for the entire family at one of his firemen friend's vacation home. Tony Canizaro had generously allowed his mentor, Martin, to have one week rent-free at his summer home in Wildwood Crest. The cost for the vacation involved only the gas for the ninety-mile drive and food. The place had a kitchen, so food costs would be cut down even more. The high boardwalk prices could be avoided, although Marty enjoyed walking the boards and spending some money for boardwalk food on at least one night during the week. Marty and Mark especially enjoyed the pizza, fudge, and Alpine tropical drinks, especially the creamy coconut milk.

The last remaining obstacle was transportation since the family owned no car. Martin Senior walked the four blocks to work, and Kathleen and Cassie also walked about seven blocks to the Quartermaster/Defense Logistics Plant on Oregon Avenue, so there was no overwhelming need for a car. Besides, parking was tight along the narrow streets and closely packed row homes.

Martin Senior was able to borrow a Chevy station wagon from his older brother, Jack. The car was barely large enough to fit the entire family. Kathleen and Catherine would take the bus down or hitch a ride with one of their friends to make a little more extra room. The station wagon was big and accommodating but not that big.

The entire family looked forward to the hour-and-a-half drive to the shore. The cool ocean breezes and the pounding surf at the beach were a welcome change from the stifling late summer heat that hung like a wet blanket along the row home-lined streets of the city. It was a nice change of pace to look forward to before the month ended and the kids had to get ready for school.

The ninety-minute trip from Philadelphia across the recently built Walt Whitman Bridge into the flatlands of Southern New Jersey toward the ocean was interrupted by several choruses of "Are we there yet?" from the younger siblings. The harassed father, Martin, tried to interest the family by remarking how flat South Jersey was and related his wartime experiences in various training camps throughout the Continental US.

"Look at the surrounding countryside. It is flatter than a dinner dish. No hills or tall buildings in sight unlike Philadelphia."

Marty was the only one slightly interested, and he had heard it all before.

"Try to get some sleep," begged Veronica in a vain attempt to quiet the constant whining and the "When are we getting there?" questions. "You will be more refreshed for all the fun we will have at the beach."

Marty ignored most of the complaints by daydreaming about the positive impact Frank Thomas would have on the Phillies and all the work needed to finish his pride and joy, the monster movie. Marty was able to tune out his younger siblings' plaintive pleas of

"How much longer until we are at the beach?" His two daydreams kept him occupied for most of the trip. The two youngest sisters, Margaret and Theresa, were the only quiet ones because they slept for most of the trip.

The entire family perked up when Martin Senior grandly announced that they were very close and that now was the time to roll down the car windows and "smell the ocean air."

Mark and Marty opened the back windows to let in the salty air, which was very prevalent and exhilarating, almost as strong as spaghetti sauce but not as tasty.

The station wagon glided across the low-lying marshes, and the children became even more excited when Mark spotted the large Ferris wheel looming over the seaside resort. Soon everyone in the car could see the roller coasters on the boardwalk and the homes and colorful art deco hotels of Wildwood.

"It will not be too much longer," said Martin to his children. "We will unpack first and check out the place, and then Mom will make us some lunch."

The family arrived at the beach house, which was actually located three blocks from the ocean but close enough for a rent-free week at the shore. The timing was almost perfect. While unpacking, Cassie and Kate showed up after walking from the Trailways bus station and helped carry the boxes and suitcases into the two-story wooden house with its charming front porch and rocking chairs, quite a rarity for the South Philadelphians.

Cassie seemed more pensive than usual, like she was either deep in thought or trying to vent something deep in her soul. Even the younger children noticed the unusual quiet demeanor of their energetic older sister and "second mom."

That night during the family dinner, the family discovered what preoccupied Cassie. The news turned out to be quite a shock.

After finishing the delicious Veronica-cooked meal of chicken cutlets, brown potatoes, and corn, Cassie stated she had something important to say.

Mark thought what else was new since Cassie was never known to withhold her opinion on any subject. She also never sugarcoated her thoughts no matter how much it hurt anyone else's feelings.

Cassie began, "Well, I am glad everyone is sitting down because what I am about to say and do might be slightly surprising."

Everyone's ears perked up, even the littlest daughters sitting on their parent's lap.

Martin was getting a little impatient with all the suspense.

Cassie sensed this and just blurted it all out.

"Well, I've decided not to attend Immaculata College this fall."

Before Veronica and Martin could voice their objections, Cassie continued, "I have been accepted into the Columban Sisters and will be entering their novitiate."

The family was collectively quite stunned. No one spoke or made any movement. There was an awed silence. It was finally broken when Kate stood up and gave her twin sister an affectionate hug and said, "We love you and are so proud of you."

That seemed to break the spell and stir the family into action.

Veronica also congratulated Cassie and gave her a lingering embrace.

Martin Senior still seemed in a daze but recovered enough presence of mind to say, "When will you be leaving?"

Cassie replied her departure will be around Labor Day.

This was not the complete story; the family received another jolt when Cassie announced what type of order she was about to join.

After the initial surprise wore off, Martin and Veronica assumed their daughter was entering the Immaculate Heart of Mary (IHM) Sisters, a local order that specialized in teaching. More than likely, Cassie would be a grammar school teacher in one of the numerous archdiocesan schools throughout the City of Philadelphia and the adjoining suburbs. They did not at first realize that Cassie did not actually say she was becoming an IHM sister but was intent on joining the Colomban Sisters, a missionary society that serves in the world's poorest areas.

Martin Senior was beginning to absorb the full impact of Cassie's decision. Grandfather Adolph was a monthly supporter of the Columban Fathers and Sisters and received their mission magazine throughout the year, along with numerous other Catholic Church charities. That must have been the initial spark for Cassie's vocation.

"Are you positive this is what you want to do, Catherine?"

"Yes, Dad. This is not a spur-of-the-moment decision. I have given it a lot of serious thought and contemplation as well as many prayers. Haven't you noticed all the correspondence I have been getting?"

"Not really," Martin sadly confessed.

Veronica actually was aware but thought all the mail was for a school project.

"Why were you keeping it such a secret?" asked her father.

"Well, I wanted to be absolutely positive. I did not want any outside badgering or questions. I thought it best to think and pray about it on my own."

Martin had recovered enough from the unexpected shock to tell Cassie, "Well, we certainly will pray for you."

Martin was now beginning to absorb his daughter's fateful decision. Cassie would not be close to home if she became a missionary nun. She could be stationed anywhere in the world, most likely South America or Africa.

Most of the younger children did not realize the full impact of Cassie's pending departure. It would hit them very hard in the coming weeks.

Cassie hoped her news would not dampen the family's vacation.

"Nonsense," said Veronica. "We will make it the grandest and most memorable family vacation ever! We will cherish every second together."

Veronica had to stop. She feared if she said anything more, her voice would crack, and she did not want this to be a sad occasion.

Her father came to the rescue.

Adolph spoke up and told Cassie, "You will make the entire family proud. You are an answer to one of my many petitions to the Almighty. To have one of my grandchildren as a religious . . . how magnificent and wonderful! I know it will be difficult at times, but you will be fine."

That seemed to revive the family's spirit again, and the somber mood changed to vacation mode once again.

Marty had to admit he was impressed. He never thought Cassie had that much character and integrity, that she could be so dedicated and holy. Admittedly, she did try hard—helping her mom doing laundry, vacuuming, mopping, changing diapers. Cassie was an indefatigable worker and a good athlete. She was the center of her high school basketball team at St. Maria Goretti. Despite her average size, Cassie was a tenacious defensive player and aggressive rebounder, so she undoubtedly did have grit. She just had to work on her personality, which could be harsh at times—at least, that was the impression of her younger siblings.

Mark put it best when he first discovered her desire to become a religious sister. "Well, she certainly is mean enough to be a nun."

Mark was incorrigible in class, and his exuberant antics were enough to gain the attentions of many of the nuns, who had to discipline two platoon size classes of unruly inner-city kids. How else could they keep order?

When Marty reflected more on his sister's decision, Cassie's bombshell did kind of make sense. Cassie, despite her rough edges, was selfless and uncomplaining. Marty always thought Kathleen would be the nun in the family, which was why her having a boyfriend was such a surprise, but life doesn't always make sense as Marty's dad often said. Needless to say, her parents and grandfather were thrilled with the news the more they reflected upon it.

The rest of the week went according to previous vacations at the shore.

The weather was decent for late summer, just a few stray thunderstorms in the late afternoon and a passing early morning shower.

Marty began the day with his grandfather, who walked the entire two-mile Wildwood Boardwalk. The trip to the southern end of the boardwalk was about a mile from the vacation house, so the entire round-trip walk was six miles, about two hours of exercise, which started at six in the morning. The amusement piers and the wide beaches and the far horizon of the Atlantic Ocean kept up interest during the walk.

Marty had to adjust his sleep schedule because he usually stayed up late during the summer, sometimes going to bed as the sun rose, but it was well worth waking up early to spend time with his grandfather.

During the walk, not many places were open, but Marty found the boards busier than he imagined with numerous bike riders that amiably cruised past Adolph and his grandson.

The smell of freshly cooked bacon and eggs wafted enticingly through the ocean air.

"Smells good, doesn't it, Marty? It is very tempting to walk in and grab a seat and eat a leisurely breakfast while watching the pounding ocean surf. One of my favorite pleasures. But we need to resist the temptation. Your mom will cook up a storm when we get back to the beach house."

Marty really enjoyed the early morning walk and forced himself to go to bed early so he could accompany his granddad again the next day. Soon it became a habit while at the shore during the walk. The early dawn walks also hatched an audacious plan that Marty and his grandfather concocted during their time together.

The family made it to the beach on most days but only in short spurts. Most of the kids did not like the abrasiveness of the sand, including Marty. It was nice to jump in the ocean, get wet, allow the waves to crash into you, maybe even do a little body surfing. After that, it was time to dry off and go back to the beach house to relax.

Cassie and Veronica were the only true sun worshippers in the family. They remained at the beach for several hours. Everyone else made the obligatory short visits before and after lunch.

Veronica would have preferred to stay all day along the ocean shore. Cassie felt the same way, but duty called, and they both went back to make and serve lunch.

Marty felt a little sorry for Catherine. This was probably going to be her last chance for a nice tan before she donned the nun's habit where the only sunburn she could possibly get was on her nose, and even that was remote. Every other part of her body would be completely covered in black, or so Marty assumed. Every religious order had different habits, but most seemed to be dark in color.

The McAlynn family settled into a comfortable summer vacation routine. The boardwalk was avoided on most nights to save money, but Martin Senior did take the younger children a few times to play at the arcade. One night they even went on a few rides at the Amusement piers. It was a pleasant collective memory, made a little melancholy by Cassie's imminent departure.

Marty gladly helped out his Dad on the Boardwalk nights, and actually enjoyed it. He loved how little Margaret would hold her entire hand in Marty's fingers.

However one night, a particularly distasteful assignment fell by default into Marty's lap.

Veronica and Martin deserved a night out. Martin was planning to meet some of his fireman friends. Cassie and Kate had prior plans to meet with some high school classmates at the same time.

A babysitter was needed for the evening, and Marty drew the short straw. Mark was a possibility, but he connected with some neighborhood friends also in Wildwood for the week. Grandpa Adolph went to dinner with his daughter, Bernadette, in North Wildwood. There was no other choice. Marty unfortunately had no other plans and was unanimously selected by default.

Marty hoped to salvage the night and head to the Boardwalk with the little ones, but this plan was vetoed by his mom.

"They have already been there enough for the week. I think you should take them to the movies. There is a brand-new Disney movie that just came out, *Mary Poppins*. It is supposed to be very good. It is getting rave reviews."

Marty grimaced and thought, *Oh no! Not a Disney movie!*

He enjoyed them when he was a kid, especially *The Shaggy Dog* and *The Absent-Minded Professor* with Fred MacMurray, but he was going into high school now.

"Mom, it is not a cartoon, is it?"

"Not completely. There are some animated sequences, but there are live actors in it."

Veronica sweetened the pot by saying Dick Van Dyke was the star. The older part of the family were fans of the *Dick Van Dyke Show*, which they never missed when it was on every week.

Marty was wavering, but what really made it better was when his mom said, "Guess who else is in it? Elsa Lancaster! Wasn't she the bride of Frankenstein?"

That did it! Marty was now more than willing to take his younger sisters and brothers to the movie. He also read the latest issue of one of his favorite magazines, *The Castle of Frankenstein*, which reviewed it very favorably. Plus, the younger siblings would really enjoy it.

Marty took Marie, Teresa, Margaret, and Joseph to the theater for the six-thirty show. It was longer than he thought, almost two and a half hours. The movie ended around nine. They had about a mile to walk back to the house. Marty decided to buy them ice cream to give the younger ones some extra energy for the trip back. The kids thoroughly enjoyed the film and probably did not need the sugar boost. They were so excited and kept talking about the movie and started singing about spoonfuls of sugar as they almost skipped back to the vacation home.

Marty had to admit the show was very good. Even the songs were memorable. The kids kept singing about feeding the birds and an unpronounceable long word that was about to become world-famous. Marty did not mind. All the songs were catchy tunes. This kept them occupied for the long walk back. The kids did not even whine about not stopping at the arcades or buying trinkets from the stores lining the Boardwalk.

Walt Disney worked his magic once again.

Chapter 19

A Walk to Remember

Delsea Drive (Route 47)-connecting the
Jersey Shore with Philadelphia.

As usual, the vacation week raced by faster than Superman chasing the Flash to the moon. The hands of time could not be stopped, and in what seemed all too soon, the station wagon was packed for the trip back home. Cassie and Kate were getting

143

ready to head to the bus station when Grandpop Adolph and Marty sprang an amazing surprise.

Adolph announced, "There is no need for Cassie and Kate to take the bus. Cassie is not the only member of this family to have a surprise up her sleeve. Marty and I have already discussed what we plan to do. We are well prepared, and we can't be talked out of our plan."

Martin Senior had no patience for more secrets, so he interrupted. "What in the world are you talking about?"

"I am about to do something I have always wanted to do but never could because of family obligations."

Veronica and Martin were completely puzzled. What goal could an eighty-one-year-old man still want to achieve? Before they could further ponder this question, Adolph answered, "Marty and I plan to walk back to Philadelphia from here."

If Adolph had said he wanted to suit up as an astronaut and fly to the moon, the shock and surprise could not be greater.

"What!" said both Veronica and Martin in unison.

Adolph was undeterred and proudly said, "You heard right. It makes more sense than you realize. There will be more room for Kate and Cassie in the car now. We can save bus fare. Plus, it will be nice for Cassie to take another long family trip back home, especially considering her future plans."

"There is *no way* on God's green earth we can allow that to happen," said a determined Martin.

He was reinforced by his horrified wife.

"Pop, come on! You cannot be serious! Maybe forty years ago it was feasible but not now!"

"Forty years ago, I had twelve children and an invalid wife, plus a six-days-a-week job with very little vacation time. This is a great opportunity. You don't know what next year will bring. What makes it even better is now I have a walking comrade to keep me company. Marty and I will make a good team. You of all people should not doubt my stamina, Veronica."

"It is not that, Pop. It's just that . . . well . . . you are not young anymore. You have to be realistic . . ."

144

Veronica was getting desperate. She was losing allies. Most of the kids liked the idea.

Mark also volunteered to go along, but Veronica's icy stare eliminated that possibility.

"Pop, I will worry too much. How long will this crazy idea take? It is over ninety miles."

"I figure three or four days. I have plenty of cash for food. We can sleep under the stars . . ."

"But what if it rains?"

"I have enough for an occasional motel if the weather is terrible. We have backpacks. We'll carry plenty of water. Remember I am an old soldier."

"Pop, but that was almost fifty years ago! Talk some sense into him, Martin. Please!"

Martin was slowly warming to the idea and becoming more intrigued.

Martin thought to himself and realized it was not that crazy an idea. *Why not? Let the old man pursue his dream. Marty will be a godsend to him.*

Veronica sensed she was losing the battle, but she persisted. "Martin, say something!"

But her husband was becoming more and more receptive to the idea. Sometimes you have to respect a long-simmering dream. Martin was doing some quick figuring and believed it was a possibility, provided his father-in-law and son stuck to a specific route.

"Let them do it. It is not like they are walking to Canada or across Death Valley. We have friends and relatives who can check up on them along the way. My brother, Mike, lives in Jersey now over in Pennsauken. He can help . . . Pop, you guys can do it, but you have to stick to a specific route and not deviate from the main road, which will have to be Route 47, the Delsea Drive. There are plenty of small towns and restaurants along the way."

"Yes, that's what I figured also. Plenty of woods, farms, fruit stands, and restaurants, so we won't starve."

Veronica could not believe she was losing the argument. She gave it one last try.

"Martin! Please!"

"It will be okay. Your dad and son are not crossing the DMZ in Korea. The South Jersey farmland is pretty safe last time I checked, except for the Jersey Devil, who might still be wandering the back roads of the Pine Barrens, but the Delsea Drive is too developed for any shenanigans on that end."

Adolph clinched the discussion with a biblical quote. Well, if I remember this old saying from the Bible. I believe it is from Isaiah . . . "A highway will be there, a roadway, and it will be called the Highway of Holiness. The unclean will not travel on it, but it will be for him who walks that way. And fools will not wander on it."

What could Veronica say to that?

Adolph and Marty finalized the route on the map and told Martin their exact route of march.

So it was all set.

Marty grabbed his backpack. His grandfather had a smaller one but more compact.

"Well, Marty, are you ready for a grand adventure? The hardest part of the journey can be the first step, so here we go."

Adolph told Veronica they would make collect calls every night to update their progress. The rest of the family wished them luck and waved goodbye. Mark still wanted to tag along, but Veronica was not about to lose that argument.

The first few miles were joyous to Marty. The challenge and excitement masked some lingering annoyances that would become all too evident during the journey. Marty enjoyed the march over the bridge that connected the barrier island to the mainland with the salty air of the ocean still prominent like the smell of freshly baked tollhouse cookies on Christmas Eve. The slight breeze caused the tall grass in the marshes to sway back and forth like a waving, cheering crowd at the ballpark.

The run-down, shabby white paint peeling fishing boats docked along the water's edge looked like they endured one rainstorm too many, but the crews seemed to maintain their enthusiasm. At least, that is what it looked like to Marty as the fishermen gave an encouraging wave of support to the unlikely backpacking duo.

Grandpop Adolph was adamant on maintaining a certain regimen, sticking to his five decades old World War I training, and insisted on ten-minute rest stops every hour. Marty still felt energetic and wanted to keep walking to retain their momentum, but Adolph said this is how the US Army trains, and who could argue with the US Army's undefeated war record?

During the walk, Marty enjoyed looking at the variety of miniature golf courses that appeared with regularity along the road, a last-ditch effort to lure beachgoers with another memory of vacation fun times.

Marty was amazed at their diversity and grandiosity. Each one tried to top the other with spectacular themes. Most had waterfalls or bubbling, cascading colorful water gushing over man-made volcanoes or mountains. Some had jungle themes with gorillas and giraffes; others had pirates complete with sailing ships and one-eyed scoundrels flashing menacing swords. These attractions kept the walk interesting, but the golf courses soon thinned out like wheat during a drought as they trudged farther from the resort town.

With the disappearance of these family entertainments, Marty could now feel the sheer physical effort was beginning to wear him down. The initial joy and excitement was giving way to concrete reality. Walking around the neighborhood was one thing, but a long-distance hike carrying a heavy backpack was a horse from another fire department, as the new Eagles head coach, Joe Kuharich, once said.

It was not so much his feet and legs that bothered him, but rather his aching back and shoulders were the main culprit. His shirt was drenched and sticky with well-earned perspiration.

Grandpop seemed effortlessly at ease. His backpack was lighter, but he was over eighty years old! It reminded Marty of the scene in *Treasure of Sierra Madre* when Bogart marveled at the "old goat" Walter Huston's physical stamina climbing the mountain trails in Mexico.

His grandfather's words were not comforting. "No matter how strong your legs are and how well conditioned a hiker you think you might be, the backpack will ride you more mercilessly than a Mongol cavalryman on his horse. There is no escaping this grim reality. You just need to accept this discomfort. Offer it up to God and get a few poor souls out of purgatory. Make the best of it, Marty. Soon it will be second nature to you, like a cross that a good Christian gets from God that you will just have to put up with."

The old man and the teen kept walking through the mercifully cloudy afternoon. Soon the sun was dipping closer to the horizon, and the two started looking for the night's rest stop.

"No sense walking during darkness. Let's not give a weary driver an excuse to hit us by accident. I promised your mom we will be extra cautious."

There was a small diner in the quaint little town of Dennis, so Adolph made a collect call home and reassured Veronica all was well and that they were stopping to sleep for the night.

The phone call went better than Adolph originally feared. His daughter seemed more at ease and accepting with the trip.

Grandpop found a nice secluded patch of woods well off the highway near a lake campsite. The trees were thick but spread evenly about four to five feet apart, thick enough to stop a car from accidentally plowing into their bivouac site. The two hikers filled up their bottles and canteens from an old-fashioned water pump from an underground well. Marty felt like a pioneer from a John Wayne Western as he plunged the red metal handle several times to gather some water from the faucet. After a few up-and-down pumps, the water flowed like a waterfall as the water gushed out.

The first bivouac in the Pine Barrens of South Jersey.

Dinner was some mushed but still tasty bologna sandwiches that Veronica dutifully prepared at the last minute.

"We will feast tomorrow night at the Egg Harbor Lake Diner and treat ourselves to a four-course meal with all the trimmings. How do you feel, Marty? The first day is always the hardest, using muscles you never knew you had. This kind of activity was normal one hundred years ago, but we are much softer now—too much TV and too many automobiles."

Grandpa further said he felt sore and a little stiff but in a good way. "This is telling my body I am still alive."

Marty, with the suppleness of youth, felt amazingly well, especially his legs and feet. No blisters or corns. His shoulders were feeling much better with the backpack off.

Adolph continued, "We did pretty well today. Time to wrap it up. The earlier we get to bed, the sooner we can start walking again and take advantage of the dawn's cooler weather before the afternoon's sun starts to wear us down."

149

Marty was fine with that. The rest of the evening, he listened to some of Grandpop's World War I Army stories. Marty was getting more and more groggy. It was tough to keep his eyes open. He soon gave into the delicious comforting feeling of closing his eyes and drifting into slumber land.

Marty woke up several hours later and heard his grandfather's rhythmic snores, which were much louder than he imagined since grandpa slept on the third floor.

Otherwise, the forest was peaceful and dark. Very dark. It was a black world with very little light. The night sky above could be glimpsed in between the tall, straight-as-an-arrow pine trees. Marty was amazed at the number of stars he could see. They were as bright as the glitter on his mom's homemade doll dresses—sharp specks of brilliance pasted on the velvet sky.

The bugs were annoying. Unbelievably irritating! They had to be swatted away to an alarming degree. It almost ruined the beauty of the nighttime sky. Marty remembered his grandfather, thinking ahead as usual, did pack some insect repellent. Marty took it out from his outside pouch of the backpack and smothered it on his neck and arms for some relief.

He could not sleep right away, so he daydreamed in the night about werewolves prowling the nearby woods. Marty even wondered about the mythical Jersey Devil. How true was it? Every legend has a basis in fact. Marty heard some sounds snapping on the forest floor— the cracking of twigs, the rustle of bushes. This set his imagination in overdrive and sent chills up his arms and spine. No horror film ever frightened him as much as lying on the ground in a dark forest deep in thought about werewolves and mythical monsters.

The comforting presence of his sleeping grandfather was a tremendous relief and caused him to drift back into a relaxing sleep.

When his grandfather woke him up, it was still dark, but dawn was approaching.

It was time to begin day two of the journey.

"Come on, Marty. We are burning sunshine. Time to get moving. Let's take advantage of the day's freshness before it ages into the afternoon's withering heat and humidity."

Marty stretched his arms and legs and crawled out of his thin, astronaut-light sleeping bag. He groggily rolled it up, drank some water, brushed his teeth, devoured a Clark bar, and filled up more water bottles from the pump.

In a matter of minutes, the duo walked on down the forested road like Bilbo Baggins and the dwarves in *The Hobbit*, a tale that Marty's grandfather often talked about and read to his grandkids on cold winter nights with its many thrilling adventures of fighting orcs, dragons, and reclaiming lost treasures.

Marty felt refreshed and strong. The restful night worked wonders. His aching shoulders and back felt much better. In a matter of hours, the hikers were beyond the small towns of Cape May County and entered the lake and forest country of Southern New Jersey. The bright blue lakes were a pretty contrast to the abundant green world of pine trees that lined the road and surrounded them like a benevolent mother embracing her children.

During the walk, Marty daydreamed a lot. His grandfather was strangely quiet, often deep in thought, but occasionally something would trigger a long-lost memory, and Adolph would narrate an interesting story from his long life.

After a solid ten hours of walking covering a distance of twenty-five miles, the two hikers were ready to pack it in for the evening. They looked at the map and found a nice spot just to the west side of Egg Harbor. This allowed them a chance to enjoy a sit-down meal at the local diner. Marty noticed the headline from the *Philadelphia Inquirer* that happily announced the Phillies were pulling away in the National League pennant race with the help of Frank Thomas, who slugged another homer.

There was a pay phone, so Marty could make a collect call and talk to his mom.

"How much longer do you think?" said Veronica, still anxious for the trip to end sooner rather than later.

"Probably another two days. Grandpa says we are making really good progress."

His mom thought not soon enough, but she bit her tongue, as she could sense the joy in Marty's voice as well as her dad's. She figured they were actually enjoying the walk as strange and inexplicable as this appeared to her.

This would turn into the high watermark of their journey and the last truly satisfying moment of the journey with one exception. That night and the following days plunged them into a morass of driving rain, sleepless nights, and relentless heat and humidity, not to mention the constant harassment of large, biting green flies.

The night actually started well. The Egg Harbor Diner had a delicious meal with all the trimmings. Marty demolished a bowl of spaghetti and a generous helping of chicken parmesan washed down with pink lemonade and topped off with pie a la mode. The farm fresh ice cream smothered the slice of pie in mouthwatering abundance. Marty could barely see any sign of the apple pie underneath the giant scoop.

His grandfather had a lighter fare—a cheeseburger with home fries and a cherry pie.

"Might be a good idea, Marty, to brush our teeth here in the diner bathroom now before we get started again. It will be just woods and a few farm stands for the next twenty miles."

They both felt bloated after the generous meal, but there would still be about ninety minutes of daylight left, so they could easily walk off the stuffed feeling in their stomach.

As they walked out of the rustic diner, Grandpop smelled moisture in the air and saw dark clouds hovering over the western horizon.

"This does not bode well, Marty." The twosome kept walking before the heavens opened up.

They were able to walk four more miles before the rain pelted them like arrows from an Indian attack in a cowboy movie.

Luckily, there were plenty of woods to duck into for shelter, but Marty and Adolph kept walking. Adolph looked in the distance for a good place to camp out. Marty and Adolph did not carry a tent, only a couple of ponchos, and were planning to just sleep under the stars.

Adolph spotted a large wooden billboard about a mile away.

"We will head to that landmark. It should afford us a bit of shelter from the storm."

The short walk seemed much longer. The wind picked up and caused the rain to slash their front, both sides, and back. There was absolutely no relief from the storm's wrath. Marty and Adolph were totally drenched upon reaching the billboard. The huge sign advertised sun tan lotion ironically enough. The reverse side was an ad for the movie, *Mary Poppins*.

"We could sure use her umbrella now," said Marty.

As grandfather hoped, there was enough overhanging wood to provide some protection from the fierce wind and sweeping rain.

They were completely soaked, but at least, they would not get more and more drenched. It was a slight solace to the weary travelers.

"At least, we will not get any wetter," said Grandpop. He also had some solid advice from his Army medic experiences in the training camps of the AEF (Allied Expeditionary Force).

"We really need to keep our feet dry. Our body heat will dry out our shirt and pants, but we can't allow our feet to stay wet. Take off your socks and put them inside your shirt, next to your skin."

"But they are dirty and smelly," said a worried Marty.

"Do it anyway! We are not visiting relatives or going to the opera. We need to put on some foot powder and some dry socks. This will prevent a horrible injury called trench foot, which was a big problem in the Great War. My medical training really drilled this medical reality into us. Trench foot is caused by constant wetness. The feet become red, swollen, tender, and very painful. At all costs, we want to avoid that horror. We have too many miles to still cover."

"Say no more, Grandpa. I understand completely."

Marty and Adolph settled as best they could for some fitful but restful dozing. Marty and Adolph took some brief naps but never were able to fall into a truly restful slumber.

Marty and Adolph could not wait until the sky lightened at dawn.

Marty dozed off, and when he awakened, he could see a fiery horizon blazing in the east that looked like a forest fire, but it was high in the sky, and Marty knew this was a good sign. This was all they needed to start day three of the grand adventure in good spirits.

Their clothes had dried decently during the night, and the dirty socks were as dry as toast. Grandpa Adolph told Marty to put these socks in a separate pouch. It would come in handy as they hiked down the highway.

"If your feet feel wet, don't hesitate to stop and change them, even if it has to be yesterday's socks. At least, they are dry."

One thing really struck Marty as he walked down the road. He was totally amazed at the number of dead animals lying on the side of the highway. They came in all shapes and sizes, ranging from small snakes and turtles to raccoons and skunks, even a decaying cat and dog on occasion. The smell was local fortunately. There was no overwhelming stench until Marty came right up on the dead carcass. During one particular mile-long stretch, Marty counted twenty-one dead animals.

The lonely road stretched for miles with trees
framing both sides of the highway.

"If we had a dime for every dead animal we see on the ground, we could buy your dad a brand-new Chevy," said Adolph. "It is a good life lesson. You need to be on your toes at all times, always be on the lookout. Try not to daydream too much. I know that is one of your favorite pastimes, but you have to look where you are going. Otherwise, you will be squashed like these poor creatures we see all over the road."

The rain was out of the area for now, but the heat of the sun was unrelenting like a fly buzzing around a picnic dinner. The humidity was also becoming more and more oppressive. The grand adventure was starting to turn into a great ordeal, but Marty and his grandfather plunged ahead, each deep in their own individual thoughts. Adolph reflected on his long life, his marriage, his children, and it brought forth a fount of bittersweet ponderings. Marty did not possess such a wealth of memories to keep him occupied as they forged onward. He thought of the future but only to the end of summer. Marty still dreaded the onset of high school, so he concentrated on his two great summer obsessions—baseball and his monster movie.

The silence did not bother either of them. They enjoyed their solitary thoughts.

The walk down the lonely South Jersey roads was not a numbing drudgery all the time. The milk of human kindness was surprisingly evident just a few miles down the highway.

After a long two-hour stretch of walking with nothing but dense trees and flat farmland to observe, Marty and his grandfather came to a tennis court seemingly out of place in this very rural part of the state. It was the first glimpse of a rare housing development recently built in the area.

An older couple, Carl and Noreen, in their early sixties were finishing up their friendly tennis match and, while wiping their perspiration with a white towel, gave an enthusiastic greeting to the hiking pair.

"Where are you two heading?" asked the man with a friendly interest.

"Philadelphia . . . or bust!" answered Grandpa.

"Really! Where did you all start?"

"Wildwood by the Sea!"

"Wow! That is impressive. I guess you are about halfway there now."

"Yes, that is what we figure."

Grandpa decided to take a break earlier than he wanted to. Why not? The couple seemed nice enough and sincerely interested. The trip was not designed to be a mindless trek of mile after mile with no time for improvisation. Why not experience life and the people you meet along the way? It's a nice microcosm of life's journey.

It turned out that the older couple were veteran backpackers themselves, having walked several sections of the Appalachian Trail in New York and Pennsylvania as well as Yosemite and Yellowstone out west. The conversation was very pleasant and provided a nice respite for the two tired hikers. After the brief conversation, both groups departed with a friendly wave and an exchange of good luck.

Marty and Grandpa started to walk away from the tennis courts.

Carl, after a gentle prod from his wife, Noreen, called out and asked, "How would you like some breakfast? You can hop in our car. We promise we will drive you right back to this same exact spot so you can still claim you walked the entire distance."

"Thanks, that is very kind. We are not fanatics. It is the journey, not the destination, that really matters."

Grandpa Adolph was enjoying the unexpected encounter.

Marty was also more than happy. He was overjoyed at the prospect of a home-cooked breakfast.

Marty and his grandfather got into Carl's red Valiant sedan, and the car drove about fifteen minutes west off of Route 47 deep into the fertile farmlands of the Garden State. Carl and Noreen's home was near a peach orchard and a cornfield. The house stood by itself and at night would look uninviting because of its Victorian starkness and isolation, but in the daytime, it looked more like Ma and Pa Kettle than Norman Bates' infamous motel made famous in Hitchcock's *Psycho*.

Noreen and Carl were gracious hosts, and Noreen cooked up a killer breakfast of eggs and ham, along with some buttery biscuits and freshly squeezed orange juice. Marty could actually watch Carl cut the fruit in two and squeeze it into the glass. Marty felt a little guilty at the thought that it might have been the best breakfast meal he ever had, especially in light of his mom's delicious Sunday morning feasts. Maybe it was just the circumstances of the long walk and the unexpected invite that colored Marty's perception at the absolute joy of this particular meal. The wonderfully fresh orange juice factor might have been a major tipping point. Marty was trying his best not to hurt his mom's feelings even in his deepest, most private thoughts.

Before they departed, Carl gave Marty and Adolph some freshly plucked peaches and plums from his backyard.

Carl also gave Marty a fisherman's hat. It was goofy-looking, and Marty would never wear it around the neighborhood, but Carl thought it would come in very handy.

"This will give you some protection from the sun, young man."

Marty was grateful and had to admit Carl had a point. His nose and forehead were beet red over the past two days, and the hat will not make the sunburn get any worse.

Carl had another helpful suggestion.

"Why not take a dip in our pool? It will refresh you and wash away some of the grime."

Marty and Grandpop Adolph were more than willing and fortunate that Veronica did pack their bathing suits because "You never know," as she was fond of saying.

They gave each other a "Why not?" shrug and eagerly accepted the offer. Their departure was only delayed for about thirty minutes, but both felt so much better and reenergized.

"I think I can walk all the way to Pittsburg, now," said a rejuvenated Marty.

"Let us not get too carried away, Marty. Philly will be good enough," said an equally revitalized Grandpa.

True to his word, Carl and Noreen dropped off the two hikers at the tennis courts, and they resumed their long march to the Delaware River.

The August sun blazed the road and their bodies. The goofy fisherman's hat proved to be a godsend. It deflected much of the sun's searing heat. The brief breakfast stop was also providential and provided enough endurance for Marty and his granddad to plow through the late morning and early afternoon heat.

The terrain was still flatter than a kitchen table and less forested. Farmland relentlessly surrounded them on all sides. The occasional family farm stand was a welcome respite with its cold cider and baskets of fruit. At one stop, Marty was eyeing the sumptuous array of ripe gold and red peaches and noticed one of the biggest peaches he ever saw. It was easily two fistfuls wide, about the size of a softball, not a baseball. Perfectly plump and ripe to eat.

Marty asked how much this one peach would cost, and the kindly saleslady said, "Just a smile."

Marty could not believe his luck, but she was sincere, and Marty carefully picked up the peach. Grandpa overheard the conversation and thanked the woman but also bought a few extra peaches and cold drinks to help the small business and subtly thanked the lady for her unprovoked kindness.

Marty walked outside and sat on a curved log seat and enjoyed the juicy peach that was as tasty and as good as it looked.

Further recharged, the two hikers continued on Delsea Drive and saw a sign that indicated Philadelphia was thirty miles away.

"We are getting closer and closer. We should arrive by noon or early afternoon at the latest. Too bad we can't take the Walt Whitman across the river. It is more modern, but there is no pedestrian path on the bridge like the Ben Franklin or the Tacony Palmyra. This will add several miles to our trip. We live in an age that downplays the old-fashioned virtues like walking and enjoying the great outdoors unfortunately, Marty."

Adolph was mulling over the possibility of changing plans slightly. He was seriously considering calling his son-in-law, Martin, and having him meet them at the New Jersey side of the Walt Whitman Bridge in Audubon. This would eliminate a further seven to eight miles hiking through Pennsauken and Camden to reach the more pedestrian friendly Ben Franklin Bridge. It would also save them another two to three hours of arduous walking. This move was making more and more sense. Adolph was not sure how his grandson would react to the change. Would Marty be a purist, insisting on hiking every single mile, or would he be more of a realist, realizing the spirit of the hike was what really counted—the fresh air, the open sky, the friendly encounters? Adolph would broach the matter later that night after the collect call home to inform the family of their progress.

It was now the end of the third day. Although understandably tired, Marty was actually getting stronger. His legs felt fine. His back was becoming more and more accustomed to the rucksack. The only remaining annoyance were his shoulders. The backpack straps still bit into this part of his body, but he was accepting the burden and took his grandfather's advice and offered the pain up for the sake of the poor souls in purgatory.

Adolph was still game but understandably not as spry. The miles were beginning to take their toll on his aging frame. Inwardly, Adolph hoped to end the trip in Gloucester City at the western edge of the Garden State and not Camden. South Philadelphia was right across the river. Adolph thought he could convince Marty that it was best to end the hike in sight of their neighborhood. It was not their fault the Delaware Port Authority did not have the foresight to add a pedestrian pathway across the Walt Whitman Bridge. *Just another concession to our car-obsessed modern age*, thought Adolph.

If they continued north toward the Ben Franklin Bridge, the Center City Philadelphia skyline could be seen, and that would be quite a thrill, but the walk would need to continue past Center City and head south another three miles in order to return home. The added miles would total about ten miles—completely unnecessary and gratuitous in Adolph's mind. The spirit of adventure and the camaraderie of the hike were what really counted. He was sure he could convince Marty of this wisdom.

The afternoon wore on, and the shadows lengthened across their path. The rural open spaces soon gave way to suburbia with its consecutive one-after-another small town after small town with no obvious break between communities. It was getting harder to locate a quiet patch of woods to sleep and bivouac. Too much congestion. The two might have to find a motel and call it a night.

As if in answer to Adolph's thoughts and incipient prayers, a Navy blue pickup truck with prominent USMC stickers and Leatherneck Bulldogs pasted all over the vehicle pulled up alongside them on Clements Bridge Road in the town of Runnemede. The driver, wearing a cowboy hat, a flannel shirt, and state trooper super dark Foster Grant sunglasses and sporting a salt-and-pepper beard and a gracious smile, asked if the two men needed a lift.

"No thanks," answered Grandpa. "We plan on making it all the way to Philadelphia."

Marty and grandpa were bracing for the usual incredulous reaction of "You mean you really want to walk?" But the driver seemed impressed and said,

"That's cool, man. I get where you are coming from. I was in the 'corpse' for a number of years in the infantry. All those long twenty-five-mile humps were actually one of the highlights of my USMC service."

Greg was his name, and he was intrigued by the unlike duo of an old man and a young teen travelling together. He asked, "Where are you guys sleeping tonight? No way you are going to make it to Philly before nightfall. I can save you some hotel money. I have plenty of closet space . . . Just kidding! There is plenty of room. I really want to know what makes an old-timer like you tick."

Grandpa needed no convincing. Marty was also interested also. Greg turned out to be a more fascinating character than his shabby appearance let on, as they would soon find out.

Marty and Grandpa clambered into the back of the open truck bay. The trip was short, about fifteen minutes. The brushing breeze was an invigorating dose of freshness like a plunge into a swimming pool. The highway had lost its rustic appeal many miles ago, and the truck cruised past blocks of detached homes and front lawns all lined up in drab post-World War II sameness.

Greg's home was not much to look at. It was actually more like a shack, but there was plenty of open space with an ample front and backyard. The front lawn was about twenty yards deep, and the backyard extended almost half a football field into a dense thicket of pine trees. Greg apparently had a green thumb and cultivated a bountiful garden with tomatoes, peppers, cucumbers, and snap peas. He even had an orchard of sorts with some apple, plum, and cherry trees.

There were plenty of machine and car parts piled up in his detached wooden garage, which was actually bigger than his home.

"I like to tinker," said Greg. "I fix things and sell them for some extra cash."

"What do you do for a living?" asked Marty.

"I do odd jobs but mostly work as a janitor at a nearby school. I also teach martial arts to some local kids. It helps pay the bills."

"Is it enough to support a family?" said the ever-practical grandfather.

"Probably not. I live alone. Never married. I was in love once, but it takes two to tango. After that, I thought I had a religious vocation. I wanted to go to the most poverty-stricken hellhole and serve the poorest of the poor, but I wandered, dithered . . . overthought . . . and never pulled the trigger. And here I stand ten years later."

Greg briefly drifted into a silent melancholy, as if these thoughts dredged up some long-lost painful memory, but he quickly recovered his customary confidence.

"Well, let me light up the grill and put on some rat burgers." Greg paused before going out onto the patio to gauge their reaction.

Adolph was too tired to pay attention, and Marty seemed oblivious. Greg realized his joke fell flatter than the plains of Kansas and focused on grilling hot dogs and hamburgers.

The small house had several crucifixes and holy pictures. There were pictures of several Popes, the Blessed Mother, and the Holy Family.

"I guess this guy must be pretty religious," said Marty to his grandfather.

"More than likely," replied Adolph. "That is a good sign. At least, we know he is not an ax murderer."

The house was very cluttered, mostly with books and magazines spread haphazardly over tables and chairs, giving the place the look of a disorganized library. Marty, being the son of a fireman, was cognizant of the burning potential of all that paper.

The house did not have a strong musty smell. This surprised Marty. In fact, the air had a crisp and pleasing aroma of mint and basil. Marty soon spotted the reason for this. Right outside the living room window were a couple of overflowing mint and basil bushes.

Greg came in and asked if they ever tasted deer meat.

To Greg's surprise, Grandpa answered no. Marty, of course, being a born-and-bred city boy, also replied negatively, "What! You guys have not lived until you taste my nicely seasoned deer jerky."

Marty asked, "What does it taste like?"

Without missing a beat, both Adolph and Greg answered almost in unison, "Chicken!" and the two men both dissolved into boisterous laughter.

Marty did not see the humor in the reply but was glad the meat tasted similar to chicken and not liver or, God forbid, fishcakes.

The meal was very good, and even the deer meat was palatable.

For dessert, Greg brought out some Tastykake chocolate cupcakes.

The after dinner discussion soon focused into some serious matters. No mention of the Phillies or current movies. The two men talked about politics and history.

Marty looked at the photo of the Popes and recognized Pope John XXIII and Pope Pius XII, but he did not know the white-haired Pope to the left of Pius XII and asked who it was.

Greg answered, "That is Pope Pius XI. He was the Holy Father right before World War II started. He wrote a ringing denunciation of Nazism in one of his encyclicals. Not that people listened. They rarely do. I am seriously thinking of taking down the portrait of Pius XII."

"Why in the world would you do that? He was a great Pope in a dangerous time," said Grandpa in an incredulous tone.

"That is what I used to think, but there is a new play out called *The Deputy* that accuses him of collaborating with the Nazis."

"What! That is so untrue! It is pure Communist propaganda."

Marty never saw Grandpa so animated. Not even after a thrilling come from behind Phillies' win matched his intensity at this moment.

Adolph continued, "Don't people know he opened up monasteries and convents to hide so many Jewish refugees? He ransomed gold from churches to save Jewish lives. Most estimates claim his actions saved hundreds of thousands of lives. I have read over eight hundred thousand lives were spared from the Nazis. Golda Meir and Albert Einstein were deeply appreciative of the Vatican's efforts, and they should know. In fact, the Chief Rabbi of Rome converted to Catholicism due to the Pope's heroic example. He was a beacon of light in a very dark time."

"Wow! I never knew that. That is encouraging. Why is this not public knowledge?"

"Who knows? One could fill the Library of Congress with what is not reported in newspapers."

"The Holocaust is hard for me to reconcile with a benevolent, loving God, especially with all the innocent children as helpless victims. It has really tested my faith, I'm afraid, although I am still a believer."

"The problem of evil has always been a monumental roadblock to sincere seekers of God's existence. We have to also remember all the good and glorious things in life and balance that with the horrors of life. If there is great evil, there has to be an even greater good."

"Yes, but what bad things did young children commit? Why should they suffer? What was their crime?"

"St. Thomas Aquinas wrote that the sun shines on executioners as well as martyrs. It is one of the great mysteries of our earthly life."

"Well, if I make it to the pearly gates, that is one question I plan to ask the Almighty."

"I am sure you will make the cut," added Adolph in a gesture of hope. "Keep the faith. What else can sustain us?"

"A couple of steaks and some cold beer can also keep me going," replied Greg, trying to change the conversation to a lighter topic, but Adolph was undeterred.

"Try not to get too influenced by the major newspapers and TV channels. They always emphasize the negative—murders, robberies, wars. Your problem is you spend too much time reading *The New York Times*. All the news that fits . . . the liberal worldview. I will send you a subscription to my favorite newspaper, *The Wanderer*. It was originally a German Catholic weekly that has since branched out into English. It will keep you informed and faithful."

"Thanks. I could use some reinforcement in my faith. Living alone does take its toll sometimes. I am sometimes a prisoner of my own loneliness."

"It will certainly fill a basic need. We all need reinforcement in our faith."

"Well, speaking of basic needs. I could sure use a cold beer. How about a nice brewski?"

"I have never been known to turn down a cold beer, even during Lent," said a joyfully eager Grandpa.

Greg apologized to Marty. "Sorry, young fellow. I take it you are too young."

"Not really," said Grandpa. "I had my first beer when I was five, but that was a different time."

Marty was not interested. He had sipped beer and hated the taste. Besides, he had seen too many drunks obnoxiously wandering the neighborhood on Saturday night, and the sight turned him off to any thought of alcohol.

Greg talked for several hours and had actually lived quite an interesting life in Marty's eyes. He was a Marine and fought in Okinawa, the last great battle of World War II. Greg also volunteered at various Church-run homeless shelters and soup kitchens over the years. In addition, he also spent a few years at a Jesuit Indian mission on a reservation in Montana.

"Sounds like you have lived a priestly life throughout the years anyway. Why did you not make the total commitment and enter the seminary?" asked Grandpa.

"Good question. Too bad I can't give you a good answer. I met a wonderful woman and plunged passionately in love, but it was totally unrequited. She became a nun herself, but sadly she died in the Congo of some fatal disease. What a waste of a beautiful person, both outside and inside," Greg said this with a mixture of bitterness and wistfulness.

"A well-lived life can never be measured in time. I am sure her goodness still exists in the lives of those she served. Even now your memory of her still resonates. We can sense that in your voice and demeanor. Let's raise a toast and a prayer in her memory. What was her name?"

Greg was touched and almost choked up, but he managed to say her name without breaking down.

"Julie Dougherty."

"Well, let's raise our glass, our hearts, and our prayers to God in honor of Julie Dougherty. An unsung hero and an unknown saint. The Church celebrates her feast day on November 1."

Marty was trying to figure out how she could be unknown and yet still have a Feast Day but quickly realized Grandpa was referring to All Saints Day, a holy day of obligation that honored all the unknown saints throughout history. The day was perfectly situated right after Halloween. Catholic School kids could enjoy trick or treating with the delicious knowledge they had the next day off. The wisdom of the Church always amazed Marty.

Marty raised his glass of ginger ale, while Greg and Grandpa lifted their frosted mugs of Ballantine.

"You are quite the philosopher old-timer," said Greg in appreciation for Adolph's thoughtfulness.

"Well, I have known a little sadness in my own lifetime. What person has not? My wife and I lost our first daughter at age one. She choked on a pretzel. She died in my arms as I helplessly tried to save her."

Marty never knew that. He knew Grandpa lost a son the day after Christmas in 1944 during the war but never knew he also experienced another child's death at such a young age. Marty noticed Grandpa had tears welling up in his eyes even after the passage of so many years.

"Believe it or not, her name was Julie also," said Grandpa.

Both men nodded pensively and said a silent prayer to a long-ago unforgotten memory.

"Well, as the Hail Holy Queen prayer says, we live in a vale of tears," said Greg.

"Yes," continued Grandpa. "Into each life, a little rain must fall. Hope we are not depressing you, Marty. We have to face reality. Sorrow is part of life. It is important to remember that life on earth is not our true home. Our real destination is heaven. We get glimpses of heaven while we live but just the merest shade. Sorrow helps bring us back to our true goal, or at least, it should."

Marty could not relate to all this talk of sadness and lost love. He had never experienced the death of a close relative. This would change in another month's time.

Marty asked Greg if he had a local newspaper. He was anxious to see how the Phillies fared last night in Chicago against the Cubs.

Greg said he did and looked for the *Inquirer* in the kitchen.

He came back in, and Marty quickly scanned the sports page and was delighted to read that the Phillies crushed the Cubs, 8–1, with another pitching gem from Chris Short.

Grandpa thought this was the best time to spring his idea on Marty of avoiding all the extra miles of walking to reach the Ben Franklin Bridge and settling on walking to the Walt Whitman and getting picked up by Martin Senior at the edge of the Delaware River in South Jersey.

Marty had no problem with the change in plans. After all, it was not a contest or race. He was also anxious to return home.

Greg overheard the plan and gladly volunteered to meet them at the base of the bridge, and drive them across into Philadelphia.

"It really is no problem. I will be glad to do it."

Grandpa was appreciative, and Marty liked the idea that they could still walk another couple of miles from the Pennsylvania side of the Walt Whitman to their home on 15th Street. It would give the final leg of the journey an appropriate end. Riding back home in a station wagon had an anticlimactic and unworthy feel. It would also eliminate the need for Marty's dad from borrowing a car again, so it seemed meeting Greg was more than a fortuitous coincidence but a true blessing.

Greg asked what time did they think they would reach the base of the Walt Whitman. He helpfully estimated his house was about twelve miles from the New Jersey side of the Walt Whitman bridge access lanes.

Grandpa did some quick estimating and said, "Well, we usually cover slightly less than three miles per hour. Marty has been very considerate and slows down his pace enough for me to keep up. I also insist on the old Army routine of taking a ten-minute break every hour. So with that in mind, we should take roughly four hours to get close to the bridge. Does that help?"

"Okay, I will start calculating when you leave my front door and figure out your arrival time and hang around close to the area."

Greg eliminated any chance of miscommunication when he helpfully suggested their rendezvous point be at the Nick's Roast Beef sandwich shop located just a stone's throw away from the entrance ramp of the Walt Whitman Bridge on the Black Horse Pike.

"Great idea. Sounds like a weiner," said Grandpa, using one of his catchphrases that always amused his grandkids but made his daughter, Veronica, groan and roll her eyes.

Yes, Marty reflected, everything was falling perfectly into place; his grandpa fulfilled one of his lifelong dreams, and Marty was proud to be part of it, and the Phillies still had a solid lead on top of the National League. The family enjoyed a wonderful week in Wildwood. Could life get any better than this?

The next morning began bright and sunny, and Marty and his grandfather slept the sleep of the just. Greg cooked a light breakfast of eggs and buttered toast. They thanked him and began the last leg of the journey that commenced four days ago.

Greg said he would be at the sandwich shop at noon. Grandpa looked at his watch and saw the time was eight fifteen in the morning. Plenty of time to make the final amble.

"*Vaya con Dios*," said Greg in his southwestern Spanish learned in the pueblos of the Indian Reservations.

Marty and Grandpa plodded on down the Black Horse Pike, passing the innumerable stores, churches, camera shops, car washes, gas stations, bakeries, pizza parlors, delis advertising the area's best hoagie and cheesesteaks, photographer studios, barbershops, and of course, the ubiquitous diners in all shapes and colors ranging from futuristic space-age design to the standard old-fashioned silver stainless steel railroad car. The commercial establishments unceasingly lined the highway on both sides. Not the most scenic route, but it signaled the end of the journey was near.

There was a movie theater at the intersection of the Black Horse Pike and Kings Highway. Marty glanced at the marquee that trumpeted that *The Agony and the Ecstasy* with Charlton Heston and Rex Harrison was held over for the second week.

"We go past two more diners, and we will be at our meet spot," said Grandpa, anxious for the end of the journey. It was memorable but tiring.

The signs for the Walt Whitman Bridge were prominently displayed in large twenty-foot green squares and luminescent white lettering.

Nick's Roast Beef was in view with its huge painting of a roast beef sandwich overflowing with melted cheese. They heard Greg shouting and waving as they approached the parking lot.

"You guys are like Swiss watches!" Greg said as Marty and Grandpa linked up with him in the parking lot. "Greenwich could take lessons from your punctuality."

"When you live as long as I have and walked as many miles, you get a pretty good feel for distance and time."

"Do you want a Nick's Roast Beef? I hear it is really good. I'll even crack open my wallet, blow away the cobwebs, and foot the bill."

Grandpa, mindful of Greg's almost monastic style of living, gracefully declined. "No, Greg, you have been more than kind. It is our turn to repay you for your hospitality. Let's sit down and grab a pleasant lunch before our paths separate once again."

Grandpa was wonderfully touched by Greg's generosity and bittersweet life. If circumstances permitted, they could have become great friends, but Grandpa knew they would not see each other again once they crossed the river.

All his melancholy thoughts were in the background as the threesome devoured their delicious lunch.

Marty, enjoying a rare restaurant experience (he invariably only ate his mom's cooking), quickly devoured his sandwich despite its large size. He looked up with still hungry eyes and saw Grandpa and Greg patiently, almost delicately, slowly taking their time munching their food. Their slowpoke style of eating almost irritated him.

Grandpa was well aware that Marty was a growing boy and that he possessed an enormous appetite, so he asked, "Still hungry, Marty? I've seen you in action. Don't tell me you have had enough? Could you eat another one?"

Marty's slight irritation at the older men's excruciatingly slow eating style soon evaporated in gratitude with Grandpa's insight.

Both Greg and Grandpa laughed at Marty's eager response and his zestful dispatch of another Roast Beef sandwich.

During the car ride across the mint green suspension bridge with its soaring towers and looping hanging steel cables, Marty sat in the back seat and looked north to the Philadelphia skyline. The stone statue of the city's founder, William Penn, atop the iconic City Hall stone tower was a tiny speck in the distance. His dad had once told him that a car, albeit a small one like a VW Beetle, could drive around William Penn's Quaker hat. It was hard to believe that such a large statue could look so small on top of the tower.

Marty also observed the huge number of cars that were packed in the parking lots bordering the banks of the Delaware.

"Look at all those foreign cars imported from overseas," said Greg as if he was reading Marty's thoughts. "Good thing we have the best car industry in the world. Otherwise, those cars could put a lot of people out of work."

Greg could fix just about anything but was cognizant of the high price of foreign car parts.

After paying the toll that Grandpa insisted on taking care of, the pickup truck dropped off Marty and Grandpa right off the exit ramp at Front and Oregon.

"You sure you don't want me to drive you to your front door? It will only take a few extra minutes. I've got plenty of time."

"No thanks, Greg. The final two miles will be the icing on the cake. We will be appropriately tired when we enter the front door. Besides, it will not look good if we come out of a truck after supposedly walking ninety miles from the shore. We need to look as if we walked a few miles and earned a well-deserved rest."

"I can certainly understand that. Well, old-timer, it has been a real pleasure."

Greg shook Grandpa's hand, and both men nodded in a brotherly understanding.

Greg turned to Marty and gave him a comradely pat on the shoulders and then shook Marty's hand.

Marty always remembered his dad's advice of a strong handshake. First impressions count, so Marty wanted to do it right.

Greg was impressed. "Nice handshake. It was definitely no limp dead fish grasp. Always a good sign. Good luck in high school. It won't be as bad as you might think. Pay attention to your Latin class. It will really build your vocabulary."

Greg turned away and entered his truck.

"Don't believe everything you read in the newspapers, especially *The New York Times*," said Grandpa.

"What can I say? A momentary weakness. I should have known better, as that new Beatle song sings about." Greg joked.

Marty found it surprising that Greg was hip enough to know about the Beatles latest hit.

Marty and grandpa began the final leg and walked down Oregon Avenue, a narrower and more residential version of the Black Horse Pike, toward home. The only difference was that Oregon Avenue had more cheese steak establishments than diners. Only a short mile and a half remained to complete their long journey that bonded Marty and his grandfather and created memories for Marty that would last a lifetime and fulfilled one of Adolph's most cherished goals.

Martin felt like a conquering hero as he strolled up 15th Street. Most of the younger kids knew what Marty was attempting and were fascinated.

A gaggle of kids, mostly friends of his younger brothers, kept hammering questions at Marty.

"How tired are you?"

"Do your feet hurt?"

"Did you get to see the Jersey Devil?"

Marty was tempted to exaggerate and say that he did run into the mythical creature but decided all the adulation he was receiving was satisfying enough.

The youthful questioning continued until they both reached the front door and walked into the vestibule.

The first person to greet them was Cassie, who said with a mixture of pride and awe, "Well, the Wandering Warriors have returned. Mom and Dad will be thrilled to see you both returned safe and sound."

His grandfather also felt a surge of pride, and as he sat down to rest his weary legs, he asked, "Cassie, how about a cold beer! Marty, you sure earned a cold one, but your mom would never allow it, even though she has been drinking beer since she was ten, but don't tell her I told you that."

"Don't worry, Grandpa. I have no desire for a beer. I can't stand the taste, but I will go for a nice cold glass of root beer."

"You heard the lad, Cassie. Dig into the icebox and find something so cold that the can will be dripping in frost."

Cassie, surprisingly enough, did not complain about getting a drink for Marty. Normally, she did not like to be a servant for her younger siblings, but she had to admit she was proud of her little brother.

Chapter 20

A Close Call

The paterfamilias of the household, Martin Senior, was a Philadelphia fireman for over fifteen years. He was lucky in all those years battling blazing fires from the refineries along the Schuylkill to the row house tenements of North and West Philly and never suffered any serious injury.

Until today.

A four-alarm fire was raging in one of the warehouses near the Delaware River just south of the newly built Walt Whitman Bridge. A beverage-flavoring business caught fire in a two-story building. Martin and his rookie partner, George Zammora, were on the second floor putting out the last flames of the smoldering inferno and were about to leave the charred floor when Martin's feet dropped through the weakened ceiling. Martin grasped part of the floor and was suspended for an agonizing few seconds. George attempted to grab hold of Martin before the floor gave way. The wood flooring snapped, and Martin fell twelve feet to the first floor. Before finally falling, Martin tried to grab hold of the floor, but the piece also broke off and landed to his right as Martin crashed to the floor with a hard impact. The pain in his right leg was intense. He broke his fall slightly with his left hand, which lessened the force on his upper body. Above him, George was able to stop before he also fell through. George immediately yelled for assistance.

Martin had enough presence of mind to holler up at George to backtrack and carefully get off the second floor. He wanted to prevent George from falling and also to prevent debris from falling down and adding to his injuries.

"Are you okay, Martin?" yelled George as he gingerly retraced his steps.

"Not too bad. My leg hurts. Don't think I can get up."

"Hang in there. I'll get help."

Help quickly came for Martin as his fellow firemen rushed to get Martin out of the damaged building.

Veronica was baking a coconut cake for Marie when she heard a loud knock on the door. Andy Borremeo, the Philadelphia policeman who lived down the block, wanted to personally break the news to Veronica. Andy knew Martin's injury was not life-threatening, but it was serious, a possible broken leg and a sprained wrist. Andy wanted to stress this information to Veronica to lessen the shock when he told her. Andy, as a trusted friend and neighbor, would be the best person to assure her Martin was going to be all right.

When Andy gently broke the news, Veronica almost dropped the cake-crusted spatula and the dish on the kitchen floor despite Andy's best effort to put the most favorable spin on the news.

"Martin's hurt, but he will be okay. He's at St. Agnes. I can take you there now, Veronica. My car is right outside."

Veronica was not thinking too clearly, but the older girls stepped up and told their mother to go. Cassie and Kathleen told their mom to leave. The twins would stay with the younger kids, and even finish the cake.

Grandpop Adolph came down the steps, absorbed the news, shook his head in a sympathetic manner, and gave his daughter a comforting hug.

"Martin will be all right. I'll say a rosary for him," Adolph told her as added encouragement.

"Cassie, go with your mom. Keep her company. Kate and I will stay with the younger ones."

Veronica rinsed her hands, and Andy drove her the four blocks to the hospital on Broad Street.

The old gentleman took charge at the family home with calming reassurance.

"Kate, get the younger ones inside. I will tell them what happened. No sense letting the kids get the information from misinformed friends and rumors."

Kate immediately went outside and started gathering her younger brothers and sisters.

She quickly spotted Marty, who was walking along Porter Street.

"Marty, find Timmy and Ted . . . make it quick . . . we all need to go home now. Grandpa will explain."

Kate hesitated. Her grandfather was right. The kids might find out about their dad from hearsay and inaccurate comments. She thought hard on whether to tell Marty. He was mature for his age, so she decided to tell him.

"Dad was hurt, but he will be okay. Find everyone and have them come home now! Try not to tell them what happened, if possible. Grandpop will tell everyone. It will sound better coming from him."

"Okay, Kate." She was not only Marty's favorite sister but also his favorite person in the world besides Mom and Dad and Grandpop. In Marty's eyes, she could do no wrong. She was as nice as she was beautiful, in a sisterly sort of way, of course. Her gentleness and kindness were always an inspiration, and whenever she acknowledged Marty's existence, his disposition brightened. A smile from Kate could change Marty's dark mood after a depressing Phillies or Eagles loss into a heavenly field of colorful sunshine.

Marty would do anything to help out his beloved sister, Kate. He would even do the dishes if she asked him.

Her twin sister, Cassie, was different. She was a lot meaner and blunter. Marty acknowledged she helped a lot around the house, but couldn't she be a little nicer about it?

Armed with Kate's mission, Marty scoured the neighborhood for his younger siblings. He pulled Tim out of the corner candy store and Ted out of the Hollingers' house.

Marty outdid himself in rounding up his younger siblings. He knew Kate would be impressed, and that pleased him immensely.

Marty was able to gather the troops without giving a reason. Fortunately, none of them heard about their father's injury, and no one asked what was going on.

The whole McAlynn gathered into the living room. Grandpop took charge in his usual gracious and dignified manner.

"Kids, first of all, your dad will be fine. He was injured during a fire. He is being taken care of at St. Agnes Hospital. Your mom and Cassie went there to see him. We should hear from them very soon, so don't worry too much. It is a good time to start praying. Prayers can never hurt and can only help. Let's say a few Hail Marys."

The prayers helped the younger kids over the initial shock. After a couple of Hail Marys and Our Fathers were finished, the youngest children, Joey, Theresa, and Margaret, started to tear up.

The grandfather walked over to the three youngest and gave them a reassuring hug. The kindly gesture seemed to help.

Now the waiting game began. This was harder than they all thought. The children kept asking, "When is my mom coming back? What is taking so long?"

Grandfather Adolph was able to calm their fears for a while, but when no word was forthcoming about Martin's condition, Adolph decided to send Marty Junior and Mark to the hospital to gather some information. They had strict instructions not to stay long but to check with their mom, find out their dad's status, and come right back.

Kathleen also wanted to go, but Grandpop said, "No, Kate. I will need you here to help with the little ones. They need some motherly comfort that only you can give."

Marty and Mark were glad to get out. It was depressing hanging around the house and not knowing what was going on.

Marty and Mark walked out into the humid night air and practically ran the four blocks north to the solid gray fortress-like hospital that looked like a castle from Ivanhoe.

They went to the right floor and went inside. The two brothers were able to find Cassie and Veronica. Their mom had tears in her eyes, but she was not crying hysterically. *That was a good sign*, thought Marty.

Cassie did most of the talking and said Dad was being well taken care of. He was almost ready to receive some visitors.

"Grandpop told us not to stay too long. We need to return as soon as possible and let everyone know how Dad is doing." Marty was determined to accomplish his mission.

They waited a few more minutes, and the kindly nurse came over and said the family could see their father/husband.

Marty and Mark did not plan to stay long, but they wanted to see their dad for themselves and see how he was doing.

All four slowly walked to the patient room with a serious sense of dread and anxiety. As they walked around the corner and craned their necks to peer into the room, the sight both shocked and relieved them.

Martin Senior was sitting up in his bed with a big smile on his face, which made them all feel better.

However, seeing the big white Mummy-like cast on his left foot was quite a shock and initially took all four aback.

They all froze before entering the room, but Martin called out, "It looks worse than it actually is." His voice sounded strong, and that tipped the moment in a more positive direction.

Veronica walked in and went to her husband's side. Cassie followed, and they both gave Martin a grateful hug. Marty and Mark walked closer but just looked on.

Martin tried to further cheer the family up with news about the next edition of the *Philadelphia Bulletin*.

"It looks like I will be in the front page of the *Bulletin*. A photographer snapped a photo as the nurse helped put the cast on my leg. The reporter asked for all of my children's names, so all you guys will be mentioned in the story."

Martin Senior seemed to be in excellent spirits despite his injury. His wife, Veronica, was visibly relieved.

"What is even better," said Martin, "was that the cast won't be on too long, maybe three or four weeks. I'll be on light duty after that, so I should be able to spend more time at home."

Marty and Mark were tempted to stay longer and relish their visit, but Marty remembered his marching orders from Grandpa. He needed to inform everyone back home about their dad.

Marty said, "We are heading back. Grandpop and Kate and the rest of the gang were really worried. Glad you are doing better, Dad."

Marty and Mark left the hospital in a much better frame of mind than when they entered and walked down fifteenth Street. After crossing the busy thoroughfare of Snyder Avenue, Martin could smell the tantalizing smell of the Greek hot dog restaurant. Both brothers were tempted to buy a couple, but they had no spending money in their pockets. The Mario Lanza museum was close by inside a local record store. Marty planned to visit the place one day. He recently saw one of Mario Lanza's movies with Vincent Price, which was probably the main reason Marty watched the film, which had a lot of singing—too much in Marty's opinion, but then again it was a Mario Lanza movie.

The next day's *Evening Bulletin* prominently displayed on the front page a photo of Martin Senior smiling with a pretty nurse working on his cast. It was a thrill to see the whole family mentioned by name in the caption. There was not a whole lot to the story. Martin was mentioned as a heroic fireman injured in the line of duty with a wife and ten children to add further human interest.

What was even better for the family, a few hours later, was when their dad hobbled in the front door on crutches after he was discharged from the hospital. The injury put Martin on light duty, so the kids would see a lot more of him in the coming weeks. It also meant he would be around more at the house for the Phillies' stretch run to the National League pennant.

When Martin Senior plopped on the chair, his younger children flocked around him as if he was royalty holding court. The children were so relieved their dad was home, and they wanted to savor the moment.

Grandpop came into the room after a decent interval to allow the kids to bask in their dad's presence. Adolph garnered everyone's attention and said, "We are all very grateful for your dad's safe deliverance from the terrible fire. He has a very dangerous job and protects our city. Let us show our thanks and say a prayer to God in joyful thanksgiving."

Nobody groaned or made a face, not even Mark, who often found all the "God talk" very tiresome. "Don't we get all that from the nuns at school all day?" he would often complain but not this time! Mark was praying with such intense piety that the most devout saint would have difficulty in emulating.

Chapter 21

The Glory of Summer or Confession Is Good for the Soul

To a young child, and even a teenager, summer was a glorious time. You could sleep in and be on no fixed time schedule. When you finally dragged yourself out of bed, your only responsibility was to figure out what friend to pal around with and what game to play. Would the choice be a pickup baseball game at Marconi Plaza, a half ball match on 15th Street dodging cars that drove down the block or flip baseball cards against a house ledge? Perhaps a rollicking contest of prison escape, touch football, and/or other outdoor fun limited only by the imagination.

The only limitation was on Sunday morning, but there were enough different Mass times for a lot of flexibility. Marty and Mark normally stayed up all night for the five-thirty Mass, but if they fell asleep early and the movies that night were terrible, they could catch the 10:10 Mass in the upper church, but that was a high Mass and extremely long, so they did their best to avoid that Mass. However, there was a nine and eleven-o'clock Mass in the lower church, which allowed them more options. The tremendous flexibility was liberating and not very burdensome despite Mark's chronic complaining.

The only other potential impediment to a stress-free summer week was Confession, but that was normally on a Saturday afternoon, usually around four thirty. The kids on the block could still go down to the park and play a doubleheader in the early afternoon with ease before trudging off to the church.

In some ways, the trip to the dark confessional was a refreshing break, especially on a scorching hot afternoon. This was true for the boys but not for the poor priest who had to endure the boy's athletic smell in the confined space. The sweat stuck on your clothes like glue in a scrapbook and was uncomfortable causing some chafing. It was actually a blessed relief in more ways than one to walk from the open humid air of the park at Broad and Oregon into the lower church. Entering the cool basement of the lower church was soothing. It was even darker in the confessional booth and felt refreshing, except for the nervousness of confessing to the priest behind the screen. For most kids, it was a good thing to see a long line since it could mean the priest was too busy dispensing penances and did not have much time to dwell on individual sinners. In this case, a quick, painless, least embarrassing penance was practically guaranteed. If the line was sparse, the confessor could spend more time with each particular sinner and pay more attention to youthful foibles.

One late Saturday afternoon, the neighborhood boys had played a tough doubleheader and came home pretty tired. Mark played his heart out in the outfield running down a lot of pop fly balls and was dog-tired. He collapsed on the couch. Mark knew his dad was at the firehouse. He was hoping his mom would not force him to go to confession that day. Mark really thought he could get away with it, but he did not reckon with his formidable grandfather.

"You are not going to Confession? Why in the world not? Don't you want to be pure in the sight of God?"

Mark tried hard to justify himself and said, "Grandpa, I went two weeks ago. I have not been too bad lately, just ask Mom. I have not broken many Commandments. I'm only thirteen years old, how many sins can I commit in just two weeks?"

"That is not the point. It is also a spiritual exercise. Don't you want to be a good baseball or basketball player?"

"Sure."

"Well, in order to be a good hitter or to perfect a good jump shot, don't you have to practice?"

Mark hesitated. He could clearly see where his grandfather's logic was leading but had to answer truthfully, "Yes, it does take a lot of practice to become a good fielder and hitter."

"Well, it is even more important in religious matters. To become physically strong, you need to lift weights. In order to run fast in track, you need to pound out the miles and sprint around the football field. With God, it is the same thing. To be worthy, you need to have discipline and make little sacrifices. Sometimes they are small, and only God and your conscience know what you gave up. There are times when you feel like cursing up a blue streak at someone bothering you or making your bed or cleaning dishes when no one is around to see what good deed you accomplished. That is real virtue. Start small, and it leads to greater holiness. After all, what is your ultimate goal in life? Isn't it to get to heaven?"

Mark was tempted to say a .300 batting average and a lifetime supply of Tastykakes, but he kept his wise guy comments to himself and felt he had to agree that heaven was the big prize.

Grandfather Adolph continued, "Just start small and take little steps, and it will lead to greater virtue. Keep your eye on what is really important in life. Come on, I'll walk over to church with you. We still have time."

Mark thought Grandpop was always looking for an excuse to take a walk. It seemed he was walking morning, noon, and night, even during the coldest winter day or the warmest summer evening.

Mark tried to change his grandfather's mind.

"No need to come, Grandpa. I will be fine. After all, what sins could you possibly commit at your age and all the praying and God stuff you do."

"You will be surprised. Besides, even the Pope goes to confession once a week. If it is good enough for the Holy Father, it is certainly right for us to follow his example."

How could Mark argue with that remark? He put away his baseball glove and walked out with Grandpa to travel the four blocks to church. Marty overheard the conversation and felt obligated to also go to Confession.

It was still July hot, but there was a refreshing late afternoon breeze. Mark and Marty were still a little sweaty from the two hard-fought games. Marty also walked a few extra blocks further south to check out the woods where the werewolf scene would be filmed. They hoped to film on it on Monday. The next day was Sunday, and the Phillies were playing an afternoon game themselves, so there would not be too much time to do much of anything else. Sunday was just too jam-packed. Monday was the best time. Both brothers were looking forward to the use of the new mask.

The two grandsons and their grandfather walked into the lower church. The dark coolness of the church was bracing after the short but hot walk from home. They worked up even more of a sweat, and the church's cavern-like solitude chilled them, but it felt reinvigorating.

The confessional booths were near the back. Just a few people were waiting in line. Marty and Mark both thought the same thing and hoped they would get a nice priest who would not give them too hard a time for their transgressions. They also wished the priest's name was on the booth to see who the priest was before entering since some priests were more understanding of childhood foibles.

Once again, they were inspired by their grandfather, who knelt in the pew and said a short prayer before standing up and heading toward the confessional. Fearless and devout as ever, Adolph led by example.

As Adolph, Marty, and Mark came out of the lower church, the slight breeze that greeted the trio as they walked to church was gone. They felt the intense late afternoon heat. Summer held the city in its sultry grip with little breeze to relieve the heat and humidity.

The walk down Ritner Street encountered a few Italian delis and a variety store or two and a very unusual phenomenon in this section of Philadelphia—Bambergers, a German bakery deep in the heavily Italian neighborhood.

The smell as one walked by was fresh and heavenly. It was best not to stop and look at the window display unless you had money to spend. The temptation was too great. The raisin bread, fruit tarts, donuts, and cakes were provocatively arranged to grab a pedestrian's attention. Often, Marty would go way out of his way to avoid Bambergers sights and smells because of his lack of pocket change. He did not want to become disappointed at not being able to taste the Garden of Eden-like pastries.

Grandpa Adolph seemed to read both of his grandson's minds. In addition, he wanted to reward the boys for taking the time to go to confession on a leisurely summer day. As the three approached the bakery, the soul-pleasing aroma overcame Marty and Mark with an overwhelming desire. They looked at their grandfather, and he had a wide grin that seemed to say, "All right, boys, take a look in the window. I will buy," which was precisely what happened.

Marty and Mark almost ran into the store. This was, indeed, a real treat. There was so much to look at, and it was so hard to make a choice between the snowy white powdery Bavarian creme puffs, the sumptuously colorful strawberry and blueberry tarts, or the overly large, hot, right-out-of-the-oven donuts of dazzling variety.

Mark went with the creme puffs, while Marty chose the Black Forest Cake dark chocolate donut. Their granddad picked the glistening, super sticky but delicious cinnamon bun. The saleslady was going to pack them in a neat white box, but the boys were too anxious to bite into the unexpected treat, so they each grabbed their pastry and devoured it on the way home.

In between bites, Adolph imparted a theology lesson. He pointed to a nearby home that was being renovated and pointed to some embedded nails in wood.

"You see those holes that are open? When a nail is pulled out, it still leaves a gaping hole. That is like sin. When you go to confession, you are taking nails out of your soul, but sin still leaves a hole and a mark. Your penance helps because it is like yanking the nail out. How do you fill in the hole? That is where indulgences come in. They are like spackle that closes up the hole and makes the soul clean and whole."

"I was always curious why we needed indulgences," added Marty. With their taste buds still savoring the soft, fresh donut, the meaning and importance of indulgences were permanently implanted in Marty and Mark's mind. Maybe that was their grandfather's point as they continued the walk home. This was God talk that Mark could actually enjoy—a religion lesson topped off with a mouthwatering dessert.

After polishing off the pastries, Adolph and his two oldest grandsons were about a half a block from home. Their little stroll sparked a question in Mark's always curious mind. Growing up in South Philadelphia, one knew to avoid certain neighborhoods. Territorial gangs were eager to either protect their turf or give their idle hands something to do.

Marty and Mark had a bad experience last year coming out of the Lehigh Avenue subway exit en route to Connie Mack Stadium to watch the Phillies game. It was about eleven in the morning, early enough to avoid game time congestion, so not many spectators were milling around. The boys were hoping to watch some batting practice. If they arrived later, the additional fans in the street would have made them less of an inviting target. As it turned out, the local gang should have waited for better pickings. Marty and Mark did not have any money on them, their sole possession only a large brown paper bag lunch their mom had packed for them.

That was their only food to sustain them for the game, so Marty and Mark were like Spartans defending Thermopylae to protect their lunch. They had no choice. If they did not put up a stiff fight, they would have been too hungry to enjoy the game, and it was a double-header to boot!

During the tussle, Marty's bag ripped, and an apple and Tastykake Coconut Juniors fell to the ground. The sight of his disintegrating lunch bag further enraged Marty. He felt like Samson battling the Philistines and was somehow able to push two of the gang members against the front steps of a home along Lehigh Avenue. Marty saw an empty trash can and grabbed the top and used it as a shield to further push the attackers away. Mark found an old milk carton container and used it as a club to beat away further assaults. The brothers' furious counterattack shocked the gang, and when the muggers saw the slim pickings of the brown lunch bags, the group concluded it was not worth the effort and soon gave up and slithered away.

"It is not worth it, man! Those kids are crazy! Let's get out of here," Marty and Mark heard one of the gang members say to the others as they walked north on 16th Street.

Marty asked Mark if he was hurt.

"No, just a scrape on my elbow. How about you?"

"Nah, I'm fine. Just a little bruise on my knuckles."

Marty picked up the apple and rubbed it on his T-shirt. The Coconut Juniors was squashed but still unopened, which meant it was still perfectly edible.

As a result of this painful experience, Marty and Mark were always mindful of wandering into the wrong neighborhood. They were aware of their grandfather's daily walk to work from North Philadelphia to West Philly and were curious enough to ask, "On your walk to work, did anyone ever bother you, Grandpa?"

"No, I guess I was lucky, or my guardian angel kept a close watch over me. I also avoided the small side streets. Too many punks lurking around the smaller streets, hanging out with something to prove. I always played it smart and stayed put on the main streets—Allegheny Avenue to Broad Street and then down to Market. Too many witnesses on the larger avenues, plus there were a lot of commercial establishments. There were always a lot of people milling about, entering and buying from all the stores along the route. I'm sure it helped that I said a couple of rosaries as I walked and plenty of Aspirations."

No matter what the subject, Grandpop Adolph always managed to put a Catholic angle on everything.

Just before they entered the house on 15th Street, Adolph asked, "Are you boys still planning to watch one of your monster movies tonight?"

As was their usual habit, Marty and Mark made a determined effort to view both Double Chiller Theater and Hollywood's Finest, which was normally another horror film, usually a good one from Universal Studio's Golden Age. However, tonight's lineup was just so-so. The first movie was *The Monster That Challenged Mexico*, which Marty had already seen and thought the monster was worth watching—it was a hairy, caterpillar-looking beast that was thirty feet long

185

with fire-breathing tentacles—but the movie took its time getting to the monster scenes. The second film was totally forgettable, even by Marty and Mark's already low standards: *The Lizard Monster from the Mojave*. Poor special effects, just a scaly lizard made to look as big as a school bus. Marty lamented the current Hollywood trend of using reptiles to stand in for giant monsters or dinosaurs and preferred the ground-breaking stop motion animation of Willis O'Brien and the current master of this exciting technique, Ray Harryhausen.

The third movie was much better with Lon Chaney, Jr., but it was one of the *Inner Sanctum* series, which were more of a mystery story and not really about monsters. So tonight's lineup was fair at best and weak at worst.

Adolph sensed Marty's reply was a little ho-hum and almost disinterested.

"Do you boys really want to stay up that late? You both do not seem too enthused about what is on TV tonight."

"Well, we more or less do it just to keep up the tradition," replied Marty, curious to figure out why Grandpop was so interested.

"Well, if the movies are not that great tonight, would you two like to go to the Phillies game tomorrow afternoon? I think Bunning is pitching."

Marty and Mark were both excited about the prospect of going to a game when the Phillies were in the thick of a pennant race. They had not seen a game at the ballpark yet this year. What made it even better was that they would not miss any good movies on TV that night. It was an unbelievably happy set of coincidental circumstances.

"I was going to ask your dad when I purchased the tickets a few weeks ago, but his injury has him in a cast, so he cannot get around much, so he thought his two older sons should accompany me. What do you think?"

"That is great! I always wanted to see Jim Bunning pitch in person."

"Okay, it is all settled then. We will go to the nine-o'clock Mass and then eat some of your mom's delicious bacon sandwiches for breakfast and then take the subway to the game. I will bring my genuine Alpine walking stick to ward off any intruders (Grandpop

186

was well aware of last year's incident). I suggest you boys get a good night's sleep. Do you think you can manage to be in bed before midnight on a Saturday night?"

"It will be tough, but we will give it the old college try."

"I knew you boys would not want to pass up a game with the first-place Phillies! Gosh, that sounds so good when I actually say it. Still hard to believe it is this late in the season, and our team is still leading the pack."

Chapter 22

A Summer Afternoon at Connie Mack

The iconic scoreboard in Right Centerfield.

After attending Mass and eating breakfast, Adolph and his two grandsons left the house with their enormous bag lunch—twelve ham sandwiches with mustard, some soft pretzels, and an assortment of Tastykake chocolate cupcakes, peanut butter Tandy cakes, Coconut Juniors, and butterscotch Krimpets.

They walked the four blocks to the Snyder Avenue subway station, the southern limit of the ten-mile underground Broad Street line that cut through the middle of Philadelphia. The trio descended the grimy gray steps, and almost immediately the fetid smell of urine and mildew assaulted their noses, but they quickly got used to the foul stink. Marty was carrying the large Acme shopping bag that contained all three of their lunches and folded the top even tighter as if to keep the noxious stench off of the food. He planned to guard its contents like a chivalrous knight defending a maiden's honor.

They were fortunate to find a seat together in the rail car. The overhanging, plastic straps along the ceiling for standing passengers reminded Marty of *King Kong* when the giant ape tore down a section of New York's elevated line, corralled a moving train, and pounded on the steel car.

There was no need to use the straps today. The subway car was practically empty. Adolph and the boys were leaving at the right time before the crowds made for more congestion. After a twenty-minute train ride, they arrived at Lehigh Avenue, their destination stop. More and more people had entered the subway cars during the trip. Marty thought that was good. More people heading to the game meant less chance of getting jumped by the neighborhood bullies. There was always safety in numbers.

Marty was reading the *Philadelphia Bulletin* sports page during the ride and looked at the current leaders in batting average, home runs, and runs batted in (RBIs). The later was one of Marty's favorite statistics, a good indicator of a ballplayer's value in a clutch situation. He noticed his grandfather had several small Catholic Church pamphlets that dealt with sin, conversion, loneliness, and ultimate happiness and salvation. Adolph had several of these pamphlets, along with some prayer cards. He placed a couple of the religious booklets in the seats next to him, and when the train reached their final stop, Adolph prominently placed a few more in the seats they were vacating.

As they stood up to leave the train, Mark asked his grandfather why he was doing that.

"You never know who might be in great need to read this material. It is a small way to comfort some suffering person, and maybe even save a soul."

As they walked up the dank station and ascended to the bright late morning sunshine, they were joined by many other subway riders from different cars with the same destination in mind—a glorious day at the ballpark watching the first-place Phillies.

Grandfather Adolph pointed out to his grandsons the car wash establishment across the street on the south side of Broad and Lehigh. It had no distinguishing features other than a fifteen-foot high red-and-yellow neon sign with bold letters saying, "CAR WASH." It was a flat one-story series of garages.

"Do you know what that place used to be?"

Marty knew the answer but played along with his grandfather's efforts at small talk. His dad told him that it was once the site of the Phillies' old ballpark, Baker Bowl.

Adolph continued with a nostalgic look in his eyes, "I saw Chuck Klein bang out many extra base hits and a few homers in that old ballpark. I remember one year when Chuck Klein, probably the greatest Phillies slugger of all time, won the triple crown and particularly recall one season when he drove in one hundred seventy runs and, believe it or not, did not even win the National League RBI title that year because the Chicago Cubs' Hack Wilson set the all-time RBI record for a single season with one hundred ninety. No ballplayer, except for Lou Gehrig, has even come close to breaking that record. It stands along with Joe DiMaggio's fifty-six consecutive game-hitting streak as one statistic that will never be broken."

"Aren't records made to be broken, Grandpa?" said Mark, repeating a familiar saying in sports.

"That's what all the sportswriters claim, but I will bet the horse farm those two marks will stand until the end of time."

The two teens looked at the boring, nondescript building and uninspired open space and found it hard to imagine a grass ballfield, and bleachers once stood there with all that baseball lore and history.

The Phillies' current home, Connie Mack Stadium, originally named Shibe Park, was the home of the Philadelphia A's (Athletics) for forty years before they moved to Kansas City. The park was renamed in honor of the Philadelphia A's legendary manager for fifty years, Cornelius McGillicuddy, popularly and mercifully shortened to the memorably iconic Connie Mack.

Marty was always curious why his grandfather was a Phillies fan instead of the Athletics, who were far more successful than the sad-sack Phillies. The A's had numerous Hall of Famers like Lefty Grove, Mickey Cochran, and Jimmy Fox. In the late 1920s, their team was so talented that they ended the Murderers Row legacy of the 1927 Yankees with three consecutive American League pennants and two World Series titles from 1929 to 1931. This was the start of the Great Depression, and the lack of tickets sales forced Connie Mack to sell all of his great players. This was not the first time Connie Mack had to sell his best players to stay financially afloat.

Grandfather Adolph could never give a snappy answer or a good reason why he was so loyal to the perennial National League door-mats other than the team was six blocks closer to his 2nd Street home. Maybe the Phillies had more German ballplayers when Adolph first became interested in America's pastime. It was very strange. Who could say why a fan becomes so attached to a particular team. At least, you could say Grandpa Adolph was not a frontrunner.

It was gratifying to see that in 1964, ten years after the Athletics shockingly left town and went to the Midwest, Adolph's long-suffering fidelity to the team was being rewarded in spectacular fashion. In late July, the Phillies were still very competitive and in a seesaw battle for first place with the San Francisco Giants.

The six-block walk to Connie Mack was uneventful, the growing crowd contained enough manpower to discourage any isolated muggers, and each individual set of groups glided happily to 21st Street and Lehigh. As they came closer, Marty could see the gray steel twenty-nine-foot-high wall of right field, like a dam blocking a river of spectators. Grandpop Adolph mentioned he sometimes watched the game from the roof of the homes across the street, but the Athletics management built the higher wall to prevent any non-paying customers from enjoying the game.

"I guess that was only fair," said Grandpop. "The team needs to make money on their product. After all, Major League Baseball is a business."

Shibe Park, now Connie Mack, was a spectacular achievement when it was first constructed in 1909. Hard to believe now because the stadium looked like a fading opera star in steep decline. However, over fifty years ago in its heyday, Shibe Park was the country's first steel and concrete ballpark. The home plate entrance was designed to resemble a high-class Parisian hotel with its green onion-dome tower.

The grand Beaux Arts front entrance of Connie Mack Stadium.

As they entered the turnstile, the earthy smell of crisp peanut shells and the savory aroma of grilling hot dogs filled the air and seemed designed to tempt any spectator entering into purchasing food at the concession stands.

Adolph sensed the mouthwatering desire of his grandsons to bite into a steaming hot ballpark frank and interrupted their daydream and said, "Smells good, doesn't it? That is why I had your mom pack such a large lunch. A working class man could go broke buying food for his family here. Your mom sure knows how to pack a great lunch. There is enough food in that bag to feed a starving Chinese village. Don't worry, your boys won't go hungry."

Their seats were on the third base side of the field in the lower level. It felt a little cramped because of the overhanging upper deck and the columns that held up the structure, which also prevented an unobstructed view of the infield.

Marty preferred the more open and liberating upper deck. There were fewer obstructions, and the view was more panoramic. It was nice to have the sky above you instead of a concrete ceiling. The factories, smoke stacks, and warehouses prevalent in this manufacturing mecca base of blue-collar Philadelphia could be seen over the center field wall and beyond the black 447-foot fence of center field. The mammoth and semi-spectacular scoreboard situated in right center field provided a pleasing variety to the gray industrial vista. The old ballpark was old and creaky but still a fun place to be, like a musty attic with plenty of neat items waiting to be discovered. The gray flat roofs along 20th Street could barely be seen now that the twenty-nine-foot right field wall was built to discourage enterprising residents from placing seats on their roof to watch the game without paying the standard price for a game.

One major plus to the lower deck was that the hot sun would not beat down on your head, and the shade of the upper deck provided some small relief from the heat. One other drawback to their seats was that they were in the middle of the row. This was a minor annoyance, and Marty vastly preferred to sit at the end of the row so he could stretch his legs, but more importantly, it afforded easier access to use the bathroom or just to wander around the stadium to get different views of the playing field. Being in the middle, in order to leave the row, you had to shuffle across the narrow aisle and avoid stepping on spectator's toes as you gingerly edged to the end of the row.

But beggars can't be choosers. They were at the ballpark with their grandfather on a wonderful summer afternoon with the first-place Phillies taking the field. Did life get any better than that? What more could they ask for? Okay, maybe a bite into the still tempting choice of a Phillies' ballpark frank would have been even more ideal, but consuming five ham-and-cheese sandwiches went a long way to assuage their desire for a hot dog.

The afternoon sun burst through the dull gray morning clouds. It was really getting hot. Marty was now glad they were sitting in the lower deck and had some comforting shade. Phillies' pitching ace, Jim Bunning, was hurling his usual workmanlike game but was clinging to a slim 1–0 lead in the top of the sixth inning.

At the start of the bottom of the seventh inning, the lower deck fans saw a shocking sight. A body fell from the upper deck into the seats below! The helpless boy seemed to be flapping his arms in a vain attempt to fly like a bird.

"What in the world was that?" exclaimed Grandpa Adolph, echoing the sentiment of many who saw the stunning sight. It didn't seem possible.

For a few seconds, there was no activity, as if no one could believe a person could fall out of the stands. The frozen inaction of the crowd seemed to last longer than it actually did, and then an explosion of activity snapped the audience into overdrive.

Many bystanders rushed over to where the boy fell. Several women and men ran to the exit ramps to get help.

The bleachers along the third base side of Connie Mack Stadium.

Adolph and his grandsons were about ten rows behind where the accident happened. An orderly group of people rendered assistance to the boy and the woman he fell on. Soon some medical help arrived, and both injured spectators were quickly taken care of.

Adolph told Marty and Mark to say a quick prayer for the injured parties.

Before the Phillies came to bat, the plummeting boy and unfortunate woman he landed upon were evacuated safely. It looked very hopeful that no serious life-threatening injuries were sustained by either party. The game was not even delayed. It was doubtful any of the ballplayers knew what just happened.

After that incredibly weird incident was resolved, the game grinded on. Bunning was excellent as usual and retired eight batters in a row, but in the eighth inning, he gave up a couple of cheap infield hits, and then Willie Mays drilled a solid double into the right field corner, and before you could say, "This game is in the win column," the Phils' 1–0 lead became a 2–1 deficit.

"If Dad was watching, he would say that Bunning was about to get robbed again. Another wasted pitching gem," said Marty.

"Have faith, boys. The Phils still have two more chances to come to life," replied their irrepressible grandfather.

Mark thought his grandfather was being overly optimistic as usual, but Mark was a "natural born crepehanger" according to his mom.

The score stayed that way until the bottom of the ninth. The Phils had one last gasp, but Juan Marichal was mowing the Phillies down. They did not have a base runner since the sixth inning. Marty could just hear his dad at the firehouse complaining about Bunning's lack of run support and his usual litany of what "a hard-luck pitcher Bunning was." The Phillies' ace right-hander still had a shot at twenty wins, but by rights, he should be approaching twenty-five wins.

It looked like the Phillies were about to lose another heart-breaker. There was one out in the ninth inning when Tony Taylor revived the fans' flagging hopes with an infield hit as the second base-man beat out a slow roller to the shortstop. The team had a man on first with only one out and center fielder, Tony Gonzalez, stepping to the plate. Tony normally had good power and had a couple of twenty-plus home run seasons with the Phillies recently, but he was hobbled with nagging injuries this year and hardly played most of the season.

Gonzalez worked the count to two balls and one strike. Marty looked at his grandfather, who was muttering what looked to be a humble prayer. So much for his admonition that God doesn't care about winners and losers in baseball. Marty had to admit he was also selfishly praying. This would be a tough game to lose to the second-place Giants, their closest rivals for the National League pennant.

The tension mounted. Marichal kicked his leg high in his trade-mark fashion and threw a blazing fastball. Tony Gonzalez waited and drove the pitch deep to right center. It was a searing line drive but not high enough to clear the twenty-nine-foot right field wall. Adolph could not help but think if the wall was not raised to block row home rooftop spectators from enjoying the game, the hard hit ball would have easily cleared the fence for a homer, and the Phillies would win a dramatic come from behind victory.

But what was done was done, and the line drive caromed off the right field light tower that looked like a giant robot from a Japanese sci-fi movie. It bounced high in the air like a dolphin at Seaworld. The right fielder, Matty Alou, waited for the ball to come down into his glove. The baseball seemed to float and remain suspended high in the North Philly air. The crowd collectively held its breath.

Tony Taylor ran like a demon around the base path. The Cuban second baseman was as fleet as the road runner outrunning his coyote pursuer in the cartoons. There was no doubt he would score to tie the game. Tony Gonzalez had at least a double, and with his speed, a triple was a good possibility.

The ball finally came back down to earth but took an odd bounce away from the outfielder and landed on the warning track at the base of the wall and bounced a few times before Alou could pick the ball up.

This gave Tony Gonzalez an easy chance to dash from second base to third. Tony G was flying toward the hot corner like the DC comic book hero, The Flash. The right fielder was finally able to grab the bouncing ball, and he whirled around to quickly throw the ball toward the infield. Gonzalez kept his short but powerful legs churning like a piston. He was rounding third and took a wide turn toward home plate by the time the second baseman received the right fielder's throw.

The crowd held its breath and seemed evenly divided between fans that wanted Tony to hold up for a stand-up triple and those fans who wanted him to keep running toward the plate. The infielder hesitated with the ball when he looked toward third base, figuring the runner was about to slide into third base for a solid triple. That quick look enabled Tony Gonzalez to make it halfway between third and home. By the time the second baseman realized the runner was heading home, it gave Tony G several more steps closer to home plate. The infielder squared up and threw an accurate dart to the catcher. It was a good throw but a second too late, as Gonzalez slid safely home before the catcher could tag him out

This was a unique but thrilling event, an inside-the-park home run! Even rarer, it won the game, so it was doubly exciting.

The jubilant crowd was jumping up and down, and strangers were hugging each other. Even the usually staid and dignified Adolph was deliriously happy. He was always in a pleasant and positive mood, but he seemed even more beamingly joyful than ever.

"In all my seventy years of watching Major League Baseball, I have never—*never*—seen a game winning bottom of the ninth inside the park home run. Savor the moment, boys! It will be a long, long time before you ever see something like this again."

Marty was more and more convinced this *was* the Phillies' year. Even Mark was becoming a true believer in the Phillies' once-in-a-lifetime karma. How many good things could possibly happen in one season to one team? Earlier last month, in early July, during the all-star game at Shea Stadium, the Phillies' right fielder, Johnny Callison, won the game in dramatic fashion with a three-run homer in the bottom of the ninth inning. Even the most cynical fan in the city had to admit every sign from the baseball gods was promising and encouraging for the Philadelphia team.

The festive, jubilant mood continued as the crowd orderly filed out of Connie Mack Stadium and walked down Lehigh Avenue past the row house porches and the high brick walls of the factories toward the Broad Street Subway entrance. The happy crowd was just large enough to eliminate any fears of getting mugged along the half-mile walk to the train stop. The thrilling win put everyone in a good mood, even any would-be muggers lurking in the shadows and alleys were temporarily transformed into happy-go-lucky fans.

Winning makes brothers of us all.

Chapter 23

The Final Battle

Front Entrance of the Swedish-American Museum at FDR Park.

August was now more than one-half over. School would start in less than a month. This was going to be a major change in Marty's life. He would be leaving the safe confines of the parish school and entering the new and unfamiliar world of high school.

Bishop Neumann, the name of Marty's new school, was named after the fourth bishop of Philadelphia, who literally died on the streets of Philadelphia from exhaustion and overwork in service to his flock. After a perilous transatlantic voyage across the storm-tossed Atlantic Ocean from his native Bohemia, his charitable efforts during a short forty-seven-year lifetime ranged in scope from the isolated settlements of the unsettled Midwest to the snow-packed frigid North American wilderness of upstate New York before finally settling in as leader of Philadelphia's growing Catholic community. The good bishop had to contend with the Know-Nothing Riots and the influx of Irish fleeing from starvation in their native land. He was presently up for sainthood having performed two of the required three miracles for Vatican canonization.

Marty was a little nervous about the new school. It was almost a two-mile walk as opposed to his present two-block walk to St. Monica's at 16th Street and Porter. The longer walk did not bother him, of course, but leaving the comforts of the neighborhood did concern him a little.

His dad was more upbeat about the pending change, saying the friends he met in high school there at Neumann could remain lifelong. He painted an optimistic picture of what should be the best years of his life. Marty was still a little skeptical, but he trusted his dad, so this helped Marty deal with his impending nervousness.

With Labor Day and the start of school closing in fast and the end of summer vacation, Marty and Mark were anxious to film the final battle between the Wolfman and the Frankenstein monster. The basement was too narrow and confining, especially the ceiling with several pipes crisscrossing across the top, making the ceiling height even lower. It was so low that Marty hit his head a few times, causing the monster mask to fall off. Sometimes this mishap was caught on film, causing unintended hilarity to the spectators watching. Marty would have to edit out the scene somehow.

The cellar was perfect for the early graveyard scenes. The darkness helped obscure the fading brick sidewalls. Marty and Mark had their little brothers scoop up some piles of leaves from Marconi Plaza park and bring them to the house. They were placed on the cellar floor to resemble an outdoor cemetery. It worked pretty good but created quite a mess. Initially, both their mom and dad were upset, but Grandpa Adolph smoothed things over, and even helped clean it up. He thought the effort revealed a lot of ingenuity, and Adolph was proud of his grandkids.

"This is a good sign, Veronica. Shows some imagination. At least, they're not watching TV all day. They are not becoming sofa slugs. They show great spirit . . . Don't be so hard on them. The leaves will get cleaned up . . . That's an easy fix."

That seemed to calm down his daughter, Veronica, who adored her father, so she grudgingly relented on her initial frustration with the bags of leaves her kids tracked in from the park.

Because of all the ruckus the cellar scenes caused, Marty and Mark decided it would be best to stage the climactic fight somewhere outside. The majestic setting of the Swedish American Museum would make a great backdrop. On the surface, no objections would come from his parents, but Marty and Mark did not take into unpredictable outside forces as they would soon discover.

Mark thought they had plenty of time to film the penultimate scene. They had practiced for weeks for the fight scene, wrestling and choreographing each grapple and throw. They knocked over a few chairs and tables, but they both thought they were getting pretty good at it. One night, they received some added inspiration from a non-horror film. Marty and Mark watched an old John Wayne movie, *The Spoilers*, which featured one of the greatest fight scenes in movie history.

Luckily, they rehearsed when their parents were not home so the noisy racket the two brothers caused would not be too disturbing for the rest of the family. Kathleen and Cassie were usually not home when they rehearsed the monster fight. If Kathleen was home, she would gently tell her brothers not to get too loud or break anything.

Mark and Marty shuddered to think what Cassie would say, so they made doubly sure she was not around when rehearsing.

It seemed essential to have the fight scene outside. This not only gave them freedom from parental interference but also gave the brothers a lot more room to toss and trip and throw each other around in an exciting (they hoped!) tussle.

The museum would also double as the Mad Scientist's castle. They both thought they could pull off the fight without getting themselves injured.

One major problem remained. Who would film the fight with the Kodak camera? Their mom did a lot of the filming in the house, but the previous outside scenes were filmed by Marty and Mark, who each took turns since they played both monsters. However, the battle between the Wolfman and the Frankenstein monster would have to be done by another person. Tim was the next oldest younger brother, but he might have been a little too young. Marty didn't really want to take the chance, especially if the fight scene was going so well but was not even captured on film.

No, they definitely could not take that chance. Nothing against Tim. He was a good kid, but the cinematic responsibility was just too great.

Marty decided to recruit one of his friends from school and a charter member of the Count Dracula Society, Jimmy McConnell. They were the same age, and Marty felt Jimmy could handle it. He was trainable. Plus, he was also a big monster movie fan. They both liked watching Double Chiller Theater on Saturday night and discussing it on Monday morning at school. So Jimmy could be relied upon and knew what needed to be done behind the camera.

He did appear earlier in the movie as a burgomaster complete with a fake mustache, which unfortunately fell off in full view of the camera and film. The scene provoked a lot of unintended laughter when it was screened by his family. It took a while before Marty acknowledged the humor in the shot. Jimmy also had a small role as the "fiend," the twisted hunchback assistant to the Mad Doctor, but it was hard to get Jimmy over when they filmed, so his movie role was considerably cut.

Now Marty could make it up to Jimmy and have him play a key role in the movie as a cinematographer, a sophisticated word for someone turning the camera on and pointing it in the right direction. Jimmy seemed enthusiastic about it all and was ready to start.

Marty looked at the weather forecast and believed that Thursday would be a good day to film. Ideally, rain and lightning and thunder added a lot of excitement to an outdoor scene, but after his experience a few weeks ago in a thunderstorm with frightened kids and soaked clothes, Marty thought it was best to film in the clear sunshine with not a hint of rain. Besides, the final product looked much better on film with no dull, hard-to-see moments.

The decision was made. Thursday would be the day. Not only for the last of the filming (since school was starting soon) but also for what Marty and Mark hoped would be the moment they were practicing for several weeks and the whole point of the movie—the clawing, grappling battle between the Wolfman and Frankenstein monster.

The night before Marty and Mark rehearsed for the last time. They really believed they had it all figured out. All that was needed was the proper stage—the fight would take place on the top of the steps of the Swedish American Museum near the entrance. Luckily, the museum was not open on that day.

Because the scene was between the two monsters, no extras were required, but the younger brothers, Tim, Ted, and Joey, wanted to watch and cheer. Marty was amenable to this idea.

Thursday morning dawned, and the sky was bright and sunny. Marty wanted to leave by ten, but Mark was slow to wake up again, but the crew still managed to depart by ten forty-five. They knocked on Jimmy Mac's door, which was at the other end of the block. Mark noticed Mrs. Cassano, who lived five houses from them down the street, was her usual nosy self, peeking behind her living room bay window.

"Probably thinks we are up to no good," sniffed Mark as they passed her neatly arranged and freshly scrubbed front steps and door. Whenever a broken window occurred on the block, she invariably blamed the McAlynn family.

The boys kept walking, which probably surprised Mrs. Cassano, who was probably thinking the young group was setting up for a half-ball game near her spotless house.

They continued to walk the five blocks or half mile to the Swedish American Museum located at the edge of the Lakes, better known as FDR Park, situated adjacent to the Philadelphia Navy Yard at the southernmost point in Philadelphia.

The young film crew walked to the front of the castle-like museum and climbed a dozen or so steps to the top. The entrance door was still impressively solid and haunted-house-looking with large oval solid steel door knockers, a perfect backdrop for the battle between the two monsters.

Marty showed Jimmy how to operate the camera. He did not want Jimmy looking through the wrong end.

What else was there to do but to start the filming. Jimmy filmed two close-ups of the two fighters, and then Marty and Mark started to grapple with each other. Marty, being the Frankenstein monster, was, according to the script and movie lore, the strongest, so he pushed Mark a few times down the steps, which sounds dangerous, but Mark was pretty limber and gracefully monkey-like and safely fell down with the skill of Douglas Fairbanks and Buster Keaton. The two brothers chased each other up and down the steps in dramatic fashion.

Marty had an idea for even more excitement. The wide stairs had two large concrete side blocks with cannons about five feet above the steps. Marty wanted the Wolfman to get on top and jump down on the Frankenstein monster, just like in the original *Frankenstein Meets the Wolf Man* movie when Lon Chaney, Jr. leaps off of the Mad Doctor's lab machinery onto Bela Lugosi as the Frankenstein monster.

They practiced the stunt a couple of times to get it down perfect. Jimmy had a good idea to film the shot from different angles, so they actually did the jump scene several times. Marty and Mark thought this idea was a stroke of genius on Jimmy's part and completely justified bringing Jimmy along.

Everyone and everything is working out great, Marty thought with great satisfaction. All their hard work—the penny-pinching saving, the fight rehearsal, the late-night hours writing the script, organizing the young cast (mostly friends and younger siblings)—was starting to pay off.

After about fifteen minutes of choreographed battle, the two brothers took a short break. Marty asked the cameraman, Jimmy, how it looked from his standpoint. Of course, Marty and Mark thought it must be really spectacular, but they were a little biased. Marty was honest enough to admit that.

"I think it looks really good," said Jim. He really believed it. Tim and Joey also were tremendously enthusiastic, and even cheered some of the exciting fight scenes. Fortunately, there was no audio on the Kodak eight-millimeter camera, so the cheers could not be heard.

Marty and Mark were very pleased, but they still had to film the final move in the fight scene when the monster pushes the Wolfman against the Mad Doctor's electrical equipment that ignites an explosion, which causes the lab to set on fire and results in the entire castle's collapse in a fiery conflagration. Marty wasn't sure how he would film the burning lab. Probably he could use a miniature set, but being a fireman's son, it would make setting something on fire a little tough. Marty thought about going to a burning building and using the eight-millimeter camera to film it and then incorporate it somehow into the movie. But Marty did not want to take advantage of someone's misery just for a dramatic scene.

They had time to figure it out. He read in some of the monster movie magazines of how other fans built different movie sets with models and shoeboxes. Marty could use some of their ideas and then torch the whole contraption. Marty would let his imagination run wild and then discuss it with his dad on how to accomplish this safely.

But before that scenario could be started, the last live shot with actors had to be done. The Swedish American Museum had a metal wall that could be considered a laboratory machine—it was gray and had some knobs that could look like dials from the right angle.

Jimmy understood where to film the scene to make it look as close as possible to being scientific equipment.

So this was it! The last live shot was about to take place and just in time before school and homework kept everyone too busy.

Jimmy said he was ready, and Marty and Mark grappled once more. They grabbed each other's shoulders and spun around a couple times, and then with a big push, Marty threw Mark against the wall.

Crack! A huge problem developed!

Somehow Marty missed and tossed Mark against the side window with such force that Mark's shoulder smashed a small split in the window. The crack was not that big, and Mark said the jolt didn't hurt too much, and he appeared to be all right. But the small crack set off a loud blaring alarm!

Everyone was shocked and scared. The sound was unbelievably loud and ear-deafening.

The group did what any group of frightened kids would do.

They ran!

They ran away with great speed like Flash in the DC comic book. Mark wisely grabbed the camera from Jimmy, who almost dropped the camera in shocked panic.

The boys fled past the mammoth Naval Hospital complex and scattered down 16th Street and disappeared into the narrow blocks of row homes located north of the museum. Everyone ran as fast as their little legs would carry them—that is, everybody except Marty.

In truth, he was as scared as everyone else and initially started running, but after sprinting half a block, Marty stopped. Mark looked back, but Marty told him to keep running. As long as Mark had the camera, Marty was satisfied their precious film was safe and could be developed.

Marty walked back and decided to face the music alone. He remembered lectures from his dad and grandfather about integrity and the lack of respect kids had nowadays. Marty recalled stories his dad told of the rudeness of some of the kids in the neighborhood and some of the vandalism they caused by overturning trash cans and scribbling graffiti on walls, but what really irritated Martin Senior and got his goat were false fire alarms. Some kids thought it was funny to send firetrucks scrambling in search of nothing, wasting time and effort on a nonexistent fire.

"They wouldn't think it was so hilarious if we were out on a run to a fake location and their house caught fire. The delay could mean the difference between life and death. I've seen it, believe me. I've witnessed too many tragic young deaths, enough to last several life times," Martin Senior said this many times to make a strong impression on Marty Junior.

This was not a really serious offense. It was not a false alarm. The window was cracked and was truly an accident, but Marty felt responsible. His father's admonitions about the sad state of America's youth were still ringing in his ears, so Marty decided he would take the blame and not run away.

However, Marty was grateful everyone else got away, and he was doubly thankful that the film was safe and sound. Marty really thought they recorded some good scenes in the camera. At least, he hoped this was the case. He trusted Jimmy to get it right since he was also a big fan of the movie.

Marty sat on the step. The alarm sound was screeching and unbelievably loud. Marty had to cover his ears.

No cops were in sight. Maybe no police will show up. *That would be perfect*, thought Marty. He would give it maybe five more minutes and then leave—slowly. Marty would not run away.

He waited another few minutes and was beginning to think he would get away scot-free from this mess. Marty thought five minutes was about up, so he stood up and started to walk down the steps. He almost reached the bottom step when a police car suddenly pulled up.

The policeman was young and aggressive, filled with crime-solving eagerness. He jumped out of the car and yelled at Marty.

"What's going on? Hold up! Did you do this?"

Marty stopped and walked toward the police car in a more confident manner than he ever thought was possible when confronted by an authority figure.

"Yes . . . I accidentally cracked the window. Sorry, Officer . . . I didn't mean it."

"Well, so you were trying to run and get away."

"No, I waited a while and figured no one was showing up, so I just started to leave. I admit I did it . . . I could have run and got away, but I have to accept that I did something wrong."

"Well, that's very unusual for kids nowadays. Let me get some information. I'm gonna need your name . . . where you live . . . and then tell me exactly what happened."

"Am I going to be arrested?"

"I don't think so, but your parents will have to pay the damages, unless you have a boatload of money in your back pocket."

"My dad works two jobs as it is . . . will it be expensive?" Marty then played the fireman card in hopes that the policeman will be more sympathetic and added, "My dad is a fireman who works a few blocks from here."

"I'm afraid so."

The young officer almost felt sorry when he saw Marty's crestfallen face.

As the eager young policeman was writing down Marty's name and address, another police car pulled up behind the first car. An older officer took his time getting out of the vehicle.

Marty immediately recognized the older officer, who was approximately the same age as his dad. It was Officer Andy Borromeo from down the street. He lived on the same block but closer to Porter Street. Andy immediately recognized Marty and asked, "What's going on, Marty?"

Marty explained, and Officer Andy told the younger cop that he would handle the situation.

Bob, the younger officer, was grateful for Andy's intervention. To him, this was a boring call. There was more action in the Tasker Housing Projects, so Officer Bob decided to head in that direction so he could be one of the first to take a call if something really exciting was brewing—a fight between a couple of street corner gangs, or maybe even a robbery in progress.

Meeting Andy was a big break. Maybe Officer Andy could smooth things over with the museum people.

Marty explained what happened and accepted full responsibility. Officer Andy was impressed and thought something could be worked out.

"There are a lot of pigeons and flying geese around here. I'm sure a flock of them plowed into the window . . . probably the sunlight blinded them."

Andy walked up the steps to inspect the damaged window. In truth, it wasn't all that bad. A bunch of sun-blinded pigeons could have caused the minor damage. Just a few cracks. Nothing major.

"Yeah," he told Marty. "I am sure that's exactly what happened . . . go home, Marty . . . don't worry about a thing."

Marty could not believe his luck.

"I don't even have to pay for the damage?"

"No, it was an act of God. Strange things do happen, Marty. Believe me. I've seen a lot weirder things."

Marty thanked Officer Andy and started walking toward Broad Street, and he started thinking, *I guess old Abe Lincoln was right . . . honesty is the best policy.*

As Marty walked home, he wondered what his fleeing brothers would say as they dashed safely into the house. Their dad was at the firehouse, but Mom would be there and would notice their exhausted and excited state, not to mention that Cassie would also probably be home and just as curious.

Would they mention the alarm and the broken window?

The broken window was no big deal. Glass was constantly being broken in the neighborhood from all the half ball and softball games being played on the block. As long as the kid who broke the window owned up to it, there were no hard feelings. After all, your own house could be the next accidental victim.

Marty did own up to it, so he felt no worry from his mom or older sister. In fact, he was in a surprisingly good mood—nothing to be ashamed about. He could walk down the block without any slinking embarrassment.

Before he walked into his home, there was a group of kids lined up in front of the house, not only his younger brothers, but some of their friends were just as curious.

It was one thing to break a house window, but a museum broken window! especially one as ornate and forbidding as the Swedish American Museum had to be a lot worse. Marty saw a dozen of eyes riveted on him and could sense all the rumors that were undoubtedly swirling.

"How did you escape?"

"Were you arrested?"

"What happened?"

Before Marty answered, he saw Mark and thought he needed to know first things first:

"Mark, do you have the camera and film? Is it okay?"

Marty was assured by Mark that the film was safely in the house and that there was no damage to the camera.

"It wasn't dropped as we took off to get away . . . so tell us what happened. I thought you'd be hauled off and taken away in the back of the paddy wagon."

Marty was tempted to play it up and paint a heroic portrait but decided to tell the simple unadorned truth. Everyone was disappointed at first, but the more they thought about it, they were glad it all turned out okay.

Marty and Mark couldn't wait to mail the film to Kodak to get developed. They were convinced it would be the best filming yet, better even than the rock-throwing sequence on Penrose Avenue.

Chapter 24

Finishing Touches

Summer was almost over, and Marty also believed the movie was just about finished. The Kodak film arrived in the mail, and the filmed monster battle turned out pretty good, not as great as they hoped, but there were some dramatic fight footage scenes in front of the museum.

The push that cracked the window and set off the alarm was especially good. There seemed to be a slight spark or electrical charge maybe from the alarm or maybe from a scratch in the film. Whatever it was, Marty could use that static blip and then cut to the miniature set he was building with Mark.

This phase was becoming more fun than he originally thought. It was great to let their imagination run wild and think of what to use for the Mad Doctor's laboratory—cardboard flaps for operating tables; paper clips for electrical equipment; photos from *Life* magazine for doors, windows, and outdoor scenes such as clouds, forests, mountain landscapes, etc. Marty even used some of his younger sister's dollhouse furniture to useful effect. Marty also planned to use his beloved Aurora models of the Universal Studio stable of monsters: Frankenstein, the Wolfman, and the Hunchback of Notre Dame, Quasimodo. They would all be sacrificed when the lab was torched.

Marty talked to his dad about the fiery destructive climax. Martin Senior was still recovering from his injury and had more time on his hands than he was used to; working two full-time jobs was second nature to him. To his pleasant surprise, Martin Senior agreed to the plan as long as it was filmed under his supervision, which was a big comfort to Marty Junior. He had been in enough hot water with his fights and the broken window at the museum (which could have been much worse), so Marty did not want to risk any more problems.

His dad recommended the fire take place in the backyard. It was a typical South Philadelphia yard—no small trees or grass, just a concrete pad measuring eight feet long and five feet wide so the planned fire could be easily controlled. No chance of anything catching some sparks and causing a bad fire. Martin Senior would have some water buckets and fire extinguishers close by for added security.

So Marty and Mark worked on the miniature lab set. It was finished in a couple of days. Marty waited for his dad's approval and set up the fiery final scene, which went off pretty well. The fire extinguisher was not needed, and Marty poured buckets of water to douse the flames.

The original *Frankenstein Meets the Wolf Man* climax had a dam bursting that flooded the castle laboratory. Marty thought he could end his film in the same way. He was able to film the buckets dumping the water in such a way that it kind of looked like water from a flood. At least, he hoped that was how it would look when the film was developed.

Marty felt great relief when the movie was finally finished shooting. It still had to be edited yet from all the rolls of film, but that should be the fun part. Now he could concentrate on two more things before the summer ended—getting ready for high school and following the Phillies who were still in first place in the National League and gradually building a nice cushion against their nearest rivals!

Every baseball fan in Philadelphia and the surrounding suburbs thought they were immersed in a wonderful dream and feared they would wake up to reality one day with the Phillies mired in mediocrity. Even that, at least, was better than being the perennial last-place team they normally were.

But almost miraculously, it was no dream, and the Phillies still led the National League, now well ahead of such top-notch teams like the Dodgers (last year's World Series winners) and the San

Francisco Giants stacked with all-stars like Willie Mays, Orlando Cepeda, and Juan Marichal as well as the powerful Cincinnati Reds with Vada Pinson, Pete Rose, and Frank Robinson and the well-balanced Cardinals with all-stars like Ken Boyer and Joe Torre, and solid pitching from Bob Gibson, Ray Sadecki, and former Whiz Kid, Curt Simmons. Yes, it was still true: the Phillies were comfortably atop the National League, and their manager, Gene Mauch, was proclaimed a baseball genius. He was magically making all the right moves with players of limited ability.

Mark was still pessimistic, and their dad had weathered enough Philadelphia sports tragedies to still be a little wary, but Grandpa Adolph was still excited about the Phillies' surprising run and his delight was infectious.

"Savor this moment, boys. It doesn't happen very often with the Phillies. I remember Grover Cleveland Alexander. He was quite a pitcher in nineteen fifteen. I remember Chuck Klein was a hell of a hitter, a triple crown winner no less, but the Phils were still lousy. The Whiz Kids in nineteen fifty were a great surprise, but they flamed out pretty quick. There were young. I thought they would be contenders for years to come, but the Giants and Dodgers were just too good. This year, the Phils came out of nowhere. I don't know if lightning will strike twice next year, so enjoy this while you can. You don't know what next year will bring."

Sadly, Grandpop Adolph's words were weirdly prophetic. Next year would never come for him.

SEPTEMBER

National League Standings September 1964

TEAM	WON	LOST	WON-LOST%	GAMES BACK
PHILADELPHIA	78	51	.605	-----
CINCINNATI	73	57	.562	5.5
SAN FRANCISCO	73	59	.553	6.5
ST. LOUIS	71	59	.546	7.5
MILWAUKEE	66	64	.508	12.5
PITTSBURGH	66	64	.508	7.0
LOS ANGELES	63	66	.488	9.0
CHICAGO	60	70	.462	18.5
HOUSTON	57	75	.432	22.5
NEW YORK	44	86	.338	34.5

Chapter 25

World Premiere

It was the weekend before Labor Day, and the developed film arrived in the mail on Saturday before noon. The final scenes were on eight-millimeter film, and now the whole movie could be put together in one reel.

With Mark's considerable help and their mom's patient and invaluable assistance, Marty was able to splice the strands of film together into a coherent whole. He was surprised at how short the final product turned out, barely thirty minutes.

Marty was proud of the film. Mark and Marty worked very hard and underwent a lot of hardship to finish before the summer ended—torn masks; hair-raising, soaking thunderstorms; broken windows; ear-splitting, scary alarms; exciting Phillies games—but all that was now over, and school was still less than a week away. Marty could now enjoy a few relaxing days before the new and somewhat frightening experience of high school began. The unnerving fact of getting used to a new school and classmates was still bothersome to Marty.

Despite the film's short length, the movie was chockful of exciting scenes: angry villagers (mostly kids under ten) chasing the monster through weeds and lonely trees, the werewolf transformation scene (still a little jerky and jumpy but overall not too bad), the Wolfman's savage attacks on unsuspecting victims, the Frankenstein monster rampaging through the countryside and tossing boulders (actually little rocks) at his tormentors, and, best of all, the titanic battle between the two monsters on the wide spacious steps of the museum. Even the fiery destruction of the miniature lab and the flood turned out pretty good. Mark and his younger brothers agreed it bordered on greatness. His dad boosted Marty's pride when he said he would show the home movie to his fellow firefighters at the station the next night.

Marty thought this was a great idea. It was always good to get some independent opinion from sources outside of the family. After all, his relatives were prejudiced. Marty thought it was exciting and dramatic, but he was primarily responsible and had a large stake in it. He poured his heart and soul into the project.

Marty proudly turned over his hard-earned movie reel to his dad, still on light duty, when he left the house and hobbled the four blocks to the Ladder 49 fire station on 13th Street.

"Okay, Marty, I'll try to show your movie tonight as long as there are no fires raging in the city."

"Do you know what time, Dad?"

"If all is quiet, maybe around eight, after we eat and do some cleanup."

Marty decided he would take a walk around then and try to hang around outside of the firehouse and maybe gauge the reaction of the firemen for himself. Marty was too keyed up and excited to wait until the morning to find out the result when his dad returned home from his night shift.

Yes! That was the plan. Marty could buy some water ice from Pop's around the corner on Oregon Avenue and eat the frozen concoction while hanging outside the building. Marty had been around the firehouse enough times to know the best and closest place to stand and eavesdrop unobtrusively below the recreation room where his movie would be shown.

The Phillies' game was not on TV that night but only on the radio. Marty did not feel too bad about not listening to the whole game at home with his brothers and grandfather. He could follow the score by walking from block to block and hear bits and snatches of the game from the residents listening to the game on their front steps. Marty left at seven forty-five in the evening, and by the time he walked the four blocks to the firehouse, Richie Allen hit a two-run homer to give the Phils an early lead.

Marty could observe the firehouse from half a block away and see the fire trucks were still inside the open truck bay, so no fires were raging in the neighborhood. This inactivity also meant Marty's dad would more than likely show his fellow firemen the film.

It was close to eight, so Marty walked over to Oregon Avenue and purchased a lemon Italian ice from Pop's Water Ice. He bought a large one so he could milk the snack while hanging below the window of the fire station's kitchen/recreation room.

Marty uncharacteristically took his time eating the frozen treat. Normally, he would devour the whole icy drink in less than five minutes. Often this haste would cause a painful brain freeze that slightly slowed him down. Marty hated these painful delays and never seemed to learn his lesson. Eating ice cream or water ice too quickly caused the nagging debilitating ache that lasted only a minute, but the intense pain seemed so much longer.

Marty concentrated and slowly licked around the top of the lemon water ice, forcing himself to take his time so as to make his loitering around the wall somewhat reasonable.

As Marty hung around, he could hear some of the firemen joking around and talking about a world premiere. Marty didn't think of it like that, but in a sense, it was the world premiere of his very own film. Of course, there would be no Hollywood stars parading down the walkway or a massive searchlight shining into the night sky, but his film was to be viewed for the first time by an objective, neutral audience. His mom loved it, but what else could she really say? Her sons put in the effort, and she obviously could have been overly enthusiastic in her praise.

So Marty believed this to be a good test to see if all his hard work with Mark was going to be all worth it. Marty was able to overhear his dad tell everyone to be quiet. Why quiet was needed since it was a silent film was a mystery, but Marty figured his dad was just trying to get everyone's attention. He looked up and could see the room light was switched off.

This is it, thought Marty. *Showtime!*

Marty wished he was taller so he could better hear the firemen's reaction, but he still had a decent location and still had enough lemon water ice left (Thank God he bought a large one!). This made it seem he was just enjoying his summertime treat and not eavesdropping on the firehouse. Any passing police car would assume Marty was just standing around slowly licking his frozen dessert.

Marty could just about make out his dad explaining to his fellow firemen about his son's movie that they were about to watch. He did hear a few comments before the movie began.

"What's it about?"

"Does it even have a plot?"

"Is he your oldest boy?"

The chatter quieted down, and Marty could sense the screening began.

Marty had a nervous pit in the stomach when something exciting was about to happen. When he was a little kid, he felt this way on Christmas morning when he stood at the top of the steps and was about to walk down the stairs to see all the wrapped Christmas presents around the tree. Nowadays, he felt this way during a Phillies game when the game was on the line with a runner on third with two outs and a full count with the game's outcome hanging in the balance.

Right now, Marty was concentrating on how the firemen would react to the movie.

What he initially heard was not encouraging.

What was he hearing? It sounded like laughter and not just a few chuckles here and there but a loud boisterous burst of laughs. How could that be? The movie wasn't a comedy; it was deadly serious. What was so funny?

Marty stayed riveted to where he was. His ears were latching onto the sounds from the firehouse recreation room like a frog seizing a bug with its tongue. He felt shattered.

His big movie premiere was not going as well as he hoped. Marty hung around for another minute or so. His stay was bordering now on loitering and didn't want to arouse suspicion from any roving police cars. His ears were still sensitive, almost bordering on

Superman's super hearing, and he heard several comments from the firemen.

"That was priceless, Martin."

"I haven't had that many laughs since the last Jerry Lewis movie."

"I think you have the next Charlie Chaplin or Bob Hope with that crazy son of yours."

Marty could hear similar comments about how funny the movie was.

Charlie Chaplin! Marty didn't want to be the next Charlie Chaplain, or even Jerry Lewis. Marty wanted to be a combination of Boris Karloff and Lon Chaney, Sr. In fact, he wanted to do all those great actors even better. Marty wanted to do it all—write, act, and direct.

In short, he wanted to be the Walt Disney of horror movies, creating scary thrilling movies but still family-friendly. Not with all that smut that his dad and mom constantly complained about that were in too many modern movies.

His movies would have monsters and a lot of killings but no naked woman. Marty wanted to make clean but scary movies. However, his initial film was not the thriller he envisioned. Apparently, adults found the monster movie unintentionally funny.

Marty was a little stunned and didn't want to hang around the firehouse anymore. He had heard enough and slowly slouched and ambled his way west toward Broad Street. He passed several stores, and even the fresh chocolate smells of Lerro's homemade candy shop, and the seasoned aromas of cheesesteaks cooking on the grill did not comfort him. The Phillies were still playing. Maybe that would take away some of his dejection.

What Marty could not see in the firehouse was the following scenes that provoked unintended hilarity like the fake mustache falling off the burgomaster in full view of the camera, the Wolfman's hair falling off in clumps again in direct focus, the monster hitting the top of his head on the cellar pipes, knocking off the mask. These mishaps were not edited out and set the stage for all the laughter. Marty at first was too hurt to acknowledge the gaffes and humor. He would appreciate it more in a few months, but for now, he was devastated.

The first person Marty saw as he trudged in the front door was little Marie. She was playing with her raggedy dolls. She looked at her brother and positively beamed with delight.

"Hi, Marty. I keep forgetting to tell you how much I really liked your movie. It was really exciting. I could not believe how good it was."

Good old Marie, thought Marty. He was tempted to give her a great big hug. The tears that were beginning to flow from his eyes were halted by Marie's enthusiasm.

"Thanks, Marie. I'm glad somebody liked it."

Marty returned Marie's big smile with one of his own. He was deeply grateful for Marie's kind words.

He walked into the dining room, and the second person to greet him also cheered him up, his Grandpop Adolph.

Two things could clear his spirits: a nice talk with his grandfather and listening to the Phillies, who were firmly in first place, surging well ahead of the fading San Francisco Giants. The Reds were making their move, but they were still well behind. The St. Louis Cardinals were showing signs of life but were just barely a .500 team. No cause for concern there.

His grandfather summarized the pennant race perfectly.

"The Cards and Reds will have to win 70 percent of their remaining games to catch us, Marty, and the Phils will have to collapse like they almost did in nineteen fifty, so I wouldn't worry too much. If we're lucky, I'll try to get some World Series tickets. This is a great opportunity. You don't know how many World Series chances you can get. I've been on this earth over eighty years, and this is only the third time, so you weigh the odds."

Grandpa's enthusiasm and joy were the perfect antidote for Marty's flagging spirits. Soon his humiliation was pushed far back in his mind, and Marty was transfixed by the rare chance for a Phillies trip to the Fall Classic.

"You just never know as I have said repeatedly," Grandpa kept talking. "We thought the Whiz Kids would contend year after year. They were young enough, but unfortunately they were in the same league as the Brooklyn Dodgers of Gil Hodges, Johnny Podres, Duke

Snider, and Roy Campanella and the Willie Mays-led Giants. Too much stiff competition."

He continued, "In a lot of ways, this is true today. The Reds have great hitting with the dynamic duo of Frank Robinson and Vada Pinson. The Cards have great pitching and a few potential MVPs in Bill White and Ken Boyer, and the Giants have the great Willie Mays and two up and coming sluggers in Orlando Cepeda and Willie McCovey. The Dodgers have tremendous pitching but no hitting. On top of that, the Milwaukee Braves are no slouches with surefire Hall of Famers like Hank Aaron and Eddie Matthews. Even the Chicago Cubs are a threat with not one but three one hundred RBI hitters like Ernie Banks, Billy Williams, and Ron Santo. In fact, the only patsies in the National League are Houston and the Mets, and they are expansion teams that will only get better, so the competition in the senior circuit is fierce, but the Phillies are playing way above their heads. Let's hope this dream season continues."

Grandpop Adolph's positive analysis of the baseball season made Marty's mood less melancholy and put his movie's disastrous premiere more into the background. It brought a little more joy on this, the last weekend of his summer vacation.

Chapter 26

High School—the First Day

Marty walked down the reddish brown stone steps of his modest row home a little slower than usual. It was his first day of high school. His dad and mom were enthusiastic about this new phase in their son's life. Marty was not so sure. He liked the comforts and familiarity of his grade school class. There was one teacher, normally a nun, who taught every subject in just one classroom. No need to move from class to class. Marty felt safe and secure in his first row, last seat position that he was normally assigned from the first day of class.

That was all going to change now, as there would now be many different teachers (all male) and not only in several classrooms but also on different floors. What a pain that could be!

Marty mulled these coming changes as he trudged the lonely two miles to Bishop Neumann. He walked past familiar and comforting landmarks—the delicious aromas of the German bakery, the butcher shop where he bought lunch meat for his mom, the Carnegie library where he browsed through magazines and biographies. This is where the old gentleman who resembled Boris Karloff used to visit and could be seen reading *Time* and *Newsweek* magazines. Marty would often have to stop others from making a nuisance of themselves from staring and asking for his autograph. Marty felt bad for the old fellow, who just wanted to read his magazines in peace and not have a bunch of teenagers gawking at him, thinking he was a famous movie star.

Marty kept a slow walking pace and thought about more pleasant times. He really despised change but knew high school was the next step in his life as much as he disliked the thought of growing up. He was beginning to think Peter Pan was on to something.

Marty walked across the large strip mall parking lot, which also had the bowling alley, scene of more enjoyable times. He was now getting closer and closer to the new school. This was the outer limit of his northwest directional walk. Any further advance and the neighborhood changed. His dad, who knew the city inside and out from his job as a Philadelphia firefighter, always warned him about venturing into the high-rise urban renewal projects where he might get jumped. Fortunately, despite all his perambulations, he avoided being a mugging victim. Some of his friends were not so lucky. One of his buddies had an ice pick stabbed into his shoulder.

Marty yielded to common sense, his friends' negative experiences, and his dad's warning and never entered that unknown domain.

The high school was perilously close to this danger area, but Marty had no choice. Bishop Neumann was located where it was, but Marty would remain alert to his surroundings and avoid any potential confrontations.

The fresh, fragrant smell of Entenmann's Bakery temporarily revived Marty's flagging spirits. It rekindled memories of family birthday parties, but this heartwarming thought was soon dashed as he turned the corner, and there it was—the massive two-story brownish gray stone structure of Bishop Neumann High School. It was ominously centered between an encircling green fence topped by sharp barbed wire.

Barbed wire? Was this a concentration camp or a POW camp? Marty had just watched *The Great Escape* at the nearby President Theater on Snyder Avenue last month, and he sure felt like Steve McQueen and James Garner as they entered the German Stalag.

Marty took a deep breath and crossed the threshold onto the dark gray pavement of the school grounds. He joined scores of other wary freshman students milling around the entrance to the building. There was no official school uniform, but the teenagers were all dressed pretty much the same—dark jackets (gray or blue), white shirts, dark tie, and tan slacks.

Marty recognized a few friends from his grade school and nodded a terse hello. Many were driven to school on their first day, but Marty insisted on walking. His dad worked the night shift at the fire house anyway, so it would have necessitated his dad leaving work early and borrowing a car. Martin Senior would have gladly made the arrangements, but Marty declined. Two miles was no big deal. He was going to walk on most days anyway, so Marty might as well get used to it right away. Besides, Marty wanted to ease his way from home to school on his own terms.

The gathering group of students loitered around the yard with no real purpose. Some herded together with grade school acquaintances. No one could enter the building yet, so the boys congregated aimlessly in small clusters, waiting to get organized. No one seemed to be in charge.

That soon changed.

Marty could hear a lot of commotion and surprised murmurings that was soon directed at the roof of the building.

Marty looked up and squinted through the early morning reddish sun rising above the school rooftop. As pretty as the crimson sky appeared above the building, this did not impress him. A hulking dark figure began to emerge upon the rooftop, and that was truly impressive.

The dusky silhouette outlined by the fiery sunrise gradually emerged as a hulking figure. It was an astonishing sight. The mysterious form looked like Moses coming down from Mount Sinai with the Ten Commandments.

The dark figure became less harshly framed against the background of the sun and became more visibly identifiable. The silhouette that appeared came forth as an athletic, middle-aged priest, broad-shouldered, clean-shaven with graying temples, and carrying a bullhorn.

The burly priest lifted the bullhorn to his mouth, and his booming, resonant Charlton Heston-like voice drilled order into the waiting, chaotic cluster of students.

Soon his commands dissolved the disorder and organized the aimless mass of students into disciplined ranks. This was accomplished solely by his authoritative voice. There was no need for help on the street level ground. The priest's booming voice soon had organized groups forming up into orderly columns that entered the building quickly and quietly. Once inside the fortress-like building, another group of teachers took command of the freshmen and guided them to their respective homerooms.

Marty's first impression of high school was memorable with a combination of three movies—*Stalag 17*, *The Ten Commandments*, and *1984*—but streamlined and a little friendlier. It was a rigid order but not a Communist prison.

This impression became even more favorable when Marty entered his homeroom class and met the teacher, Father Clement Wlodarcyck, a rugged but affable, athletically lanky priest. He made the entire class comfortably at home with his quiet authority. In addition to his muscular build, he had huge hands that could easily palm a basketball like Wilt Chamberlain. A swipe from these powerful paws could knock sense into a recalcitrant student's head with ease. This was the common consensus from the awed classroom. No one dared to find out and tempt fate.

Rumors were already spreading that he served in the Marines during the Korean War, which just added more respectful fear in the students. The talk was that he fought in the Chosun Reservoir—Frozen Chosen as it was popularly called—the epic, fighting retreat of the Marines from the Yalu River in North Korea while surrounded by hundreds of thousands of Red Chinese soldiers desperate to cut the Marines off from any escape.

Marty remembered an old black-and-white movie about the battle that he saw on TV, *Retreat Hell*, with Frank Lovejoy. It was one of the few war movies that actually interested Marty. It was a stirring tribute to the heroic Marines who fought their way out of a potential annihilation, and Marty thought it was kind of neat that one of his teachers was actually part of such a historic event. Marty was determined to read more about the actual battle at the library.

He might even work up enough gumption to ask the good Father some questions about the epic retreat.

Father W, as the teacher was dubbed by the class to avoid annoying mispronunciations of his name, endeared himself even more to his class with his admission of being a rabid Phillies fan.

"It gives you a good sense of the essential tragedy of life," he joked to his students.

This attitude relaxed many of the more uptight boys. It was the first week of September, and the Fightin Phils were beginning to pull away from the rest of the National League teams. The acquisition of slugger Frank Thomas was a welcome jolt to the team and filled a glaring hole in the Phillies' lineup. It patched up their Achilles' heel against left-handed pitching since the team lacked a power hitting right-handed hitter other than rookie sensation, Richie Allen.

Frank Thomas' powerful bat reversed the Phillies' poor record against left-handed pitching. BT (Before Thomas) the Phillies were practically hapless against even journeymen lefties, but after his insertion into the lineup the Phillies compiled a winning record against southpaws. Thomas hit seven home runs and drove in twenty-six runs in less than a month. Marty calculated that if Thomas kept up that pace throughout the entire season, he would hit over 40 homers and drive in 150 RBIs. Of course, not many players could maintain those numbers throughout the year, but it did indicate how important his bat was to the surging Phillies. Unfortunately, Thomas was recently injured with an aggressive slide into second base. His injury was a concern, but his heroics had enabled the team to build up a comfortable lead in the NL standings.

It seemed inevitable that the Phillies could almost waltz to the October Classic; it was merely a matter of time. Grandpop Adolph said the Phils could play .500 ball the rest of the season and still coast to the NL pennant. What could go wrong?

As his first day in high school continued, Marty was actually enjoying the rotating class schedule. He was beginning to like the idea of leaving one classroom and walking to another. Even climbing steps to the second floor felt pretty good. Marty was jettisoning his grade school attachment to his desk for the entire school day.

Marty also liked the variety of teachers, and they were all male. Quite a change of pace from one nun who dominated the classroom from beginning to end.

Another interesting twist to high school was that his Latin teacher, Father Helmut Fritzdorf, was also a noted cheese maker and had all kinds of different cheeses for the class to sample on the first day of class. The good father even taught the class a few Latin words about the cheese-making process, thus making it educational as well as delicious. He certainly looked the part of a medieval monk with his beach-ball-sized stomach, balding pate, and boisterous laugh. Father Fritzdorf would have been perfectly cast as Friar Tuck in a modern remake of *Robin Hood*. The one annoying aspect to his class was that he was from America's Dairyland, Wisconsin, and a die-hard Green Bay Packer fan.

Another unique teacher was Mr. Greg Fallon, the World History teacher. He was young, athletic, and smoothly cool with one major claim to fame in college. As a guard at St. Joseph's College, he once held NBA great Jerry West to just six measly points in a college basketball game. This, needless to say, greatly impressed the freshman class.

The religion teacher, Father Hubert Wurzburg, had a terrific sense of humor and kept the class in stitches with his jokes and impersonations. He did a pitch-perfect Walter Brennan and John Wayne skit based on *Rio Bravo*. Marty thought he was so funny that the priest deserved a gig on *The Tonight Show Starring Johnny Carson*.

It was refreshing to be with all the boys during the day. This masculinity was reinforced by all the male teachers. Sports was on everyone's mind, of course. The Phillies' inevitable march to the World Series was the big talk, but the impending opening of the Eagles football season was also a big topic, especially with their new helmsman, former Notre Dame coach, Joe Kuharich, who cleaned house with new personnel. He even traded the Eagles' record-breaking quarterback, Sonny Jurgensen, for Norm Snead, and when asked why he switched quarterbacks, he stated with a straight face, "Trading quarterbacks is rare but not unusual."

Marty finished the day in much brighter spirits. The dread and uncertainty of the unknown were safely in the past. Marty was getting accustomed to the newness and felt more comfortable with high school, much to his surprise.

All that needless worry during the last few days of summer vacation. What a waste of effort. Maybe his dad was right after all, as he usually was. Marty hated to admit the fact, but he was almost enjoying the prospect of high school.

Well, almost. He did not want to overdo it. The school year was only beginning, but it was looking more promising and not the ordeal Marty feared.

When Marty walked home after his first day of high school, the trip was much more pleasant. He could actually enjoy the familiar sights and sounds. Gone was the unease and fearful anticipation of the unknown—meeting new classmates from different neighborhoods, a myriad of rotating teachers, the lack of a rooted classroom.

Marty walked toward Snyder Avenue, a wider-than-normal South Philadelphia street and an interesting combination of row homes and commercial establishments with various stores and plenty of places to eat, ranging from ice cream to cheesesteaks. A few school yards broke up the densely packed urban jungle. Kids were shooting basketballs into netless rims. Despite this lack of netting, each player instinctively knew when the ball made a silent swish into the basket. Other youngsters were playing touch football on the grassless open space. This play area made it tough on bare knees when a kid tripped or was accidentally tackled. This was the main reason his brothers and friends played touch and not tackle football.

Marty crossed under the dimly lit train overpass (he was glad it was not night time) that marked the edge of where he could safely walk. He passed by the President Movie Theater, his personal favorite in the neighborhood. The lobby had a unique entrance with five-foot high silver medallions of each US President from George Washington to Calvin Coolidge, who was the chief executive when the theater was built during the Roaring Twenties.

During the past summer, this was the movie house where he watched *The Great Escape* movie with his friends and brothers. Marty reflected how his initial impression of Bishop Neumann was that of a German prisoner of war camp depicted in the film, but upon entering the school, he felt more at home and was greatly impressed by his combat-hardened homeroom teacher, Father Wlodarcyk.

When Marty entered his house, he could smell his mom's spaghetti sauce simmering and cooking on the stove. His grandfather was sitting on his favorite sofa and seemed more tired than usual, but he perked up when he saw Marty come inside through the double glass front door.

"How was your first day, Marty?"

"Pretty good. I liked our homeroom teacher a lot. He is a priest, but he was also a Marine Corps veteran of the Korean War. You were in a war also, weren't you, Grandpop?"

"Yeah, in World War I, but I never had the chance to serve overseas in France. The war ended as I was about to embark on the ship that would take us across the Atlantic Ocean. Boy, I bet your teacher will have stories to tell! Nowadays, it is not that unusual for priests to have served in the military. Many find their vocation after experiencing the horrors of war."

Marty noticed that his grandfather's breathing was more labored.

"Are you okay, Grandpop?"

"Yes, just a little tired. Didn't sleep too good last night. I guess I will rest a little more until supper."

He sat down again, but even that slight effort seemed labored.

"Maybe some food will give you more energy?"

"Yes, I'm sure it will."

It was very unusual for his grandfather to be so zestless. Normally, he was a bundle of enthusiastic energy. But Marty did not dwell too long on it. Maybe his grandfather was just sleepy from a restless night. He also developed a persistent and nagging thought: did the long walk from Wildwood gravely affect his grandfather's health? It seemed inconceivable because Grandpa seemed to enjoy the trek so much and showed no visible ill effects afterwards. The walk was completed over a month ago, so Marty concluded hopefully that the walk did not cause the recent change in Grandpa's energy level, especially since he seemed to enjoy the long walk back from Wildwood so much.

Marty walked into the kitchen and greeted his mom, who also asked how his first day of school was.

Marty gave the same reply and added, "Smells good, Mom."

"I hope it tastes just as good. Your father will be home around five. We'll eat then. Hopefully, your grandpop can take a nap. He does not seem quite himself."

"Yeah, I'm sure he will perk up at suppertime and be his old self and ready to watch the Phillies tonight."

"I hope so," replied his mom, who had a more pensive look than Marty was accustomed to seeing, especially in the kitchen.

Marty hoped it was not the start of a downward slide for his beloved and irrepressible grandfather. Marty tried to shrug the negative feeling off, but he could not brush it off so easily. The unease stayed in his mind for the next couple of hours and dimmed his initial euphoria over his first day of high school.

Being back at school meant the summer was basically over. Officially, the summer still lingered, but the joy of a school-free couple of months with plenty of leisure and playtime to cherish ended. Homework needed to be done, and sleeping late until almost noon was over. Early wake-ups and a daily two-mile walk to school began Marty's day five times a week.

The only remnant left of this special summer was baseball. The Phillies were not only still on top of the league standings, but they actually widened their lead over the fading San Francisco Giants. The Cincinnati Reds and the St. Louis Cardinals turned their season around and were playing much better, but they still lagged behind the surging Phillies. The acquisition of slugger Frank Thomas was just what the doctor ordered for the Phils' glaring weakness against left-handed pitching. This comforting fact received a body blow when Thomas injured his hand during a slide into second base to break up a double play, but his initial presence allowed the Phillies to build a commanding lead in the middle of September to a comfortable six games.

The consensus throughout the city was still upbeat with the strong belief that this golden opportunity for the Phillies to reach the World Series for only the third time in their eighty-year history was almost inevitable.

That was why Grandpop Adolph's lethargy was doubly worrisome. Having your grandfather ill was bad enough, but to have such a loyal fan feeling bad on the cusp of such a great season was even worse.

"Could God be that cruel?" wondered the always pessimistic Mark as he observed Grandpop's increasingly weary condition and the fear that he was too sick to enjoy the Phillies' trip to the Fall Classic.

Marty tried to be optimistic.

"He will rally, just like the Phillies all year. No team in the majors have had so many late inning comebacks."

Marty was outwardly more positive, but inwardly he shared Mark's concern.

Chapter 27

Farewell

Grandpop's death was as sudden as his unexpected illness. He just sat in front of the TV to watch the game and never got up. He had a quiet heart attack. It was a terrible shock. The whole family knew he wasn't his old self, but everyone thought it was just temporary. He always appeared to be in tip top shape, especially with all the walking he did. He seemed the picture of perfect health. But he was now gone, and the family's numbness lasted until the funeral Mass.

Grandfather Adolph went quick and did not suffer much. He was strong and vigorous to the end and only spent one day in the hospital. Although it was comforting to know he did not linger in a coma or was wracked with pain, his death was a terrible shock to the family. It was hard to imagine that Adolf could fall so quickly. One day, he was alert and discussed batting averages, runs batted in, and various other baseball statistics with the aplomb of a sportswriter and then effortlessly ambled on a two-mile walk after supper. Sadly, the next day, he was in the hospital fighting for his life.

Marty would never forget the dreadful moment he found out about his grandfather's death.

He sensed something was terribly wrong when he came back from a neighborhood baseball game at Marconi Plaza. Kate, Marie, and his mom, Veronica, were crying at the kitchen table. Even his dad had red, moist eyes, evidence of a good cry earlier. He never saw his dad cry and always thought of him as a rock, unfailingly kind and fair but stoic.

"What happened?" said a distraught Marty to his dad.

"Looks like a massive heart attack because it came on so sudden. He complained of some severe chest pains and was rushed to the hospital."

"But he was in such great shape . . . he walked miles and miles all over the city and always looked so healthy."

"I know, Marty. He did everything right that a man could possibly do to stay healthy. He never smoked, he exercised. He did enjoy his beer but never to excess."

Martin Senior was trying hard to both comfort his son and gently explain the inexplicability of life's misfortunes and failing him on both counts no matter how hard he tried.

"Life is full of great joys but also some unbearable heartache."

Martin wanted to say more to comfort Marty, but his voice cracked, and he did everything in his power not to break down into uncontrollable sobbing.

Marty was also trying mightily to not dissolve into a cleansing bout of crying. Tears welled up in his eyes, but as he put his head into his dad's shoulder, Marty took control of his heartbroken emotions and somehow managed to not bawl his eyes out. The pain was palpable, but Marty refused to give into the agony he deeply felt.

What more was there to say? Adolph was an eighty-one-year-old man whose long life was about to end. Yes, he was a remarkable physical specimen, especially for his age, but he led a hard life: father of twelve children, husband to an invalid wife, a soldier in the disease-ridden camps of World War I, father to four combat surviving World War II sons and suffering the loss of one son who died in the Battle of the Bulge, and a blue-collar worker toiling for hours in the dusty factories of that era. All things considered, Grandpa Adolph survived a lot of adversity, and even prospered in remarkable health almost to the very end. *Not a bad run*, thought Martin Senior, but that did not comfort his sons and his brokenhearted wife, Veronica, who idolized her dad with such good reason.

Martin Senior had seen death in many violent forms: firemen trapped in burning buildings, sailors drowning in the icy North Atlantic, the charred bodies of children in deadly fires. The death of his father-in-law, despite his advanced age, hurt equally as bad. Not so much for its shocking suddenness but primarily for Adolph's soothing common sense and genuine compatibility. Despite Martin's familiarity with death, he had to agree with his older son, Marty, and never believed the old man would ever die. It seemed so out of character; he truly seemed invincible.

To add salt to an already painful wound, the Phillies were still in first place and inevitably heading to a surprise World Series appearance, and Adolf was not going to experience it—at least, not on this Earth with his family. Somehow, that seemed so crushingly sad.

This was a sentiment experienced by his grandsons; losing their beloved grandfather was terrible enough, but having the death come with the Phillies on the verge of an unexpected National League pennant and a trip to the World Series with a fourteen-year-old rematch with the Yankees was even harder to bear. It almost made Mark doubt the existence of a benevolent God. Marty thought that this was going a little too far, but it was a doubly bitter pill to swallow.

Marty had to admit the truth of his dad's often repeated advice and words of wisdom: "Sometimes life is hard and just doesn't make sense."

Marty also thought of another saying his grandfather often said: "God's ways are not our own. That Earth is not our true home. Try to enjoy your life whenever possible but don't expect total and complete happiness during your lifetime."

Adolph's two older grandsons, Marty and Mark, were two of the pallbearers. This was Marty's first time but, with his large family, surely not the last. He was in the middle along with Mark. His dad, Martin, was in the front, along with two uncles, Paul and Ed. Martin's foot injury was pretty much healed. The casket was not as heavy as Marty feared. It helped to have five others help to carry the weight. Going up the stone church steps was a little harder, but fortunately there were only twenty steps from the street, where the hearse was parked in front of the church. Marty was glad to be one of the pallbearers. He felt honored. It would be the last thing on this earth he would do for his grandfather, and this thought kept him supremely focused.

Marty felt the solemnity of the task as he went to the back of the hearse and helped guide the casket along the brass rails. He grasped the copper handles and lifted and was surprised how light it felt, but with six people carrying the load—his brother Mark, his Dad, his two uncles, and his cousin Jack Doherty—the coffin was quite bearable.

Lifting and tilting the casket up the twenty limestone steps of the church was a little tough. Marty kept thinking he was going to trip. He was grateful there was a gurney at the church entrance that the casket was placed upon. After that, there was a slow glide down the aisle to the front of the altar. Marty tried to keep his eyes peeled toward the front of the church and did not look at the mourners lining the pews. However, as he solemnly strolled down the aisle, some instinct told him to glance to his left, and Marty was heartened to see Greg standing in the pew. Greg gave Marty a sympathetic and heartfelt nod of the head. This brief silent communication was comforting to Marty. He recalled their memorable encounter during the long walk back from Wildwood and was grateful that Greg was honoring his grandfather with his presence.

Once the coffin was placed in front of the marble communion rails, a large US flag was placed to cover the oblong box. Grandpop Adolph was a World War I veteran and deserved the honor, although the war ended before he could be shipped overseas to France and into the horrors of the Western Front.

The funeral Mass began, and the priest, Father Coniglio, knew Adolph very well from his daily walks around the neighborhood. In addition, Adolph was an everyday Mass goer and a daily communicant.

During the homily, the priest extolled his life on earth and made amusing references to his daily walks and love of baseball. There were a lot of tears but also some laughs when Adolph's walking accomplishments were recited. But mostly, it was gratitude for a life well lived.

"I know all of you are deeply saddened by this good man's death, but he lived a long and productive life. His memory will continue to live in your hearts. It seems especially poignant that he won't be here with us to enjoy the Phillies' trip to the World Series, but I am sure God will allow him to have the best seat in the house. A glorious heavenly view above the ball park. No obstructions of any kind, no concrete columns, no hot dog vendors blocking the field. He will have an angel's eye view of the entire diamond and field."

This brought a few welcome laughs in the crowded church.

Martin Senior went along with the general humor of the moment, but inwardly he winced and thought that while it was true that his father-in-law was well deserving of all the high praise for an honorable life, Martin Senior was aware no one was perfect and that even the most virtuous and devout still had to serve some time in purgatory. Isn't that why the church prays for the dead?

Martin recalled a story from his own devout father, Patrick, who said that when he passed away, he wanted his family and friends to have plenty of Masses said for the repose of his soul.

"Don't *praise* me when I'm dead. *Pray* for me!" he would often say. "Even a holy saint like St. Francis of Assisi worried about the state of his soul on his deathbed, which no doubt concerned his fellow Franciscans. If he was that apprehensive, where does that leave us?"

Martin Senior certainly understood the desire to put a mourner's mind at ease about an immediate, pain-free, straight-to-heaven journey for the deceased, but Martin would have many Masses and prayers said for his irreplaceable father-in-law. Instant canonization was rare even for miracle-producing saints. This was something the living could still do for the dead—prayers and Mass intentions.

Martin Senior fervently wished he could do more to comfort his children at this sad time, but he knew it was only the opening round, the initial start of more tragedy and heartache to come. He never considered himself a pessimist but just a realist. The old phrase from the Hail, Holy Queen prayer, "a vale of tears," was searingly accurate. Life would bring much joy and laughter but also its fair share of heartbreak.

Martin had experienced many of life's tragedies during his war-time service in the US Navy. The frightening sight of flaming, broken ships torpedoed by U-boats and the frantic attempt to rescue struggling swimmers in the freezing waters of the North Atlantic had a profound effect on him. Martin recalled with horror at standing watch and watching a nearby ship being hit. He dwelled on how close he came to death if the torpedo was aimed at his vessel.

This sense of melancholy was reinforced by his career as a Philadelphia fireman when he also saw his share of tragic deaths as raging infernos snatched the young lives of many of his friends and colleagues.

Martin Senior was never hardened with cynicism to the sadness of life, but he was aware of its random sorrow. It was a tough lesson to pass on to his children, but it needed to be done.

The evening of the funeral and burial remained gloomy for the family. Even the prospects of the evening Phillies game could not lighten the mood. Little did anyone know, it portended another life lesson to life's unpredictability and was the first step in an upcoming Philadelphia Phillies disaster. The last baseball game Adolph listened to was a Phillies victory, a well-crafted Jim Bunning 3–2 victory against the Dodgers.

Phillies' fans would be stunned to realize this was their last victory for almost two weeks, and after the nightmare was over, the Phillies' dream of World Series victory washed away faster than a sandcastle at the edge of an Atlantic City beach.

OCTOBER

National League Standings October 1964

TEAM	WON	LOST	WON-LOST%	GAMES BACK
ST. LOUIS	92	67	.579	-----
CINCINNATI	92	68	.575	0.5
PHILADELPHIA	90	70	.563	2.5
SAN FRANCISCO	89	70	.560	3.0
MILWAUKEE	85	73	.538	6.5
PITTSBURGH	79	79	.500	12.5
LOS ANGELES	78	81	.491	14.0
CHICAGO	74	85	.465	18.0
HOUSTON	65	94	.409	27.0
NEW YORK	51	108	.321	41.0

Chapter 28

An Unbelievable Collapse

After the funeral on September 21, whether by a strangely cruel quirk of fate or a benevolent action by the hand of God, the Phillies' magical season began to break down. The first loose strand that began the unraveling was the heartbreaking 1–0 loss to the Cincinnati Reds on the rarest of plays, a steal of home plate.

Marty listened to the game with his dad and brother, Mark, and Martin Senior could not believe what happened.

"How could Chico Ruiz steal home with Frank Robinson, the team's best RBI man at the plate? He is having an off year for a player of his caliber, but in the past few seasons, he has had monster years, consistently hitting thirty home runs and driving in over one hundred twenty runs. It defies all baseball wisdom. I guess that is why it worked!" Martin shook his head in bemused amazement.

"It's really a shame because Art Mahaffey pitched a really good game for a change," said Marty. "But the Phils still have a five-and-a-half game lead with only eleven games left. Practically insurmountable, don't you think, Dad?"

"I hope so, but let's face it, we are talking about the Phillies. I remember back in nineteen fifty, the Whiz Kids almost blew a similarly huge lead, seven and a half games with only eleven left. It came down to a desperate do-or-die must win against the Dodgers on the last game of the regular season. The Phils needed a clutch-pitching performance from Robin Roberts and Dick Sisler's late inning home run to finally seal the deal. I hope we don't have to sweat it out like we did back then. I doubt if my heart can take it."

Marty still had a lot of optimism despite his dad's wariness. He kept up this confidence even after the Phils were routed the next night, 9–2, after a rare poor showing by the Phillies' lefty ace, Chris Short.

However, another loss to the Reds, 6–4, especially after having a 3–2 lead late in the game that withered away with a four-run, seventh inning rally by Cincinnati, caused Marty some unease, and he was now beginning to wonder about the team.

Three straight losses were worrisome, but the team had a three and a half lead with nine games left. Still comfortable, but doubt was creeping in.

The normally melancholy "chicken little, the sky is falling" attitude of Mark was surprisingly upbeat.

"Don't worry. We still have the inside straight. The law of averages is still in our favor," Mark surprisingly told Marty.

Marty took Mark's unusually sunny optimism as a positive sign. Surely the Phils will turn it around against the Milwaukee Braves on the upcoming four-game home stand.

"It won't be easy," Marty told Mark. "The Braves are tough with good hitting. They probably have three or four surefire Hall of Famers in their lineup—Hammerin Hank Aaron, slugging third baseman Eddie Matthews, and catcher Joe Torre. Not to mention the ageless Warren Spahn."

Marty slept pretty well that night and didn't worry too much about the Phillies' three-game losing streak.

As he walked to school that morning, he looked forward to Father Fritzdorf's cheese samples during Latin class. Father Fritzdorf gave his class a taste the first week of school and promised more homemade cheese during the last week of September. Marty could not believe how good cheese could taste all by itself. Marty was used to its velvety goodness on pizza or a hamburger but rarely ate cheese for its own sake. That would soon change because of his encounter with Father Fritz.

The only drawback was that the roly-poly priest was from Wisconsin and a Braves fan, so he enjoyed needling his roomful of

Phillies fans. His beloved NFL champion, Green Bay Packers, were off to a surprisingly slow start, especially after their recent three-year dominance of the NFL. Marty also believed Father Fritz never forgave the Philadelphia Eagles for beating the Packers for the NFL championship in 1960.

Most of the class thought Father Fritzdorf was just venting frustration at the Packers' poor start and the fact the Braves, despite a powerful lineup, were a disappointment again. Marty hoped the Phillies could rebound against the Braves tonight at home and take the starch out of the priest's collar. It bothered Marty that a priest could gloat at the Phillies' slide, but as his dad often said, "Priests are human too and subject to their hometown prejudices and upbringing."

This display was a little unsettling to Marty, but he didn't dwell on it for too long. He maintained his respectful awe of priests and thought highly of them as lordly ministers of God. So he was initially taken aback at Father Fritz's perceived pettiness, or was Marty too absorbed in the Phillies season and upset at the sudden change in the team's fortune? At any rate, he did enjoy the delicious cheese and dearly hoped the Phils would win this weekend against the Braves not only for the team to right the ship but also to wipe off Father Fritz's smug grin the next morning.

Marty finished his homework after supper during his customary six-to-seven-thirty study time slot he instituted in eighth grade, which left him time to indulge his couch potato TV viewing. In 1964, network prime-time began at seven thirty. This also worked during baseball season when most games began around eight, except for the West Coast.

Marty and Mark listened to the first game of the four-game set.

Mark was still unusually upbeat.

"Bunning's pitching. The Braves can hit the tar out of the ball, but old Jimbo should be able to handle them."

Their dad was working at the firehouse, and their younger brothers were more interested in playing ball at this stage in their young life than in listening to a ballgame.

The loss of their grandfather was still keenly felt.

"Grandpop would be sitting in his favorite chair and smoking his pipe," said Marty in a sentimental, wistful tone.

"Yeah," replied Mark. "Still hard to believe he is gone."

Bunning did not have his best stuff, giving up three runs in six innings, but it was a winnable game if the Phils could have given him some run support. The Phils trailed, 5–0, before mounting a three-run rally that fell short losing, 5–3.

"That is now four in a row. The lead is only two and a half with seven to go. I'm really starting to worry," said Mark.

"Yeah." Marty agreed. To add insult to injury, his Wisconsin-born Latin teacher would really rub it in the next morning.

True to form, the teacher couldn't help but needle his captive classroom audience of despairing Phillies fans.

"What is with your team, guys? Are they feeling the pressure? Mauch may not be the genius everyone claims."

What could Marty and his classmates say? It was getting pretty bad, but Marty had his grandfather's native optimism and still had hope. As his dad would say, the Phillies were still in the driver's seat. *The team could not keep losing*, thought Marty. *Not this year when everything is going so well.*

The next game proved to be a classic. The Phillies with their lefty ace on the mound, Chris Short, pitching a customary gem, had a 1–0 lead going into the seventh inning. A couple of unearned runs (what happened to the smooth fielding team the Phillies were noted for most of the season?) put the Phils dangerously behind in the eighth by a score of 3–1.

"I don't believe it," said a frustrated Mark. Marty felt the same pessimism. Could the Phillies lose another close one and make it their fifth straight loss?

Then as if in answer to their silent prayers, their year-long seasonal magic came back with a jolt.

The Phillies' MVP candidate, Johnny Callison, tied the game with a dramatic two-run homer in the bottom of the eighth.

"Shades of Dick Sisler," said Marty to Mark, remembering the many times their dad recounted Sisler's pennant-clinching home run on the last day of the 1950 season.

The game went into extra innings.

When the Braves scored two runs in the top of the tenth, it looked bleak, but the Phillies' soon-to-be Rookie of the Year, Richie Allen, tied the game in the bottom of the inning with a two-run homer.

The two brothers were ecstatic!

"There is no way the Phillies are going to lose this game now," said Marty. Two dramatic, last-ditch home runs by their star players couldn't be wasted. The stars were once again aligning in the Phillies' favor—or so the boys thought.

Sadly and incredibly, the Braves were typically tough. The game stayed tied and extended further into extra innings, and Milwaukee scored two more runs in the twelfth. The Phils ran out of miracles and lost number 5 in a row, 7–5.

"What a heartbreaker," said Marty.

The Phillies had a dwindling game and a half lead with seven left.

Could the losing continue?

Marty dreaded school the next morning.

How sarcastic and annoying would the Reverend Cheesemaker be?

But the good Father was surprisingly sympathetic.

"I have to give your team credit. They battled back in exciting fashion and showed a lot of grit. I really feel for you, guys. Losing is not fun, especially with every game now being so meaningful."

This welcome dose of unexpected support made Marty feel better. He took stock and thought the team still had two games left against the pesky Braves. They were home in the comforting confines of Connie Mack Stadium and possessed the best home record in baseball, so there was still reason for hope.

On the next night, the Phillies cruised to an early 4–0 lead and knocked out the Braves' starting pitcher in the second inning. Mahaffey was pitching well and was hurling a shutout for the first four innings. The right-hander gave up two runs in the top of the fifth inning but settled down again, and the Phillies entered the top of the eighth, maintaining their slim 4–2 lead.

"Just six more outs, and the Phils can end this losing streak," said a relieved Marty.

"Yeah." Mark agreed. "The team has never lost more than five games in a row all season, so the omens look good."

Mahaffey struggled in the eighth and was relieved by the Phillies' top fireman, Jack Baldschun, who was always exciting, to say the least. He made things tense by pitching into a jam but some-how always seemed to work his way out of it. For the most part, this was the case. Marty remembered the first game at Connie Mack his dad took him to. Baldschun walked the bases loaded in the top of the ninth against the Mets but managed a strikeout and a double play to preserve a Phillies win. It was typical of Baldschun, tense and nail-biting drama, but he usually came through.

But not on this night. The Braves scored a run to cut the lead to 4–3, and former Philadelphia Athletic MVP, Bobby Shantz, man-aged to get out of the inning in relief of Baldschun.

"This game is getting a little too scary," said Mark. "I hope the Phillies can get some insurance runs to pad the lead."

"Yeah, that would be nice. Hank Aaron leads off for the Braves in the top of the ninth. He can tie the game with one swing of the bat, so it would be nice to get some more runs. The Phils haven't scored since the bottom of the second," added a very worried Marty.

"Yeah, and Eddie Matthews bats right after Aaron, and he can easily hit one out of the park."

So the two brothers fervently hoped and prayed their team could muster some offense.

The Phillies put two runners on but failed to score in the bot-tom of the eighth, and it was all up to the thirty-nine-year-old vet-eran Shantz to get three outs to preserve a gut-wrenching win.

Aaron and Matthews did not hit home runs, but they both sin-gled to put the go-ahead runs on base with no outs.

"We really need a double play," said Mark.

Marty agreed. "That would be a godsend."

As if on cue, radio announcer Bill Campbell's voice revved up in excitement as he said, "Bolling hits a sharp grounder to Amaro at short . . . This could be two . . . Amaro scoops it up and tosses to Taylor at second . . ."

The two brothers expected the smooth fielding Tony Taylor to turn the double play.

They were horrified to hear that Taylor dropped the ball, that all the runners were safe, and that instead of two outs with a runner on third or at least one out with runners at the corners, the Braves had the bases loaded with no outs.

The crestfallen brothers could not believe it.

The situation deteriorated even further when Rico Carty smashed a long drive into center field to clear the bases. The Phillies' early 4–0 lead was now a dispiriting 6–4 deficit.

Mark and Marty just shook their heads in a wearisome disbelief.

Did the resilient Phillies have another comeback in them?

The brothers were surprised to hear that the great Warren Spahn was coming in to pitch the bottom of the ninth. Spahn was normally a starter and a perennial twenty-game winner.

Despite his surefire Hall of Fame statistics, Spahn had trouble against the Phillies this season, losing three games.

That briefly revived Mark and Marty's flagging hopes.

"The Phils seem to have Warren Spahn's number this year for some reason. Maybe this a good omen," said a desperately optimistic Marty to his brother.

"I don't know," replied the more skeptical Mark.

The Phillies' recent run of success against Spahn ended quickly, and the Braves' great lefty easily pitched a one-two-three inning.

Now the Phillies lost their sixth in a row despite building an early lead and fell again, 6–4. Their once seemingly insurmountable lead was now down to a mere half a game.

Sunday's game was the worst.

Their dad was home, and the family alternated watching between the Eagles-Browns NFL game and the fading Phillies.

When Martin Senior heard the starting lineup, he complained. "Why in the world is Bunning pitching with only two days' rest? Mauch is pushing the panic button, I'm afraid."

As if in answer to Martin's plaintive question, Bunning got shel-lacked. It was a rare event this season, but that is how the season was ending up.

Marty came to Bunning's defense.

"There were a lot of cheap infield hits." Marty argued, but the tired Bunning was lifted after giving up seven runs in three innings. By far, it was his worst start of the year.

Callison staked his MVP claim once again with three home runs, but the team still lost, 14–8.

What was even worse, their seventh straight loss dropped them out of first place for the first team since July 21 after seventy-three days atop of the National League.

"Just our luck," said Martin Senior. "The Phillies go into a tail-spin, while the Reds and Cards are red hot." Both St. Louis and Cincinnati were on long winning streaks.

Five games were left, but the Phils could still pull it out.

However, they would need some help. It looked bleak but not impossible. On the plus side, they would be playing their two closest rivals—three against the Cardinals and two against the Reds. Hope springs eternal.

As Martin Senior had stated, the Phils were in an unfortunate tailspin and now had to face the red-hot Cardinals, winners of six straight, in a critical three-game series in St. Louis. The Phils no lon-ger controlled their own destiny. They were a game behind and had to rely on the Reds losing, which seemed unlikely since they were on a six-game winning streak of their own. Even a sweep of the Cards would not guarantee the pennant since the Reds were ahead of them in the standings and also had to lose some games.

Marty still had hope no matter how slim. The Phils had to face the Cardinals' three best pitchers—Bob Gibson, Ray Sadecki, and the former Whiz Kid-turned-Phillie-killer, Curt Simmons.

Marty's fading optimism received a severe jolt in the first game of the series. Bob Gibson was his usual masterful self, and Chris Short was decent but not good enough. He gave up three runs in six innings, which was no match for Gibson, and the Phillies lost their eighth straight, 5–1. Unbelievably, the team fell to third place, a game and a half behind the Reds and now a half game behind the Cardinals, who were barely a .500 team in July.

"The Phils are deader than a vampire in the daylight," said Mark as his natural pessimism reasserted itself. "Too many variables have to happen for the Phils to climb back into first. Hard to believe. It is really . . . really hard to believe." Mark shook his head in resigned hopelessness.

Mark wanted to say that maybe Grandpop's death spared him a lot of horrible misery, and perhaps God was merciful after all, but his mom was close by, and he wisely kept this blasphemous thought to himself.

To compound the wretchedness, the Phillies lost the next two games to make the losing streak an even ten straight. Now the Cardinals were in first place with a two and a half game lead over the Phils with only three games left. Only a miracle could save the Phillies season.

Marty prayed hard for this semi-miracle. His spirit was waning faster than a deflated balloon.

Marty felt a little guilty about praying for a Phillies win. He always remembered his dad and grandfather's admonishment that it was silly to pray for a win in sports.

"God has more important details to worry about, like rainfall in a drought or a despairing sinner," was their common retort.

Marty was on the edge of despair himself over the Phillies' collapse and his beloved grandfather's unexpected passing.

Marty optimistically reasoned the Phillies were still a mathematical possibility. The Phils could beat the Reds in the last two games and tie them in the standings. What made this possibility even tougher, however, was that the Cardinals had three games left against the last place Mets, a team which had already lost over one hundred games for the third straight year. Chances of that happening were as likely as Barry Goldwater winning the Presidential election against President Lyndon Johnson in November.

Martin Senior put it all in grim perspective: "What are the odds of the streaking Cardinals losing three games in a row against the pathetic Mets?"

Martin was trying to lend a dose of reality to his heartbroken older sons. He didn't want them to get their hopes up too high, even though it was theoretically possible for an unprecedented three-way tie for the pennant.

The Phillies and Reds had the night off, but amazingly enough, the Cards' nine-game winning streak ended, and St. Louis finally lost to the Mets, of all teams.

The Phils, on the next day, at last broke their ten-game losing streak with a come-from-behind late inning, thrilling win, 4–3, which left them only one game behind the Reds.

In another dose of incredible good news, the Cards were crushed by the Mets, 15–5.

"Do you believe this?" said an incredulous Martin Senior as he walked in the front door after his day shift at the firehouse. "The Phils have a fighting chance."

Despite his hard-earned realism, Martin was beginning to think the Phillies could still pull it out like the Whiz Kids in 1950.

"WE'RE NOT DEAD YET!" blared the front page headlines of Philadelphia's three major newspapers.

It all came down to the final game of the regular season. If the Phils beat the Reds and the Cardinals lose to the Mets again, it would create a three-way tie for first place. This had never happened in the eighty-plus years of baseball history.

Could history be made on Sunday, October 4, 1964?

Was it still possible for the collapsing Phillies to fight their way back to a stunning three-way tie for the pennant on the last game of the season?

Marty, Mark, and Martin Senior, having a rare Sunday afternoon off from the firehouse, looked forward to the one o'clock games. The family attended the 10:10-AM Mass, and their dad splurged a little for the special occasion by buying two dozen doughnuts at Bamberger's, a mouthwatering assortment of Bavarian crème, chocolate, vanilla, and snow-powdery jelly donuts. This treat was in addition to the normal Sunday breakfast routine of bacon sandwiches on freshly baked, soft-as-a-pillow dinner rolls at Cacia's Italian bakery.

So the family enjoyed the best of both culinary worlds—Germany and Italy.

Veronica cooked up enough bacon to feed the First Marine Division. It was barely adequate for her five growing boys.

Sunday morning was the only time the family would normally eat a normal breakfast together. On most mornings, the usual fare was milk, cereal, and a banana, due to the constraints of school and work.

This extra treat made the Sunday morning especially memorable. The prospect of an exciting and potentially historic Phillies game added to the uniqueness of the day. Kate came home for the weekend from Nursing school, which added more joy to the afternoon. There was one major drawback—Cassie was not there, as she already began her novitiate with the Columban Sisters in Nebraska. The whole family commented on her absence, even her younger brothers who often resented her perceived tyrannical reign. Marty already realized how helpful she was around the house, and now his brothers were becoming more aware of her good points.

Veronica asked Kathleen if she had heard from John Stanton, who was starting his Naval training at the Great Lakes Naval Base.

"I have received a couple of letters. He is doing okay."

"Does he still want the Naval Academy appointment?" asked her dad.

"Oh yes. Definitely. He believes he will be able to enter the prep school after basic training."

"That will be good," said Martin. "Always better to be an officer in the military if you have to go in and perform military service."

Martin was reflecting on his World War II years as an enlisted swabbie.

Marty noticed his sister had a sad, wistful look when she talked about her boyfriend. It brought back painful memories of the infamous incident on the Protestant Church steps down the block, something he was still ashamed of, even though everything seemed to have worked out for the best.

After the stomach-satisfying breakfast, the older brothers and their dad settled down to watch the game.

Bunning was the starting pitcher. He was having a terrific year but did have a couple of rough outings lately during the ten-game losing streak.

"Jim Bunning is pitching on his normal three-day rotation, so we can expect to see better results, just like Chris Short yesterday, who pitched much better and seemed more like his old self with proper rest." Martin predicted.

It turned out to be an accurate assessment. Bunning was sharp and steady and pitched as well as he did throughout the season. The Phils took an early 3–0 lead in the third and piled it on in the middle innings with Richie Allen hitting his twenty-eighth and twenty-ninth homers of the season.

Bunning pitched a six-hit shutout for his nineteenth victory. The Phillies' victory put them in a tie with Cincinnati. The last piece in the hoped-for comeback was the Cardinals-Mets game.

How were the Mets faring? Could they beat the Cardinals for the third straight time?

The family's hopes were briefly raised when the Mets took a 3–2 lead into the fifth inning.

Marty could not believe what was happening. If the Mets maintained their lead, the seemingly impossible would come true—a three-way tie for the pennant and a revival of the Phillies fortune.

However, that was the high point of their tenuous hope. A power surge by the Cardinals in the late innings erased the slim New York lead, and the Cards cruised to an 11–5 win and sole possession of the National League Pennant.

"Well, boys, that is it. The final nail in the coffin for the season," said Martin, who could see the severe disappointment and the inescapable reality and the bitter sting of final defeat on his two sons' faces. That was it! The Phillies' inevitable march to the October Classic was officially over. He tried to cheer them up with an unexpected gesture.

"What do you think if we went down to the airport to greet the team when they arrive from Cincinnati? Let's face it, no matter how it ended, the Phillies had a great year. They gave us plenty of thrills. In all honesty, they actually played way above their heads."

Martin knew baseball inside and out and had no doubt the Cardinals, Reds, and Giants had far superior talent on their respective rosters. Still the Phils came so close, and Martin wanted his sons to savor the near miss. Who knows what next year will bring?

Veronica overheard the planned trip and seconded the idea. Her younger children would enjoy the takeoff and landing of the airplanes arriving and departing at the Philadelphia Airport in the former swamp along the Schuylkill River.

"Why don't we make it a family affair. Let's bring the whole gang. I'll pack some food, and we will make it into a family picnic."

"Sure, why not?" said Martin, who originally wanted the trip to be a father-son experience but had to concede to his wife's superior logic. Everyone was getting older. How many family trips remained with Cassie in the convent and Kathleen in nursing school? Martin called his brother, Jack, to borrow his station wagon again.

Luckily, Martin had several brothers and sisters in a five-block radius that could lend his family a car for a short period of time. The family did not own a car since Martin could walk to work, and Detroit did not make cars big enough for his entire family. Parking was difficult in the cramped confines of South Philadelphia anyway.

The Philadelphia Airport was a short fifteen-minute drive. Martin would use his contacts at the airport firehouse to gauge when the team would exactly arrive and the best place to park. No use waiting around too long, especially since he was using his brother's car. Most of Uncle Jack's kids were grown up and out of the house, but Martin did not want to inconvenience his older brother too much.

Martin gathered his clan together. Cassie was in the novitiate, and Kate had to go back to the nursing school dormitory, which left enough room for the two youngest children—one on the seat and the other on the floor.

These were the days before mandatory seat belt laws, so the family could cram two adults and eight kids in the station wagon—three in the front, three in the back seat, two on the floor, and two in the open trunk space. There was actually room for two more passengers, so two of Mark's friends crammed into the back.

Martin Senior was not sure how the Philly fans would react to the shocking losing streak that cost the team the pennant, and it deeply concerned him with his young family in the area. Would there be a torrent of abuse and four-letter words? The season was so golden for most of the year. The summer was magical, but in one ten-game disastrous stretch, the Phillies blew a seemingly insurmountable lead.

Martin remembered with sadness at how the Phillies fans treated local homeboy, slugger Del Ennis, a perennial, power-hitting all-star who routinely smacked twenty-five to thirty homers and drove in over one hundred runs in a season but who was unmercifully booed by the fickle fans. It bothered him when the crowd hooted and hollered when Ennis struck out with runners in scoring position. He really hoped the Philadelphia fans would not be at their worse when the plane landed.

Martin still could not believe the collapse. He remembered the 1950 Whiz Kids nosedived in a similar disturbing manner but still pulled it out in dramatic fashion when Dick Sisler's three-run homer finally put the Dodgers away on the last game of the year.

The 1964 Phillies almost made another comeback with the final two wins against the Reds, but their rally fell a little too short. It was almost too much to expect to have the Cardinals lose three straight games versus the lowly Mets. At least, the Mets did make it interesting by winning the first two games to briefly revive hope in Philadelphia.

Martin pondered, how would the fans react to such a topsy-turvy season? Would the fans boo, curse, and make an ugly scene? Would they throw fruit, beer cans, and assorted other trash? Martin really hoped this would not happen.

Martin felt this way not only for his young family's sake. He didn't want them to view such a bad exhibition of poor sportsmanship. But he also hoped this would not occur for the player's sake. For 150 games, the team played way above their talent. In truth, the Phillies were probably the fourth best team in the National League in 1964. The Reds, Cardinals, and Giants had excellent starting pitching and solid hitting. Each team was loaded with all-star talent. Even the weak-hitting Dodgers were World Series champs only a year ago when they swept the powerful Yankees in four straight games with their superior pitching headed by the dynamic Koufax-Drysdale combination.

Somehow, Gene Mauch made all the right moves, tinkered with the lineup, shifted players, and stunned the baseball world for over three months.

Sadly, it all fell achingly short.

Martin hoped and prayed for the best.

When the McAlynn family arrived at the airport, Martin Senior was pleasantly surprised to see so many fans lined up all along the runway fence.

What was even more surprising were the positive signs that showed love and support for the team. Most said, "Thanks for a Great Year," and "Wait Until Next Year."

But how would the majority react when the plane landed? Martin could only hold his breath and pray for the best.

As the plane coasted out of the sky, landed, and slowly rolled and taxied, Martin looked around at the sea of faces and breathed easier. He did not see any swelling anger in the crowd. No one had tomatoes or bananas poised in their hands. It was looking more and more like it would not degenerate into an ugly confrontation.

The aircraft came to a complete stop, and the door opened. The first person off the plane was the manager himself, Gene Mauch.

Martin was impressed, and it reminded him of an incident he read about in World War II concerning the Japanese surrender. The first American plane that landed on Japanese soil was a tense affair. How would the Japanese react to the hated American enemy? After all, American planes had devastated Japan's cities in relentless fashion. Uncertainty and fear were paramount. The first person off this plane to set an example of brave leadership was General Douglas MacArthur, who led the island-hopping campaign in the Southwest Pacific. Martin read that Winston Churchill believed it to be one of the bravest acts in the entire war.

In a somewhat similar sense (but not as historically important), Mauch was displaying the same type of courageous leadership.

As the Phillies players came down the steps of the ramp, the crowd's reaction was positively inspiring. There was enthusiastic applause and a lot of backslapping. Cheers, not jeers, were the order of the day. Martin Senior smiled and felt a great sense of gratitude and pride for his hometown.

No one would have blamed the stunned and saddened fans of Philadelphia to have vociferously booed the team. What a historic collapse! All the thrills and hopes for a great World Series and a chance to avenge the 1950 loss against the Yankees were dashed in unbelievable fashion.

But the fans came out in the thousands to cheer for a 95 percent successful season.

Any person can be noble and cheerful when everything's going right. The true test of character comes with how you react to devastating and unexpected failure. The real proof of integrity is revealed in defeat, not victory.

Martin was overjoyed to see that the often mocked fans of Philadelphia passed the character test in inspiring fashion. He believed it was a terrific life lesson, and he was deeply grateful his family experienced this.

Life does not always work out the way you wanted it to. Disappointment abounds, and it's best to get used to life's ups and downs. Life is like a roller coaster, filled with soaring highs and crushing downturns. Enjoy the ride up and the view and realize the downs will not last for long either. It's a good perspective on life to get a person through the joys and travails of life. Sports is actually an excellent introduction in what to expect and endure in a person's lifetime.

For Marty Junior, the end of the regular baseball season meant the real end of summer. Unofficially, summer closed on Labor Day when summer vacation ended with the start of the school year. Officially, according to the sun and the Gregorian calendar, summer ended two weeks ago on September 21. Ironically, it was the start of the Phillies' ten-game downfall and Grandpop Adolph's funeral.

In Marty's mind, the memorable summer of 1964 was now over. For a while, it looked like the summer would extend into the middle of October with the Phillies battling the Yankees for baseball supremacy. But sadly, this was not to be. The baseball "gods" thought otherwise.

Still, it was a wondrous summer. Marty indulged his creative instincts with his movie. For most of the summer, the Phillies were in first place. In the end, his intended horror classic was a laughing stock to all who watched it, and the Phillies came up a game short. His older sisters surprised him. Cassie, in a reversal of roles with Kate, entered the novitiate, and Kate fell in love with a Marine—a dizzying chain of events that kept Marty's head spinning. Worst of all, Marty lost his beloved mentor and grandfather. It was certainly a summer to remember.

His dad summed it up best with his roller coaster analogy. Marty took it to heart and promised to enjoy the ride up and brace for the fall when it inevitably came.

Marty was snapped out of his melancholy thoughts by the loud cheers and applause as the Phillies came off the plane. He shared his dad's feeling and was proud that the crowd did not castigate the team. When all was said and done, it was a great ride, just like the summer of '64 overall. As Grandpop Adolph always said, "It is the journey, not the destination, that makes the best memories."

Marty also liked to think that his grandfather's indomitable spirit was still present in the cheering crowd. It made the encouraging moment even more satisfying and happier. It was a bittersweet moment but certainly one to cherish. It was certainly an experience to recall and savor in the years to come.

About the Author

L eo Mount is a native Philadelphian and a retired DEA Special Agent, who also served in the US Army and the US Marine Corps. Leo currently lives in Stratford, New Jersey with his wife and four children.

About the Illustrator

R ebecca Mount grew up in South Jersey drawing and watching cartoons. She has worked on children's shows such as *Abby's Flying Fairy School* and *Speed Racers* and is now working on an Indie game with some fellow artists. This is Rebecca's first book as an illustrator.